Can't Erase You

Leigh Vining

Supposed Crimes LLC • Matthews, North Carolina

ISBN: 978-1-952150-05-0

www.supposedcrimes.com

This book is typeset in Goudy Old Style.

To my little soul mate, Pepé.

Chapter One

Phil Thompson slowly drove his Chevy pick-up down the driveway and adjusted the volume on the CD player. The original cast recording of the Broadway play *Cats* made him smile. He pictured his fourteen-going-on-twenty-five-year-old niece climbing into the passenger seat and rolling her eyes at his taste in music.

The sixteen-foot utility trailer hitched behind the truck was loaded with carpeted cat trees that he'd built in his free time. The tail end of the trailer scraped the driveway as he turned onto the quiet street. He waved at his retired neighbor, Chuck, who'd helped him load up. Lucky for him, Chuck was an early riser even on Saturday.

Spring mornings in the California desert had been cool. With the breeze blowing in through his open window, today felt warmer than usual even at five thirty a.m. His sister's apartment wasn't far, and with any luck, his niece would be ready on time for the two-hour drive from Apple Valley to Los Angeles. He wanted to set up and be ready to sell his assortment of towers at the cat show as early as possible. Making extra money was just one reason he looked forward to these weekends. He also enjoyed the hustle and bustle of the show hall and being around cats and cat people. Besides those two reasons, it was also a chance to spend quality time with Eve.

At a stop light, he glanced around, taking in the world around him—so deserted with only a couple other vehicles in sight, as if he was one of only a few people left on earth.

A few glimmering stars still remained, too bright to fade just yet. Silhouettes of the distant mountains to the south became visible against the early morning sky. He used to know the fashionable, high-class neighborhood out there so well—the golf course, man-made lake, panoramic view, tennis courts, security patrol, and the country club with the fine dining. That place didn't enter his mind very often now. The last time he remembered giving it more than a passing thought was on his thirtieth birthday—five years ago. After Eve and her mom had sung "Happy Birthday" over the phone, he'd ended the call and seen the old man's face staring up at him from the local newspaper on his kitchen table.

William J. Fisher, long-time resident of Apple Valley, died in Auburndale, New York...

He sure hadn't shed any tears. Tapping his fingers on the steering wheel, he wondered how long Doris Fisher had lived after moving to New York. The obituary had said she'd preceded her husband in death. How long had she lived after her diagnosis? He sighed. But that was all water under the bridge.

When the light turned green, he came back to the present, glanced out to the south one more time and continued on, pushing the depressing thoughts of the Fishers out of his mind.

He turned into the parking lot in front of the building on Apache Road and looked up at the second-floor apartment with the porch light burning by the door. Parking under a lamppost, he checked the time—five minutes later than what he'd told them. Maybe he should have called to say he was on his way, but since lights were on inside the apartment, he figured Eve would be out any second. He waited patiently with the engine running since blowing the horn at such an early hour wasn't a good idea. In less than a minute, the living room drapes moved as if someone was peeking out. A moment later, Gail came outside with Eve following, but his niece quickly dashed past her mom and bounded down the stairs.

Eve rushed up to the truck, her long blonde ponytail swinging from side to side. "Hey, Uncle Phil, you're late." She pulled open the passenger side door and tossed her backpack onto the floor.

"Good morning," he said, waiting for her reaction to the music.

She climbed into the truck, rolled her eyes, and then waved her hands as if she was conducting an orchestra.

"Good choice of music, Uncle Phil," she said with a little giggle.

He smiled and leaned back.

Gail appeared at Phil's open window and cleared her throat.

They both turned to give her their full attention.

She wore a baggy gray sweat suit and her light auburn hair framed her face in unruly curls. "Uh, how about turning the music down so I can say hello to my favorite little brother."

He turned the volume down a couple notches. "I'm your only brother, but thanks anyway." Stretching his head out the window, he gave her a kiss on the cheek.

She kissed him back and then looked over at Eve. "Have a good day. Call or text me when you get a chance."

"You have a good day too." He rolled up the window, and Gail waved as they drove off.

Ten minutes later, they were parked outside a McDonald's with their order of Egg McMuffins, juice, and hot chocolate. Eve removed her zip-up sweatshirt, revealing the T-shirt Phil had bought her at the last cat show—a Tuxedo kitten with the words *I do what I want*.

"Looking good," he said with a grin. "That shirt fits your personality."

"Thanks, and what about you?" She reached over and peeked inside Phil's open jacket to check out his shirt underneath. "Real men love cats," she read out loud. "Good choice, I love it! And, are you growing a beard again, Uncle Phil, or haven't you had time to shave lately?"

He stuck out his chin and rubbed the scraggly hair. "I'll have you know I've been working on this for a couple weeks. Don't you like it?"

"Yeah," she said thoughtfully. "It's cool... and there's not even any gray in it... yet." She giggled and sipped her juice.

He raised his eyebrows. "Gray? I'm not old enough for gray hair."

"Dream on. You're only four years younger than Mom, and she's been covering her gray for years."

"Well, I'm not surprised. Kids are known for making their parents age." He gave her a sideways glance and then took a sip of his hot chocolate.

"Touché." She giggled, and then she got quiet and started fidgeting with the strap of her backpack.

"Hey, talk to me," he said.

She turned to him, a deep furrow marring her brow. "I wish I was old enough to get a job."

"What do you mean? I pay you for helping me at the shows,

and you pick up some money baby-sitting, don't you?"

She shrugged. "I mean a real job, at least part-time."

"What do you need a real job for?" He took a bite of his Egg McMuffin.

"I wish I could help us get a bigger place to live. Mom says we can't afford anything else. She hardly has space for her art, and besides that, no pets allowed, and I want a cat sooooo bad."

He smiled, reached across the cab, and rubbed her shoulder. "I know, honey, it'll all work out in time."

"And Mom gets depressed because she wants to be a successful artist before she turns forty, and time's running out."

Eve finally unwrapped her breakfast and took a bite, like sharing that burden with him had lifted a weight off her shoulders.

They ate in silence for a few minutes and then Eve paused, holding the last of her Egg McMuffin. "The apartment is sooooo crowded with Mom's easels all over the place."

He wanted to lighten the mood. "Are you sure you want to move because of the paintings, or is the real reason because you want a cat?"

Eve broke into a smile, ate her last bite, and crumpled her wrapper. He winked at her and stuffed his trash into the McDonald's bag. Eve placed hers inside, rolled down the window, and threw the bag into the trashcan next to the truck.

"Slam dunk," Phil said.

She blew on her fingernails and rubbed them on the front of her shirt. "When you're hot, you're hot."

Phil smiled. "I know where you can see all the cats you can handle. Let's get going." He started the engine and drove toward the freeway.

The beautiful orange and red hues of the sunrise lit their way.

Phil drove to the rear of the municipal auditorium on Southern Avenue and scoped out the back door area to stop and unload. Eve unbuckled her seat belt before he even came to a full stop.

"Hang on, let me get parked," he said.

"Is Michael going to be here today?" Eve lifted one eyebrow.

"Yeah. He said he'd help us unload the trees..." He narrowed his eyes at her playful half-smile. "What's that look for?"

"Look, what look?" She pressed her lips together.

"Like you're about to suggest—again—that Michael and I would make a good couple, and I tell you every time that I'm not interested in him."

"Well, I think he's interested. He's always flirting with you." She batted her eyes and grinned.

"He's a friend, well, not even that, just a person I see at the shows, and that's as far as it goes. He's too young for me anyway. I think he's only in his twenties."

"Uncle Phil, you need to date. When are you ever going to find someone so you won't be lonely?"

"I go out sometimes, and who says I'm lonely—I'm not lonely—now come on, let's get moving."

"Okay, okay." She opened the passenger door.

He got out of the truck and when he moved to the back of the trailer Eve appeared at his side.

"Do you badger your mom like you do me?" He untied the ropes holding the cat trees, trying to work fast since they were parked in an unloading zone. "Never mind, don't answer that." He shook his head and smiled.

"I'll run inside and check in," Eve said, disappearing in the blink of an eye.

He had the ropes off by the time Eve returned with Michael in tow. "Hi, Phil, I'm here to save the day," Michael said with a big smile.

"Hey, Michael, do you have your tables set up yet? I don't want to take you away from getting your stuff organized. Eve and I can get started here."

"I can help, no problem. I've been here for a while."

He could have sworn Michael blushed. Something seemed different about him today. Was it his hair? His clothes? He actually was a good-looking guy, and he always seemed in a good mood.

They began hauling the cat trees out of the trailer. Eve stayed at the truck while he and Michael each took one end of a tree and carried them, one at a time, into the building and set them in the space where he and Eve would spend the day.

When all the towers, big and small, were on display, Michael excused himself. Phil left Eve on duty so he could move his rig to a designated parking space. Vendors were setting up, others placing their decorated cat enclosures on tables. On his way out the door, he dodged a group on their way in carrying their ribbon contenders in cages. The excitement of the day had begun.

After parking, he grabbed his messenger bag, went back inside, and hurried over to Eve and the cat trees. "Don't forget to call your mom and let her know we're here."

"Already texted her—all taken care of. Do you want something to drink?"

"Sure, a Coke would be good." He took out his wallet, pulled out a few bills, and handed them to her. "If you're hungry get a snack."

"Do you want a snack?"

He shook his head. "No, just a Coke for me."

"Okay, be right back. Watch my backpack."

Eve disappeared into the crowd, and he ran his hand over the carpet on one of his cat trees. His mind wandered to what she'd said about her mom earlier. At least Gail had a goal in life, and he had confidence in her that someday she'd make it big as an artist. His sister didn't need to be paired off to be happy, and from what he could tell she was quite content with that decision. She was a great mother to her sweet daughter. He'd never be a father, and that fact always got him down, so he quickly pushed the thought away. Plus, he was a carpenter and barely made enough money to make ends meet. Building these cat trees on the side helped, but wouldn't make him rich. And even worse, he had no one to cuddle up with besides his two cats. Unlike Gail, he hadn't consciously chosen to stay single for life... that's just the way it'd worked out.

He toed the bottom of the cat tree—well made—nice and sturdy. At least what he built made cats happy, and he smiled in spite of himself. He was usually the only person selling large towers with plush carpet and unoiled sisal rope. Across the room near the front doors, a vendor displayed small corner units with cubbyholes in them. Another man, who was set up along the far wall, had what he called refined cat towers—very stylish and modern looking, but he didn't seem to sell very many. Maybe his price was too high, or maybe no self-respecting cat would be caught dead on one. Some people might find them artful, but they didn't have much functionality in his opinion.

Phil's station was smack dab in the middle of everything, hopefully where people would notice his cat trees. After reaching into his bag, he pulled out some mini American flags and a couple flags with cat faces. He displayed them on top of some of the towers to draw attention along with a little notice he'd printed up advertising special orders. Then he set his business cards out on a small display table Michael had brought over when he'd helped him set up.

He looked around for Michael's cat food booth. To his right there was a large group of people heading down the aisle between vendors, and he was pretty sure that was Michael's dark spiked hair and he was probably busy making sales. Just then a customer stopped to look at the trees, so he slipped into his salesman mode.

Before Eve had even returned with their drinks, he'd sold two towers. Not only that, but the first woman had two sons who carried their purchase away like it weighed nothing, and the second sale was to a man and woman with a son, so they didn't need help carrying theirs either.

Eve handed him his Coke, and he drank half of it in a few gulps. When he noticed the aroma of food in the air, he wished he'd asked Eve to bring him a snack after all.

"You didn't get a snack either?" he asked.

"No, I'll just wait for lunch. Why, are you hungry now? I can go back and get you something." She sipped her drink.

"That's okay, I'll be all right."

By noon they'd sold half of the cat trees, which pleased Phil. They had three setting off to the side marked *sold* waiting for the customers to take away before closing time.

"Are you getting tired, honey?" he asked, leaning against one of the cat trees.

"No, are you?"

"No, but I could use some lunch."

Before Eve had a chance to answer, Betty, who Phil called the T-shirt lady, appeared. "I came to say hi—how are the two of you doing?"

"Good." Eve hugged the older woman.

Phil smiled. "Selling a lot of shirts today?"

Betty hugged him. "I can't complain. I'm doing pretty good so far... I see you two have your shirts on."

Phil smoothed his out and stood up straight with his shoulders back. "It's a real nice shirt, I enjoy wearing it."

"It suits you..." She admired Eve's shirt. "And you, young lady, look very nice in yours."

Eve smiled. "Thanks, Betty."

"Hey, I thought I'd offer to watch your section if the two of you want to look around for a bit and get yourselves some lunch. I've got my daughter helping out today."

Eve's smile got bigger, and she looked like she was ready to skip right up the aisle. She widened her gaze at Phil, waiting expectantly for his answer.

"If you're sure you don't mind, we'll take you up on that offer. We won't stay away long. If you need anything, just text or call."

"Will do, now go look at some cats and get something to eat." She shooed them away.

"Thanks, Betty," Phil said.

"Thank you, Betty." Eve slipped on her backpack.

Phil walked up the aisle toward the show ring, and Eve bounced along by his side and pulled on his arm. They approached Michael's tables, and Eve said, "He always has samples of food. You need some for Batman and Robin."

They stopped in front of the cat food display, and a guy he'd never seen greeted them. "Can I help you with anything?"

"Where's Michael?" Eve glanced around the booth.

"Right here," Michael said from behind. He stepped around them to the other side of the display table. "I just took a little walk for a minute to stretch my legs. How are sales today?"

"Good, doing good," Phil answered. "We're on our way to get lunch. Betty's watching the towers."

"Can we have some samples for Batman and Robin?" Eve asked.

"Of course." Michael grabbed a generous number of little bags. "Gary, can you hand me a paper bag for these?" he asked the unfamiliar guy working at the booth. "Uh, Phil, Eve—this is Gary. Gary—Phil and Eve." Gary shook each of their hands and smiled.

He seemed pleasant, but Eve looked up at Phil with a downcast expression.

Michael placed the samples into the small bag and handed it to Phil.

"Well, Michael, thanks a lot for these—nice to meet you, Gary," Phil said. "We'd better get going. Don't want to take advantage of Betty's generosity."

"Okay, have fun." Michael put his arm around Gary.

Eve didn't bother to say goodbye. She took a deep breath and had a pained expression on her face. After they were out of earshot she started in. "Now look, it's too late. You didn't move fast enough, and he got away."

"Don't scold me. I told you I wasn't interested in Michael..." He wasn't really sure how he felt. Maybe he should have gotten to know him better to see if they might have more in common besides their love of cats. He was a nice guy, after all, but so young and they didn't live in the same city. Now it was too late. It just wasn't meant to be, but he was sorry that Eve's bubble was burst.

"Come on, honey, perk up. We'll go look at the cats, and you'll forget all about Michael." He squeezed her shoulder.

"Gary's not as good-looking as you." She pursed her lips.

He smiled. "Thanks, nice of you to say."

Eve finally smiled, tugged on his hand, and pulled him along. "Let's go see the cats from the no-kill shelter first."

They reached the rescue cat section with an array of people peering into the two rows of cages. As they worked their way through the congestion, Eve admired and spoke to each cat. Her love and compassion melted Phil's heart. He felt bad that they couldn't adopt one for her.

He rubbed her shoulders and said, "Someday you'll be able to have one."

"I know. It's nice so many are getting homes, even though not in mine." She sighed.

Over the loudspeaker the announcer called for Siamese cats to be taken to judging ring three—first call.

"Hey, do you want to go watch the judging for a few minutes?" Eve glanced up at him.

"Sure, but we'd better not stay too long. We need to get something for lunch and then get back to our space so Betty can get back to her T-shirts."

They meandered along, taking a few minutes to look at cat merchandise along the route to the judging ring. Eve stopped before a jewelry table and fixated on the bracelets.

"Do you see anything you want?" Phil asked.

"I think Mom would like this, don't you?" She held up a beautiful stretch bracelet with a very impressive tiger's face.

Phil leaned over and peered at the tag. "Says it's a Japanese good fortune bracelet."

Eve looked inside the gift box and read the leaflet. "Represents strength, good fortune, success, and protection from negative forces." Her blue eyes sparkled. "This is perfect! I love it, don't you?"

"Yeah, it's nice, and she'd like it. I'll go in on it with you. She deserves it."

"Really? Thanks, Uncle Phil."

They paid for the bracelet, and Eve stuck it in her backpack. When they neared the show cats waiting in their elaborate enclosures with fancy printed material, bows, and other adornments, they had to stop a couple times to let people with Siamese cats pass by unhindered, otherwise, they might earn dirty looks from the owners for frightening the cats. Phil liked seeing the purebred cats, but he always wondered why so many folks opted to spend so much money instead of adopting the unfortunate homeless cats from the shelters.

"Last call for Siamese cats to ring three," the announcer's voice boomed over the speaker.

Eve darted off to get a closer look at a beautiful Himalayan cat in a cage decorated with paw print fabric. He moved over to join her in the Himalayan section and nearly bumped into a guy carrying a Siamese cat. The cat was gorgeous—huge, wild, bright blue eyes. Its seal point coloring brought out the blue even more, and Phil hoped he hadn't scared the poor creature too badly. Then, he noticed the man's smoldering dark eyes as he scrutinized him through a pair of dark-rimmed glasses. Their gazes locked for a second causing his heart rate to increase. At first, he expected the guy to tell him off for getting in the way, but then the man hurried by toward ring number three.

He stood there in stunned silence. The man's eyes reminded him of a time gone by, when things were simple and innocent. Craning his neck, he tried to catch another glimpse of the guy, but he'd faded into the crowd. How could a pair of eyes look so much like... His hands were shaking, but why? He'd never seen the man before, but there was something familiar about him. Was it possible? After all, it had been years since he'd seen the guy who used to be his... his everything... He wouldn't even know what he looked like now.

He caught up to Eve, who had moved down the aisle of Himalayans and was bent over peering closely into a cage. "Hey, we'd better get our lunch and get back. I don't want to keep Betty waiting," he said.

Eve straightened and stared up at him, her eyes widening. "What's wrong? You look like you've seen a ghost."

He just stood there at a loss for words, still distracted by the odd encounter.

"Uncle Phil, you're scaring me, your face is so white. Nothing happened to Mom..."

"No, no... nothing like that. I'm sorry, honey. Uh, I don't know why I look weird. Nothing's wrong." He ran his hand down his face.

"You're probably hungry—let's go get something." She tugged on his arm.

He tried to calm down while they walked to the food vendors, but he couldn't get those dark brown eyes out of his mind. They were so familiar... so was the man's height and build—compared to him, the guy appeared to be a couple inches shorter and about fifteen pounds lighter.

"Uncle Phil, you're still pale. Come sit down." She took his hand and steered him to a small table with a couple of chairs. "Tell me what to get for you, and I'll go get in line. You sit here and rest."

The smells coming from the food stands made his stomach growl. From his chair he scanned the lunch choices. "I think I'll get Chinese, but I can go get it with you. I don't need to sit down." He started to stand up, but Eve nudged him back down.

Brushing her hand away, he stood up. "Stop. I'm perfectly okay, just hungry. Now chill out, please."

Eve gave him a narrow-eyed, reproving stare, as if she was a teacher and he was her obstinate student, but they walked over to the line together.

While they waited for their food, Eve smiled and relaxed. He assumed he must have more color in his face now. The whole incident with the strange man was stupid, and he couldn't believe he'd overreacted like that.

They took their lunch back to their booth, thanked Betty, and set their food on the little display table to eat and wait for more customers.

Phil finished his meal, and he cracked open the fortune cookie. He held the little paper in his fingers reading the words to himself as he ate the cookie.

Be on the lookout for coming events, they cast their shadows beforehand.

He stuck the message into his pocket when a man who had bought and paid for a cat tree earlier came to retrieve it. He helped the customer haul his purchase out to his van while Eve stayed behind finishing her lunch.

When he returned, Eve was busy showing a young couple one of the cat trees. She engaged with them like a professional saleslady, asking about their cats, telling them how much fun they'd have watching them play on it. She was so confident, poised, and friendly. Gail would be proud. And, she made the sale. Smiling, he stepped in to help her fill out the sales slip and collect the money.

The man and woman insisted on carrying the tower out on their own. He watched them maneuver the large tree with three big perches down the aisle without bumping into anyone.

Eve tapped his arm, and he noticed her eyes were focused off to the right. She whispered, "There's a man staring at us—don't look."

He lifted one eyebrow. "Uh, how do you know he's staring, and how can I see him if I don't look?"

She furrowed her brow. "I meant don't just turn and look real quick. You know, be nonchalant."

"It's probably someone wanting to look at the towers."

He casually followed Eve's gaze and drew in a breath. The Siamese cat guy he'd almost collided with earlier—the man with the dark brown eyes—stood near a display of litter boxes about forty feet away.

"It looks like he's trying to hide behind that display of self-cleaning litter boxes," Eve whispered, as if the man could hear her. "He's peeking out—this is weird."

"I don't think he's staring at us," Phil said, but it actually did seem like he was.

Is the blood draining from my face again?

He flicked his gaze to the man a couple times to try for a better look, but he simply could not tell if this could be who the guy kind of resembled.

Some customers appeared, and he had to give them his attention. Eve joined in to help show off the trees and one woman placed a custom order. By the time he took down the information, the brown-eyed man was gone.

During the last few hours of the day, he tried to push the guy out of his mind and concentrate on selling the last of the cat trees, but he had the urge to walk over to the Siamese cat section and take another look at the man with the brown eyes. Just when he got up the courage to go over there, his heart started to race, so he decided to let it go. What was the point? Even if by some stroke of fate it happened to be the person he used to know, they had nothing to say to each other.

By the end of the day, there were only a few towers left. A sense of relief filled him as he counted the sales receipts. He really didn't want to return for a second day. On Monday, he'd be starting work at a new job site, and he could use a quiet Sunday to relax.

Driving away from the municipal auditorium, Phil turned to Eve and asked, "Do you want a snack before we get on the freeway?"

"Sure, what kind of snack?"

"How about some ice cream."

"How about a Frappuccino at Starbucks?" She toyed with the end of her ponytail.

"Uh, well, I guess they have those without coffee."

"I drink coffee."

He turned to her, caught her eye, and considered her statement for a second. "Are you sure... Your mom says it's okay?"

Eve laughed, "Well, yeah..."

"Okay, then, Starbucks it'll be. Who am I to argue."

Phil located a Starbucks with little trouble and parked where they'd be able to see the truck and trailer from inside. He suggested a non-coffee drink, but Eve wasn't having any of that, so they ordered Java Chip Frappuccinos. After their order was called, they took seats near the window.

Eve studied him intently.

"Did I spill some already?" He brushed his fingers over his shirt.

"No, you're all right," Eve said. "I mean, your color is better now—not all white like earlier. What was wrong with you before lunch anyway?"

"Nothing was wrong. I don't know what you're talking about." He took a long, fast drink from his straw, which caused a sharp headache. "Damn." He pressed his hand against his forehead.

Eve rose partway out of the chair. "What's the matter, Uncle Phil?"

He smiled at her. "Nothing. Sit down. I just got a brain freeze."

"Whew, don't scare me like that." She plopped back down on the chair and took a drink.

"Why would you be scared? Haven't you seen someone with a headache before?" He pretended to be irritated.

She twirled her straw. "Considering how you looked earlier, I wasn't sure what to think... What happened back at the Himalayan cages?"

"I was hungry." He sipped from his straw.

Eve fixed a skeptical stare on him. He didn't want to explain it to her, but she wasn't going to give up.

Leaning toward her slightly, he said, "Okay, it's like this..."

She put her drink down, leaned in too, and regarded him without blinking an eye.

"When you were looking at the Himalayan cats, I almost ran into a guy carrying a Siamese."

Her mouth dropped open slightly. "Did he tell you off? Did you have a fight? Is that what happened?"

"Don't interrupt. Let me finish, okay?"

"Sorry." She blinked a few times and sat back in her chair.

"He looked kind of familiar—like someone I used to know a long time ago."

Eve leaned in again, her eyes wide, and whispered, "Like an old boyfriend?"

He looked down at the table. "Yeah."

She sat up straighter, and her voice got louder and more excited. "You couldn't tell if it was him? Didn't he recognize you either?"

"He left California for New York, and we haven't seen each other in fifteen years." He tamped down the anger he'd held on to all these years.

"Wow, no wonder you seemed to be in shock," Eve said, more subdued. "Wait a minute... that man hiding behind the litter boxes..."

"He wasn't hiding behind the litter boxes."

"Yes. He. Was. And he was definitely staring at you. Was that the Siamese cat man?"

He took a deep breath. "Yeah, that was him, but I don't know..."

"Why else would he be lurking around? To see if it was really you... I wonder why he didn't come over?" She finally took another drink of her Frappuccino. "Wait, when you saw him with his cat, why didn't you ask him if he was... What was his name?"

"Cole Fisher," he mumbled, rubbing his forehead.

"Why didn't you say, Cole is that you?"

"Because by the time I thought of doing that, he'd rushed off to the ring."

"We should have gone to watch the judging, and then you could have talked to him. Or, you could have walked over to the litter boxes to find out if it was him or not."

He shook his head. "I didn't want to talk to him."

"You're confusing me, Uncle Phil."

"Like I said, it probably wasn't even him. Can we drop it now, honey? Let's finish our drinks. We've got a long drive home."

"This is so weird..."

He sighed. "Tell me about it."

CHAPTER TWO

COLE LIFTED the cat carrier from the passenger seat of his Lincoln Navigator, trying not to jiggle Moonshadow too much. "Let's get you inside, champ. You've had a long day."

As he neared the entrance of the house, he narrowed his eyes at three large boxes in front of the door. He hadn't ordered anything, so he couldn't imagine what they were. Pushing one of the boxes out of the way with his foot was impossible—it was too heavy, so he set the cat carrier down and lifted all three out of the way. The return address on the mailing labels was New York. The packages had come from his ex.

Annoyed, he unlocked the front door and stepped inside. "Hey, Moonbeam, we're baaaack!"

After he set the cage down and quickly unlatched its door, he dashed over to the security alarm control panel and disarmed it. Moonshadow exited the cage and headed for the sofa. He watched closely to make sure the cat used one of the scratching posts positioned at either end. The rented house was furnished, and he didn't want his cat destroying the furniture.

When he was satisfied that Moonshadow wasn't going to sink his claws into the fabric on the couch, he scanned the room for his other Siamese cat. Moonbeam came slinking into the room as if he was afraid Cole had brought another human in with him.

Fat chance.

"Relax, no one's here but me and your brother." He turned toward the door. "I'll get you guys some dinner after I unload the SUV and get those boxes inside."

He carried the three boxes in and set them on the floor, not pleased at all that Meredith had sent them. He then went to the SUV and retrieved a bag of groceries he'd grabbed on the way home. Uneasy about leaving Moonshadow in the car alone, he'd hurriedly thrown food into the cart at the corner store.

In the kitchen, he pulled milk and eggs out of the bag and put them in the refrigerator. There was bread, cereal, and coffee too. In his hurry, he had made good choices. The cats soon joined him and rubbed on his legs, letting him know they were hungry and wanted dinner—like ten minutes ago.

"You've got dry food, you know." He looked at the food dishes near the back door. "Plenty there," he said. "Let me get your fresh water."

He filled the water bowl, and then he opened the cupboard where he kept the canned cat food. Both cats communicated their wishes with piercing cries.

"I'm getting it as fast as I can, guys. Hold on."

He hastily opened a can of ocean whitefish, spilling a few drops of oily liquid onto his fingers. "Yuck," he groaned, wetting a paper towel to wipe his hands.

The cats quieted down, but they didn't take their eyes off him while he divided their meal into two small bowls. When he tried to take a step toward their placemat, they wrapped themselves around his legs again, demanding in high-pitched yowls that he put their food down at once. He finally got to the back door without tripping and set the dishes down.

"You can take it from here," he said, as the two happy cats stuck their faces into the bowls of smelly food.

He poured himself a glass of wine and headed for the couch. His first swallow hit the spot, and he stretched out to unwind. Before getting comfortable, he probably should have checked the litter box, but he could do that later. He kicked off his shoes.

The day had been enjoyable—the first cat show he'd attended since being back in California. Tomorrow he'd take Moonshadow back for the final day of judging.

Would he see that guy again who'd almost bumped into him on the way to the ring? He'd been so startled at first, imagining the man might be someone he used to know. Of course that was impossible. He had no idea why he'd gone looking for him later, but he was glad he had because seeing him again proved it couldn't have been Phillip. The girl with him looked to be about the age of his own daughter, Dana, and there was no way Phillip Thompson could have a child.

He took another sip of his wine. Phillip had an older sister named Gail. The girl could be Phillip's niece. He chuckled out loud at his stupidity. The man wasn't anyone he knew. Why the thought had ever entered his mind was beyond him. Phil probably lived across the country now—possibly in Colorado. That was where they'd always said they wanted to go. Maybe he'd made it.

He set the empty wine glass on the end table with a hard clunk, and it almost fell over. Letting out a frustrated sigh, he got up and trudged over to the boxes. Standing over them and wondering what was inside, he tried to work up the gumption to open them.

Moonshadow and Moonbeam came into the room and jumped onto the couch. Maybe they wanted to see what was in the boxes too, or more likely, they wanted to jump inside once he emptied them out. The cats curled up on the still-warm cushion he'd been sitting on with contented looks on their dark little faces.

He grabbed a utility knife from the desk in the corner of the room and cut through the packing tape on the first box. After opening the flaps, he peered inside. It was filled with books—his old college books for drafting and architecture, and novels he liked to read in his free time. No wonder the box was so heavy. He cut open the other two and found more of the same. Why had she sent them?

He found his old high school yearbook among the collection. Flipping through a few pages in the middle section, he detected a musty smell. No wonder, since he hadn't opened it in over fifteen years.

He thumbed through the pages and stopped at the pictures of the basketball team. His gaze landed on the one of him and Phillip. He remembered that day like it was yesterday. They both had that crazy-in-love look in their eyes, but he didn't think anyone had ever put two and two together. To all their classmates they'd been buddies, nothing more.

They'd had everyone fooled... at least for a while.

Hard to believe this picture was taken seventeen years ago. He'd talked Phillip into trying out for the basketball team with him, and to his surprise, Phil had turned out to be a better player than he was. He searched through the pages of senior pictures and located Phillip. This was how he remembered him—young and handsome. Letting out a breath of air, he focused in on his kind, gentle, blue eyes. He put his finger over the bottom of Phil's face. He'd never seen him with a beard. The man at the cat show had eyes so much like the young man in the picture, but he'd had a scruffy beard and mustache.

After searching through the pages of high school memories, he finally found Phillip's message near the back of the book. The simple words he'd scribbled stabbed at Cole's heart even after all these years.

We'll take on this world in style.

He abruptly shut the yearbook and tossed it on the floor. That had been enough of a walk down memory lane.

Back in the kitchen, he washed out the cat's bowls and poured another glass of wine. He stomped back to the living room and went over to the boxes again, becoming more and more irritated by their presence. With his free hand, he picked up the yearbook and shoved it back into the box and closed the lid. After taking a long drink of wine, he paced back and forth in front of the boxes a few times.

Where in the hell was he supposed to store these? They were so heavy he didn't want to haul them up the stairs. Maybe he could carry them into the laundry room tomorrow. He took another long sip of wine, went to the desk, grabbed his phone, and dialed Meredith. She picked up after a few rings.

"Cole, what do you want?" she snapped.

The cutting edge in those few chastising words caught him off guard. Even for her it seemed unreasonable. He swished the wine in the glass for a few seconds and tried not to lose his temper.

Why the hell did I even call her?

"Obviously you're not glad to hear from me," he responded.

"I don't like hearing from anyone at this hour," she said, still obviously irked.

Not quite understanding what she meant, he tried to gather his thoughts. He sat down at the desk.

"It's going on midnight, Cole... I'm wide awake now though so talk. Why are you calling?"

He rubbed his eyes, leaving his glasses lopsided, so he straightened them and looked at the clock. The time difference had totally slipped his mind. "I forgot what time..."

"I'll ask again, what do you want?"

Her sour attitude wasn't helping his mood. "I called to ask why you sent all these boxes of books here," he barked.

When she didn't answer instantly, he continued. "I thought you understood that I didn't want anything sent until I'm in the new house. Now I'll have to haul these boxes over there. I don't need them here."

"Oh, you poor thing. Are they inconveniencing you?" she spit out.

He started to answer, but she spoke over him. "I needed the space—they were in my way, so I packed them up and sent them. Would you rather I'd thrown them out? I'm moving my office to the den, and the books needed to go."

"Well, I don't want you to send anything else—not until I'm in the new house."

"Yes, dear... certainly," she said snidely.

"It's lucky no one walked off with these. I was gone all day, and I came home to find them on the porch." He finished off the wine.

"Are you drinking?" she asked.

He ignored the question and looked over at Moonshadow and Moonbeam sleeping peacefully. He tried to speak in a calmer voice. "Dana can come this summer even if the new house isn't ready. There's an extra bedroom here. The new house is running on schedule though—a carpenter is starting in the kitchen on Monday."

"Doesn't sound very safe there in Oak Hills if you're surprised the packages remained on the porch today. If need be we can postpone the visit."

He clutched the phone in anger. "Don't look for excuses. There's no reason to wait. Like I said, I expect the new place to be ready, but if it's not, this house is fine. A girl her age would find a lot to do around here. And, it's plenty safe."

"She's a city girl, Cole. To be honest, I can't really picture her out there in Oak Hills or Apple Valley for that matter."

He stood up and paced around the desk. "It'll do her good to see a different side of life, and she's coming—you know that's the agreement."

"We'll talk about it later. You might be in the mood to talk since it's only nine o'clock there, but it's midnight here."

"Yeah, yeah, you told me that... Hey, before I go, how is our daughter?" He sat down again and waited for Meredith's answer.

"She's fine. She misses the cats."

"That's another reason she should come this summer. I can take her to a cat show while she's here."

"You're going to show the cats again?"

"I had Moonshadow to a show today. That's where I was when the packages were delivered."

"I don't know why you drag yourself and the cats out like that. Don't you have enough to keep you busy?"

"You know I like doing it, Meredith. I need a distraction from work. It relaxes me, and it's not that often anyway."

"Whatever. Well, I'm not making any promises about Dana's visit now. If that's all, I'm going back to bed."

"Okay... Before you hang up..."

When the silence drew out, she asked, "Do you have something more to say?"

He ran his fingers through his hair. "Uh, I just want to say again that I'm sorry for how things turned out for us, that's all. I'm just sorry."

"Yeah, we've been through this, Cole. I know you're sorry."

"Okay, then. Well, goodnight."

"Goodnight."

He ended the call, tossed his phone on the desk, and sat there for several long minutes, leaning back in the chair with his eyes closed. The day hadn't ended on a very high note, but there was always tomorrow...and Dana *would* be coming this summer.

After climbing up the stairs and walking down a short hallway, he opened the door to the extra room and stared into the cluttered space that didn't look anything like a bedroom. Only he knew there was a bed in there hidden beneath his plans and drawings. Work stuff even covered the dresser and chest of drawers. The drafting table with a swing-arm desk lamp positioned smack dab in the middle did nothing to make the room inviting to a twelve-year-old girl. He turned away and closed the door.

On Monday morning, he'd check with the general contractor to make sure the crew arrived at his new house as planned. He might have to make some visits to the site to light a fire under their butts. The house had to be move-in ready for the summer.

CHAPTER THREE

PHIL CAREFULLY disentangled his legs from the bed sheets, mindful not to disturb Batman who was curled up by his feet and Robin stretched out along his side. They'd scolded him something awful when he'd gotten home from the cat show last evening, wanting their canned food and some attention—in that order.

The events of the day had run through his mind the entire evening. Actually, it was the brown-eyed man who'd occupied his thoughts. He'd tried to watch TV, do a few household chores, and play with the cats, but he hadn't been able to concentrate on anything. When he'd crawled into bed at midnight, the grey tabby brothers had joined him, their soft purrs lulling him to sleep. He'd slept like a rock, which surprised him considering how crazy the day had been.

Once he was able to sit up, he gently stroked both cats and whispered, "good morning," before stumbling out of bed and heading straight for the bathroom. Batman and Robin were quiet while he used the toilet and then the sink, but by the time he was ready to step into the shower, paws appeared under the door. He ignored them, and when he stepped out of the shower, the bathroom door was rattling—getting louder by the second as if they were trying to pry it open. After quickly drying himself off halfway, he peeked out the door.

Looking down at four wide, round eyes, he said, "Be right with you, hold on."

With the door ajar, he finished drying off and went into the bedroom to put on his jeans and T-shirt. The cats weren't there, so he figured they must be waiting for him in the kitchen.

Dressed and ready for the day, he joined Batman and Robin for breakfast. First, he checked their bowls by the side of the refrigerator, which were half full of dry cat food. Then, he changed the water in their big ceramic bowl and opened a bag of chicken flavored cat treats, sprinkling out several on the floor for each cat. They lived for treats.

"Live to eat instead of eat to live," he said to the pair as they crunched.

I should talk.

He reached for the box of Cocoa Krispies cereal and filled his bowl. Fixing something heathier took too much time. Besides that, cooking wasn't something he enjoyed much.

Opening the refrigerator, he brought out the Cran-Strawberry juice and milk and set them on the table. Next, he filled a plastic measuring container with water and poured it into the coffee maker. He flipped the switch, and while the water dripped into the carafe, he stepped into the laundry room just off the kitchen to clean the litter box. Once that was done, he went outside to grab the newspaper from the yard. Back in the kitchen, he washed his hands and then plopped down in the chair at the table to finally eat breakfast and read the paper.

From where he sat, he had a good view of the cat tree next to the living room window where Batman and Robin were settling down for their first nap of the day. A lazy Sunday—just what he needed before the new job began early Monday morning. He spent some quiet time reading and watching the cats.

At ten o'clock, he wandered out to the garage to cut out perches for cat trees, including the ones for his custom order. He opened the garage door, and while he set up his sawhorses outside in the driveway, he waved at Chuck next door, wondering if his neighbor was going to ask to borrow something. The man never seemed to have the right tools for his do-it-yourself projects, but he got in his car and left, so Phil went about his work uninterrupted. His mind wasn't totally on what he was doing though.

Seeing that guy at the cat show who'd looked similar to Cole had gotten him thinking about the past, and that was something he hadn't done much of in a long time. Keeping all that buried had been the best thing for him, and now, letting it get in his head was not in his best interest, not by a long shot. If the golf course community where Cole used to live hadn't found its way into his mind yesterday, maybe the guy wouldn't have reminded him of Cole at all.

He couldn't make sense out of the jumbled-up thoughts in his head. They were too bizarre—too painful. Cole lived in New York and was happily married. Yeah, right. He'd never for one minute believed that was a real marriage. But, the fact was, Cole couldn't have been at that cat show yesterday.

"Shit." He threw his hammer across the yard. "Why am I thinking of this now?"

He stomped into the garage and headed to the back, stopping in his tracks next to a big green canvas tarp covering what used to be his most prized possession. Maybe it still was. Why else had he covered it up to keep it safe?

Shortly after dropping out of college, he'd rented this house, and only uncovered the car a few times a year, just long enough to slap a current tag on the license plate and to fire up the engine to check the battery. With no intention of using the car, he felt kind of foolish changing the battery, airing up the tires when needed, and paying insurance, but just in case he ever wanted to drive it, he could, and that made him feel better in some strange way.

He yanked at the tarp, pulled it off, and piled it in a heap next to his beloved red Z28 Camaro. After kicking at the dusty tarp a couple times, silence filled up the space in his garage-turned-workshop before he crept slowly to the driver's door. He opened it, peeking in as if a ghost from his past might fly out and grab him. Taking a deep breath, he slid into the black bucket seat and put his hands on the steering wheel, closed his eyes, and leaned back against the headrest. Memories of when he was a teenager becoming a man flooded in as if they'd happened yesterday. Good ones and bad...

He'd gotten the used car in the middle of his sophomore year in high school—bought it with mostly his own money that he'd saved up for years doing odd jobs and working part-time delivering pizzas. Gail had loaned him the rest, and he'd paid her back each month until they were square. This Camaro was worth every cent. His dad had gone with him to look at the car and had helped him make the deal with the private party seller. Even though his mom and dad had barely been able to make ends meet, they'd made sure he had insurance.

This red sports car had been the reason Cole had noticed him. Cole ran with a different crowd, but they'd had two classes together that semester, and Phil thought he was the best-looking guy in school with his athletic build and broad shoulders. Cole's dark brown eyes framed by thick dark eyebrows were to die for. Since Phil had never seen him with a girl hanging on him like all the other jocks, he'd hoped he was gay, but even if that were true, he hadn't thought Cole even knew his name. He had never imagined in a million years that Cole Fisher would give him a second look, but everything changed the day he'd driven into the parking lot in his Z28.

Cole had a white BMW at the time—real nice in Phil's opinion, even though it was over ten years old. Later, after they'd gotten together, Cole had called it a "mom mobile." He'd been embarrassed to drive it and said he would rather have a red Camaro Z28, and that riding shotgun was way better than driving an old hand-me-down from his mother. Phil had been proud of his car before that, but Cole's admiration of it had put him straight over the moon.

He tried to picture how Cole had looked sitting in the passenger seat, young and innocent... guilty as sin. That described the both of them back then.

If this Chevy could talk...

They'd become inseparable from that first day when Cole had stopped to admire the Camaro. Phil had also realized that Cole had known his name after all, and that had surprised him. Around school, and even in class, Cole had never acted like he knew Phil existed.

But he had known.

He reached under the floor mat for the key and turned it in the ignition, bringing the car to life. When he revved the engine, it sounded fine. Suddenly, he felt like taking it for a spin. Not sure what had gotten into him, he got out and moved the tools out of the way and then pulled the car out of the garage, looked under the hood and checked the tire pressure. Satisfied that all was well, he quickly locked the house and garage before burning rubber out of the driveway. Halfway up the street his better sense kicked in and he slowed down and drove like a thirty-five-year-old man instead of a sixteen-year-old kid.

He'd been so lost in his head all day, he'd forgotten to eat lunch, so he pulled into the first fast-food place along the way and entered the drive-through. With the lunch rush over, he quickly got his food and parked under a tree to eat his burger, fries, and Coke in the shade. He should have called Eve and invited her to lunch, but she'd probably already eaten. When he was done, he'd pick her up and take her for a spin. She'd never even seen his red Camaro. She knew there was a car covered up in his garage, but he'd never shown it to her.

Shortly, he was cruising down Apache Road and then pulling into the parking lot of Gail and Eve's apartment building. He pulled into a space close to their unit and revved the engine a few times to see if Gail or Eve might hear it and look out. No one came to the window, so he turned the car off and got out. He took the steps two at a time to the second floor and knocked on door 20A.

After several seconds, the door cracked open as far as the chain lock would allow, and Gail peeked out. Her narrowed eyes widened then brightened, and a big smile lit up her face.

"What are you doing here? Come in!" She quickly undid the chain, threw open the door, and tugged him inside by the arm.

His sister wore jeans and a loose-fitting denim painter's smock, and she held a small paint brush covered in blue paint in her free hand. A pink headband held back her curly hair from her face. She was the image of an artist who'd been hard at work.

"Looks like I caught you at a bad time." Phil looked around the room at several paintings displayed on easels, wondering which one she'd been working on when he'd interrupted her.

"That's okay. I need a break." She went over to an easel and stuck the brush into a small cup of water. Phil followed and checked out the half-done painting of two horses in a stable.

"This is beautiful," he said.

She put her hands on her hips. "Thanks. I hope it will be when it's all done. I was working on the sky."

"It already is... Really. It's excellent." He glanced around at some of the other paintings—quite a collection—animals, scenery, even one of a field of wildflowers.

"Where's Eve?" he asked.

"She went to the movies with her BFF. Unfortunately she's moving at the end of the school year. Eve's so sad..."

"I hate being dense, but what's a BFF?"

Gail raised her eyebrows. "Her best friend."

"Oh, yeah, of course... Sorry to hear she's moving."

"Eve will be okay. It's just a change she'll have to get used to. Hey, I need to thank you for the bracelet. You two didn't need to get me anything." She raised her wrist and shook the bracelet, showing it off. "I know I shouldn't be wearing it around the paint..."

"You can wear it whenever and wherever you want."

Gail smiled. "You two spoil me. Are you thirsty?" She moved toward the kitchen.

"I can take you out for coffee if you can spare a little time away from all this." He glanced around the room again.

She stopped in her tracks and shot him a big smile. "Okay, sounds good. And there's something I want to ask you."

He tilted his head and displayed a half-smile. "Oh, yeah? Is it serious?"

"Well, you'll have to tell me." She grabbed her purse, paused and said, "Maybe I should change."

"You look great. Come as you are."

They left the apartment and started down the stairs. "Hey, I don't see your truck." Gail scanned the parking lot.

"I'm not in the truck today."

"What?" She cut her gaze toward the Camaro. "Oh my God, you're driving this now? Since when?" A spring immediately appeared in her step, and she headed for the passenger side and flung the door open. "What are you waiting for? Take me for a ride!" She immediately got in and put on the seatbelt. "I should have dressed better," she muttered with a smile.

"I see you still recognize the car." Phil slid in behind the wheel.

"Of course. I'm surprised it still runs after sitting in your garage so long... or have you had it out?"

"No, this is the first time in..." He lowered his head.

"Since you came back early from college?"

"Don't rub it in." He smiled weakly and hooked his seat belt.

"Sorry. Can I ask why today?"

Phil turned onto Bear Valley Road and headed toward Starbucks. "You can ask, but I'm not sure I can answer." He fiddled with the radio and settled for a country music station, turning it up loud.

They were quiet the rest of the way to the coffee shop. Phil pulled in and parked and they went inside, got their drinks, and sat down at a table. He was about to take his first sip when he noticed Gail staring at him. She didn't look away, and he remembered she wanted to ask him something.

He took a deep breath. "Uh, what's on your mind?"

Gail sipped her coffee. "Yeah... I'm not sure if there's a problem or not. It's just that Eve was acting sort of odd when she came home yesterday."

"Odd how?"

Gail shrugged. "I don't know... you can read her face like a book, and she just looked funny. I asked her how the day went, and she told me about that guy, Michael, and how disappointed she was when he turned up with a boyfriend, but I still got the feeling there was something else she wasn't saying. When I asked about the rest of the day, she seemed kind of vague."

"Was it before she gave you the gift? Maybe she was excited to surprise you."

Gail pressed her lips together for a few moments before responding. "It was both before and after. She just seemed a little off—not herself."

Phil rubbed his chin. "Well, I guess it wasn't because of the bracelet then..."

"It looks like you have an idea what was on her mind. If you do, please tell me."

"It's kind of a long story. The whole day was a little bizarre." He pinched the bridge of his nose.

"I'm listening. If it affected Eve, I need to know."

"Okay, here goes." Phil slumped down in his chair and went over the highlights and lowlights of the day at the cat show, pausing to sip his coffee now and then.

Gail hung on every word, sighing when Phil mentioned how Eve had looked at the rescue cats and had shopped for the bracelet. When he got to the part about the brown-eyed man, she sat up straight with wide eyes.

"Don't jump to conclusions," Phil said. "It wasn't him... it couldn't have been. My mind was just playing tricks on me."

"Even so, the guy standing around spying on the two of you— that's creepy. He couldn't have been looking at Eve, could he?" She rubbed her shoulder.

"No, no... it wasn't like that. Maybe he'd thought about buying a cat tree and then he changed his mind. That's what I think."

She let out a deep breath. "For you to tell Eve about Cole, you must have thought it could have been him. Why are you changing your mind?"

"Because I realized how dumb it was to even think for a second that it was him—it wasn't."

"But the guy definitely got you thinking about Cole. That's why you're driving the Camaro today."

Phil pinched his temples and sighed. "I'd really love it if we could drop the subject. I told you what happened, and that's all there is to it."

He finished the last of his coffee. Thinking about how Eve had kept what had happened at the cat show to herself, like their own little secret, made him happy inside.

Gail patted him on the hand and then picked up her empty cup and napkin. She stood up, and Phil did the same and he walked with her toward the door. They threw their trash in the bin on the way, and he held the door open for her.

Outside, he glanced at her. "If you don't need to get back right away, what do you say we drive out to the cemetery. I haven't been to Dad's grave in a while. Do you want to go?"

She looked up at him and then gave him a quick hug. "Eve won't be home for a while yet, and I can't think of a better way to spend a Sunday afternoon, so yeah, let's go."

Before stepping off the sidewalk, Gail stopped to gaze at the shiny red car. "It still looks great."

He smiled. "Yeah, even at over twenty years old."

"We're not getting any younger," Gail said. She opened the passenger door. "I haven't called Mom in quite a while, how about you?"

They settled into their seats and put their seat belts on.

"No, I haven't called her either. Seems like when I do, she's busy and can't really talk." He started the car.

"Well, it's good for her to stay busy. The move to Santa Barbara to live with Aunt Ruth was good for her."

"Yeah, it was." He pulled down the sun visor.

"I have an idea. Why don't we stop and get some flowers for Dad's grave?"

"That sounds like a plan," he answered.

Sighing, Gail said quietly, "I sure miss him."

Phil missed his dad more than he could say. At least he had a truckload of good memories to bring up when he needed them, which was more than some people had—Cole for one. He scratched his head and tried to blot out his last memory of Cole's closed-minded old man, but the red, twisted face of William Fisher glaring at him with disdain and hatred was hard to forget. Shaking his head, he pushed the unpleasant thoughts away. He'd be damned if he let the likes of William Fisher ruin such a perfect day.

CHAPTER FOUR

HOLDING A glass of wine and stretching his legs out on the couch, Cole took a sip and closed his eyes. Moonshadow and Moonbeam would have to wait until morning to see their new present. Trying to wrestle the cat tree he'd bought at the cat show out of his Navigator was just too much on this Sunday night. In the morning when he wasn't as wiped out, he'd have no problem hauling it in.

The guy he'd seen yesterday hadn't been at the show today, and he'd been a little disappointed. Seeing him again would have proved once and for all that he was not Phillip. Plus, he could have checked out the guy's cat trees a little closer before deciding what to buy. From what he remembered, they looked like carpeted monstrosities, but they appeared sturdy and well-made.

I wonder why he wasn't there today.

He was very satisfied with the cat tower he'd chosen though. The one he purchased today was more sophisticated and classier and would suit his Siamese cats perfectly. He could picture Moonbeam and Moonshadow lounging on the elegant, sleek tiers. They needed an alternative to relax on so he could keep the furniture snag free and clean.

He'd fed the cats as soon as he and Moonshadow had gotten

home, and then the two had run up the stairs, likely settling down on his bed for a grooming session. Those two loved washing each other. Moonshadow was probably telling his brother all about the ribbon he'd won to add to his collection. Moonbeam had several of his own too.

The ringing telephone next to him put an abrupt end to his musings. He set his wine glass on the end table and quickly grabbed it. He smiled at the name in the display, sat up on the couch, and greeted his daughter.

"Dana, sweetie, how are you?"

"Hi, Father, how are you?"

"I asked you first."

"I'm all right, I guess."

"What's wrong, sweetie, you're not sick, are you?" He ran his hand through his hair.

"No, I'm not sick." The silence went on for a few beats, and she finally said, "Father, I just wanted you to know that I really am looking forward to being in California this summer. I like the idea of doing things I've never done before—living in a place that's different than here."

"Well, I'm glad you're anxious to come out. I'm working hard to make sure the new house is ready by the time you arrive."

"I don't mind staying at the rented place you're in now—anyplace is fine with me. I just want to spend time with you and Moonbeam and Moonshadow."

"And we can't wait for you to be with us." He leaned forward on the couch, resting his elbows on his knees. "Sweetie, I'm sorry I had to bring the cats with me, but your mother never was good at—"

"I know. She doesn't like pets that much."

"Dana, your mother didn't say anything about postponing your trip, did she?"

"She mentioned it a couple times lately. I told her I want to go." She let out a loud, frustrated sigh. "Father, she's a city girl, and she thinks I'm like her, but I'm not."

She sounded so mature and sure of herself. Cole grinned and switched the phone to his other ear. "I'm positive we'll have a lot of fun, sweetie. You know I grew up here and I've sure missed it, and I'm glad to be back. Los Angeles isn't far in case we decide we want to get a taste of the city. I want to take you to a cat show while you're here."

"I'd love that. I can't wait for school to end. Summer this year is going to be so wonderful. I miss you and the cats so much."

"Are you doing okay in school? No problems?" He leaned back against a throw pillow on the couch.

"Everything is fine, but I'm ready for vacation and being with you."

"I want that too, Dana. I think about you every day. What about your friends—you won't miss them?"

"Everyone has plans for the summer and I'm glad I do too."

"Me too."

"I'd better go before Mother sees me on the phone and starts having a fit."

Cole detected a slight giggle, and he chuckled in return. "That wouldn't be a pretty sight."

"Okay. Well, goodnight then." Before she ended the call, he heard her softly say, "Promise you'll fight for me if she tries to change plans."

"I promise, sweetie." He set his phone down and took a deep breath.

Things were going to work out. He'd see to it.

After sitting a little while longer with his eyes closed, he left the couch and went upstairs into the extra room. He turned on the laptop he kept on a small computer table against the side wall. During the boot up, he looked around, wondering again how he'd ever manage to rearrange the space into a bedroom for Dana if his move was delayed. Making the room comfortable and appealing to his daughter was a daunting task. Removing all his stuff wasn't an option. He had a big project in the works—a new office building complex an hour away in Pomona.

His new home must be completed by the time Dana arrived, and he wouldn't take any excuses from the general contractor. He figured he could carve out some time tomorrow afternoon to make a visit to the house. And it wouldn't be a bad idea to check around the neighborhood to see if there were any kids Dana's age living nearby.

He was not going to get himself all worked up about this. More than likely the house would be ready. If not, it wouldn't be the end of the world. At least his life was a hell of a lot better now that he and Meredith were divorced. These little problems were nothing compared to the hellish life he'd lived all those years he'd been married—and watching his mother slip away... and then waiting for his father to die. His daughter had been the only bright spot during that time. She still was the best thing in his life.

He sat down at the computer and began searching for points of interest and activities in the Apple Valley area. In his teenage years, there were places he liked to go for fun, but things had surely changed, and maybe those activities were gone and replaced by others. He needed to familiarize himself with what the area had to offer and if it would appeal to Dana.

He typed *Regional Park* in the search bar. The park used to be a great place to enjoy nature—fishing, hiking, horseback riding, and camping. Would it be too outdoorsy for Dana even though she seemed open to expanding her horizons?

He looked over the photos, and all that he remembered about the place still seemed to be the same.

Some things never change.

Closing his eyes, he thought about the nights he'd spent parked out there in Phillip's red Z28. He didn't know whether to laugh or cry as he recalled all the hot and heavy make out sessions with the windows down and the smell of the fresh-cut hay floating through the warm night air... No one saw a thing except the big yellow moon above.

God, those were the days.

Suddenly longing to see the park again, he wished he'd have rented a place in Apple Valley instead of clear up in Oak Hills. He was basically hiding out here because he'd been scared of running into Phillip, even though it was a remote possibility that he was still in Apple Valley. That really didn't make sense though, because he'd chosen to build his new home in Apple Valley, a place he'd always loved. But by doing it this way, he could ease back into the area—test the waters—check it out and prove to himself there weren't any ghosts lurking around.

He wasn't sure what would make his heart ache the most—finding out once and for all that Phillip had left the state and was long gone, discovering he was still there and involved with someone, or learning he was single and getting punched in the face and told to take a flying leap.

Just seeing that guy who reminded him of Phillip at the cat show on Saturday had been enough to make his heart beat a mile a minute. Pretty dumb. He shook his head.

His life could have been so different. Goddamn his father, the ignorant SOB.

Chapter Five

"Batman, no!" Phil hollered from the doorway of the laundry room. He rushed to the countertop and grabbed the Crispy Chicken sandwich in the nick of time. "That's not your sandwich. It's mine."

Luckily the wrapping was covering his lunch, so Batman hadn't gotten any. He'd bought two sandwiches on his way home from Gail's last evening and had eaten one for his supper and saved this one to take in his lunch pail today.

He set some odds and ends from the pockets of the dirty clothes he'd left on top of the washing machine onto the counter and then stuffed the sandwich into the lunch box next to a small bag of potato chips and a snack pack of cookies. Earlier, he'd filled his thermos with iced tea.

"Where's Robin," he asked, while rubbing Batman's ears.

He received no answer from the cat, so he searched for Robin and found him in the first place he looked—curled up napping on top of the cat tree by the window. Satisfied that neither cat was locked in a closet or cupboard, he could leave with no worries.

On his way to the back door, he stopped at the counter to stick a dollar bill into his wallet and toss a gum wrapper into the trash. The wrinkled slip of paper he'd gotten out of the fortune cookie at the cat show caught his attention. He picked up the fortune but stopped short of throwing it away. He set it back on the counter, picked up his lunch pail, phone, and keys, and went out to his truck.

The fresh morning air energized him. Getting an early start was good since he'd never been to the address before so he needed enough time to find it. When the contractor had hired him, he'd told him the owner was in a hurry for the house to be finished and that he'd need to be there for as many hours per day as necessary to complete the job in a timely manner. He guessed he'd find out more today.

He estimated the house was about a twenty-minute drive at this early hour before people started on their commutes. He took the freeway for part of the distance, which was a lot faster than using the residential streets.

He exited the off-ramp nearest to his destination and turned left on Apple Blossom Lane. After driving several miles past all the stores, gas stations, and restaurants, he still couldn't find the street he was looking for. Had he gone the wrong way? He kept driving until he saw some nice new residential properties—some areas were finished and others were in the process of being constructed like the place he'd be working in.

After driving another few miles, he finally came to a large intersection marked Shadow Ridge, the name he'd been looking for, so he turned right. Shortly, nice looking, big modern houses appeared—a surprise after driving so far out in the boondocks.

He drove slowly, scanned the addresses, and determined the house was on the left side. He looked ahead as he crept along to find a partly finished home without landscaping and with work trucks parked outside.

Finally, he spotted the stucco and stone two-story home proudly standing at 15345 Shadow Ridge. The impressive house was like something straight out of a magazine. Not intimidatingly huge, but probably three times bigger than his rented house. The solar roof tiles drew his attention. And the wrought iron double front door was quite a work of art. An entry door like that made him think of the saying "a man's home is his castle." He tried to picture the place with landscaping. That would be the finishing touch.

Only one other truck was parked in the wide driveway leading up to the three-car garage, and an SUV was parked at the curb. He pulled into the driveway next to the black Ford.

Before he even opened his door, a guy, who he recognized as the contractor, appeared from the side of the garage and headed toward him. He got out of the truck and greeted Tom Anderson with a handshake.

"Good to see you, Phil. Follow me, and I'll show you where to set up shop."

He had to walk at a brisk pace to keep up with Tom, who led him along the side of the garage, through a gate, and into the backyard, which was considerably larger than the front. About seventy-five feet from where they stopped was an empty swimming pool surrounded by stone pool pavers.

"Plenty of space to set up here." Tom motioned with his hand.

They stood near a door into the house. He hoped this was the kitchen because that would help him work efficiently while building the custom-made cabinets.

"Come with me." Tom hurried to the door and opened it.

He followed and stepped into the large kitchen. A kitchen this size required many cupboards, so his work was cut out for him, but this was nothing he couldn't handle, and he looked forward to starting.

Tom rubbed his neck and blinked, and Phil got the impression his boss was anxious for things to get underway.

"I'll go get my tools set up, carry out the materials and get started."

Tom nodded. "Great. You've got your generator, I hope."

Before Phil could answer, Tom said, "Uh, I think I hear another truck—might be the electrician. Gotta go talk to him. The owner will probably show up later today. He's a little antsy to move in, and he wants to see how we're progressing, so don't be surprised if he stops by and breathes down your neck."

With that, Tom hurried off toward the front. Phil went out to his truck and a blue Dodge had parked on the other side of the black Ford. Tom and a man with long hair entered the house through the fancy front door.

Phil set his tool bags on the cement outside his truck. He hauled the generator to the backyard first, so he'd be able to run his power tools. On his second trip to his truck, the Ford's door was open. A guy in bib overalls rummaged through a toolbox on the passenger side. Phil didn't mean to stare, but the guy was making quite a racket. Suddenly, the man turned and stared back at him with his brows knitted together. With wrinkles lining his eyes, he appeared to be in his late sixties.

Phil was caught off guard and a little embarrassed for being caught staring. "Um... did you lose something?" he asked hesitantly.

"Don't you have anything better to do than to concern yourself with what I'm doing?" Between his gruff tone and the scowl on his face, he came across as an old grouch.

"Excuuuse me," Phil said, trying to hold in his annoyance. He picked up the tool bags.

The older man turned back to the toolbox and mumbled, "I can't find my damn tape measure."

He wasn't sure if the man was talking to himself or to him, but there was a tape measure clipped to the guy's pocket, so even if he might get his head bit off, he'd better take the chance and tell him.

"There's a tape measure clipped to your pocket."

The man straightened up and stepped away from his truck while running his hands all over the endless array of pockets on his overalls. His right hand stopped on the tape measure and he roared with laughter.

Phil couldn't help but smile at the unexpected reaction, and he chuckled.

The guy composed himself, took a few steps toward Phil, and stuck his hand out to shake. "My name's Howard. I'm the flooring man."

Phil shook his hand. "I'm Phil, the cabinet maker."

"Oh, so you're the carpenter. Well, I'll be doing the upstairs before I get to the kitchen—after you're finished with your part. We're on some kind of an accelerated timetable here from what I've been told, so that's why I was short with you. Sorry about that, but I don't like being rushed. I like doing a good job and sometimes that takes time."

"Yeah, I hear you," Phil said. He had no idea when this job was expected to be finished. If the owner showed up later, he'd probably learn more then.

"Well, we'd better get going. See you later, Phil." Howard shuffled off toward the front door.

Phil continued on to the back and placed everything he needed within reach. He started marking his lumber, and the kitchen door opened. A tall, good-looking guy with long blond hair pulled back in a ponytail walked out at a fast pace and turned toward the side of the house. Phil recognized him as the man who'd gone into the house with Tom earlier, and Phil found himself staring for the second time that day. Although, Howard hadn't been near as nice to stare at as this dude. The guy stopped dead in his tracks, turned, and locked eyes with him, and then broke into a friendly smile that revealed his sexy dimples.

"I'll get the electricity on in this part of the house first. That way it'll make it easier for you," he said, still smiling.

Phil swallowed hard and tried not to stare too hard. "Um, well, thanks, I appreciate that. I do have a generator though, so I can get started."

"Yeah, yeah, I see that." The hot guy glanced down at the machine. "But, well, I have to start somewhere... By the way, I'm Brad, the electrician." He gave Phil another big grin.

"I'm Phil—"

"The carpenter," Brad interrupted.

"Yeah." Phil suddenly felt self-conscious, the back of his neck heating. There was no mistaking that Brad was checking him out.

"Well, guess we'll be seeing each other around here." Brad strode away.

Phil admired the electrician's muscular physique. He was tall and looked strong. Along with his face and hair, he found him very appealing.

He focused on his work, aware he needed to work as fast as possible. So far, he'd met an interesting array of people. He wondered what the homeowner was like and when he'd show up. For some reason, he pictured an ogre who would arrive and yell at everyone to hurry up. Did he have a wife and kids? The house was big enough for a family.

He knew one thing—the owner had good taste. When Tom had hired Phil, he'd mentioned the owner had designed the house himself. Tom had given Phil a long, detailed description of the cabinets right down to the hardware. The others had probably been given specific instructions as well. He understood. If he had the money to build a home, he'd be particular too, so he intended to put his whole effort into this job.

As he measured and marked the wood, he whistled a tune, glad the weather was mild since there wasn't any shade where he'd set up. He worked steadily for several hours, only stopping now and then to guzzle some bottled water provided by Tom.

His stomach rumbled, and he checked his watch. He'd lost track of time. Deciding to stop and eat lunch, he left his work, retraced his path to the front of the house, and sat in his truck to eat. He rolled down both windows to allow the slightly cool breeze to provide old-fashioned air conditioning. After he opened his lunch pail, he set his sandwich on his lap, opened his bag of chips, and unscrewed the thermos of iced tea. While he ate, he checked out the neighborhood. The quiet street seemed like a nice place to live.

His train of thought was disrupted when Brad suddenly showed up at his passenger door holding up a brown paper bag. "Mind if I join you?"

"Fine by me," Phil answered, even though he was more than half finished with his lunch.

Brad climbed in and got comfortable in the passenger seat, sitting with his body slightly toward Phil. He pulled out a couple of pita bread sandwiches and a bag of chips.

Phil couldn't tell what was in the sandwich, but he thought he saw sprouts that Gail would like, though he tried not to stare. Brad chowed down like it was the best-tasting sandwich. He didn't care for pita bread, mainly because he always made a mess when he tried to stuff it, so he'd long since given up on that kind of sandwich.

Brad tore open the *baked* chips and took a swig of bottled water.

"Are you a health food nut?" Phil asked. He finished the last bite of his sandwich.

Brad wiped his mouth with a napkin and flashed that big smile of his that showed his dimples. "I try to eat healthy, but I wouldn't call myself a nut."

Phil's face grew hot. "Uh, maybe I could have worded that better."

Brad chuckled, seeming very relaxed. He was laid back, not trying to impress—acting like they'd known each other longer than a few hours.

He must be a people person.

"Have you lived here long?" Brad asked.

"This town and I go back a long way," Phil answered. At Brad's raised brows and expectant expression, he added, "Uh, I graduated from Apple Valley High School back in 2001. How about you?"

"I started high school the year after you graduated. I got out in 2006."

"You must like it here if you stuck around," Phil said.

"Yeah, well, it's all right. I have family here."

"I do too. I left for college in L.A. for a while, but I didn't finish and came back up here." He drank the last of his tea.

"Missed the place that much, huh?" Brad held out the bag of baked chips to Phil.

"Oh, no thanks, I have my own."

"Maybe some time we could go out after work for a beer," Brad said.

Phil smiled and tried to sound casual. "Yeah, we might be able to work something out."

They finished their food and Brad stuffed his trash into the paper bag, and Phil put his into the lunch pail next to him. They exited the truck and headed toward the backyard.

"I'll have your electricity on in a little while, Phil, but it'll probably be intermittent for a time." Brad gave him a broad smile and winked. He headed to the kitchen door.

Phil stood next to his tools and sighed. He had long ago accepted that he was doomed to go through life alone, but he needed someone to spend a couple hours with now and then, and Brad would be a nice distraction.

He began working where he'd left off. Soon, Tom and a young kid approached and stopped next to Phil's piles of lumber. He straightened up from his sawhorses and gave the two his attention.

Tom placed his hand on the kid's shoulder. "This is my son, Dillion. He'll be here in the afternoons after his classes as a gofer to anyone who needs him. He can sweep up the saw dust too. Just tell him what you need. Should help to speed you men up on your work."

"Well, that sounds good." Phil made eye contact with Dillion in an effort to welcome him even though he wasn't sure about this idea.

He hoped the tall, skinny kid, who didn't look more than sixteen, wouldn't be in the way. And Tom bringing his son to work meant one of two things—that he wanted the kid to do something constructive with his free time, or that he wanted another set of hands to speed this project along.

"I'm going to introduce Dillion around. He'll be back in a bit to see if you need help." Tom motioned for his son to follow him.

Phil nodded and watched them disappear into the house.

Within a half hour, Dillion returned, and Phil tried not to be annoyed. He really didn't need any help, and he figured the boy's presence was going to slow him down. He hadn't started sawing yet, so there wasn't anything to sweep, and trying to explain what tools he needed would take longer than grabbing them himself. Couldn't the kid help one of the others? Out of the corner of his eye, Phil saw Dillion's eyes were on him, so he stopped marking the wood and turned to him. The boy stood with his hands in his pockets, stepping from foot to foot. He looked either nervous or bored, and Phil felt kind of sorry for him. Tom had probably forced him into this.

"Uh, I don't really need help right now. Maybe you could check with Howard or Brad," Phil said. He set his board aside and grabbed another.

Dillion shrugged. "Dad said I could help whoever I wanted, so I came out here. I like carpentry work."

Phil's gaze widened. "Oh, you do? Have you ever done any work like this?"

"No, but I wish they still had shop class in high school. I'd take it for sure. My older cousin learned some carpentry in shop back when he was in high school."

Phil motioned him to his side. "Come over here, and I'll explain what I'm doing."

Dillion smiled and came closer. First Phil explained about the different kinds of wood that could be used in a project like this. The boy gave him his undivided attention, and that impressed Phil. Part way through the lesson he thought, *I've turned into my father.*

Then he showed him the lines on the wood that he'd put there and told him what they represented. He demonstrated the right way to measure and mark, and then he let Dillion give it a try. The boy grinned from ear to ear when he held the tape measure and marking pen in his hands.

"Measure twice, cut once," Phil said. He watched Dillion's technique closely, surprised at how well he focused his attention.

Phil's dad had taught him the trade. He'd been a fine carpenter and a great father too. Phil had always been able to talk to him about anything. When he was fourteen, he'd come out to his dad before he'd told anyone else. His dad hadn't been surprised—he had it figured out, and consequently his mom also knew. He'd been blessed with caring, compassionate parents—the complete opposite of what Cole had.

Phil filled his lungs with air and blew it out slowly, pulling his wandering mind back to the present. He wished Cole Fisher would stop invading his thoughts. Clenching his jaw, he set his mind on helping Dillion learn about carpentry.

After a short time, the kitchen door opened a crack, and Tom called Dillion's name. The kid lifted his head, backed up, and turned toward the door, accidently knocking one of Phil's tool bags off the top of the generator. The contents scattered on the ground.

"I'm sorry, Phil." Dillion bent down to pick up the fallen items.

"It's okay. I'll get it." Phil knelt to gather up the small tools. He glanced over at the kitchen door. "Go on inside, your dad wants you."

Phil wasn't paying close enough attention to what he was grabbing, and a sharp sting flared from his left hand. The blade of a utility knife was sticking into his palm at the base of his thumb. He jerked back, dislodging the sharp tool.

"Shit." He winced at the stinging pain and frantically looked for any kind of rag to stop the blood flow from the gash.

"I'll go get my dad," Dillion shouted, already halfway to the door.

CHAPTER SIX

COLE ARRIVED at his new home on Shadow Ridge and parked his Lincoln Navigator at the curb behind Tom's SUV. He took it as a good sign that there wasn't space in the driveway for him to park. Hopefully, Tom's crew was working hard to complete the work so he could move in soon.

The unpleasant conversation he'd had with Meredith this morning, just after hauling in Moonbeam and Moonshadow's new cat tower, was still on his mind.

Before he could get the tower in place, the phone rang, which annoyed him, and his mood only got worse as Meredith had gone on with the same old rant again—that Dana wouldn't be happy living in the desert this summer. He'd held his tongue and didn't tell her he'd spoken to Dana and that she most certainly did want to come and was looking forward to it. Maybe he should have told her, but he wasn't in the mood to get into it, which would have prolonged the conversation. He'd cut the call short, finished up with the cat tower, and gone upstairs to do some work.

When he'd come down to leave, he found the cats curled up on the sofa instead of on the tower. He'd spent a few minutes trying to coax them onto their new habitat, even rubbing cat nip on the perches, but nothing had enticed them to get off the sofa to investigate. A little disappointed, he had left, hoping they'd be on it when he returned.

He was anxious to see how things were going inside the house. The outside looked great with the chisel cut stone in tones of brown and grey with the desert beige stucco, and would look even better after the shrubs and trees were planted, but he and Dana wouldn't be pitching a tent in the yard. He stepped out of his SUV and headed directly to the front door. Before he reached for the handle, it opened, and a man stepped out.

"Hello," the older guy said. "Can I help you?"

"I'm Cole Fisher." When he got nothing but a blank stare, he tried not to sound irritated. "I own the house you're working in."

"Oh, so you're the owner. I'm Howard Salvador, the floor man."

"Good to meet you," Cole said.

"Yeah, yeah, you too. I should mention that there's quite a lot of work to do here, and I'm going to do my best, but I won't sacrifice quality for quantity."

Folding his arms across his chest, Cole sighed. "I get that. You do have help, don't you? You won't be working alone?"

Howard squared his shoulders. "I do, but these things take time. Not saying it won't be done when you expect—I just want to let you know that I'm not a magician so you won't be counting on something that might not be possible. This is just the first day though, so we'll see how things progress."

"All I can ask is that you do your best."

"That I will. If there's nothing else, I've got to get something from my truck."

"Yeah, sure, go ahead. Uh, is Tom around?"

"Right inside," Howard said, before heading to the driveway.

Cole entered the house. Two men were talking in the kitchen area, and one sounded like Tom. He followed the voices and found Tom and a guy with a ponytail looking at a light socket on the wall where the refrigerator would go. The long-haired guy left out the back door without stopping to acknowledge him, and Tom stood there frozen in place. After a second, he wiped his hands on the front of his pants and smiled, but the smile didn't appear too genuine. He offered his hand though, and they shared a quick handshake.

"Mr. Fisher, nice to see you."

"Yeah, well, I said I'd be by today."

"That you did. We're doing excellent today—first day everyone's been here, and things are going just fine." He wiped his forehead with the back of his hand.

"Well, I'm glad to hear that."

"Let me call my son in so you can meet him. He's here helping out."

"Well, that's good—can never have too many helpers."

Tom cracked open the door. "Dillion, come in here a minute, please."

He shut the door and gestured to the walls where the cabinets would go. "The cabinet maker is set up out in the yard. He's already measured in here and has all his lumber stacked outside. He's been working steady all day."

Suddenly, Dillion pushed the door open and burst through. "Dad, Phil's bleeding. Bring something to stop the blood!"

"What the hell happened?" Tom rushed to the corner of the room and pulled a small towel from a box. He hurried outside on Dillion's heels, leaving the door wide open.

Cole stood in stunned silence for a few seconds before moving to the door to see what was going on. He quietly observed as Tom bent down with the towel, handing it off to a guy kneeling on the ground. Tom's son looked very upset, rubbing his hands together and pacing around.

This isn't good—is this nitwit going to be able to work after this?

The ponytailed man joined the others, examining the hurt man's hand. Blood stained the white towel. Cole wondered if he should try to help, but he stayed put and watched a moment longer. He narrowed his eyes. The injured guy had a beard and blond hair just like the guy he'd seen at the cat show.

He stepped out the door, fixated on the scene. Tom's son was saying he was sorry. The hurt man was talking, telling the boy it wasn't his fault. That voice sounded so familiar. His gut tightened. And hadn't the boy called the guy Phil?

It can't be.

Before he could get a handle on it, Tom came over. "He's going to need stitches in his hand. I can take him..."

The ponytailed guy suddenly appeared and interrupted, "I'd be glad to take him to the hospital."

"No one's leaving," Cole said. "I'll take him, and you all can go on with whatever you were doing before. There's no reason for either of you to go. I will drive him to the hospital." He took a deep breath. "Now, everyone, calm down and carry on."

Cole looked over at the injured guy, and their gazes locked for a long moment. He approached Tom who was helping the man to his feet.

Tom said to the guy, "This is the owner of the house."

Cole stopped in front of the two men. Tom backed away and stood next to his distraught son. Cole took in a sharp breath of air. The injured blond man didn't just look like the man from the cat show—he *was* the man from the cat show.

"You're the guy from the cat show," they both said at the same time.

The reality of the situation crashed down on Cole, making him slightly lightheaded. Not wanting to make a scene, he turned away from Phil and said, "Follow me. I'll take you to the hospital in my car."

As they walked toward the front of the house, he wondered if Phillip had realized who he was too. He walked briskly to the SUV, trying to formulate something to say once they were alone in the car. Though he longed to turn around and take in the sight of Phillip after all these years, that wouldn't be the right thing to do. Number one, he needed to get him to the hospital, and number two, well, he might just find out what Phil had been thinking about him for the last fifteen years and possibly get that punch he'd thought about every now and then.

He unlocked the doors and got into the driver's side. Phil struggled to open the passenger door while keeping the towel wrapped on his hand. Cole started the engine, and as soon as Phil was in the seat, he pulled away from the curb and drove slowly up the street. Phil attempted to put on his seatbelt, but he wasn't doing a very good job of it. Cole checked his rearview mirror for traffic and when none was in sight, he came to a stop right in the middle of the street and reached over to help him hook the seatbelt. In doing so, he brushed against Phil's wrist and hand. That brief contact sent sparks shooting through his body, confirming what he'd already known—that Phillip Thompson had never been far from his heart in all the years since they'd parted. He received a cold stare in return for the help.

Yeah, he knows it's me.

Cole continued driving, his shoulders tense. Who would be the first to break the ice? Phil was sitting stiffly and staring straight out the windshield. He'd always been stubborn, so Cole cleared his throat, wishing he had some water, or better yet, a pack of gum. Then he could offer a stick to Phillip, preferably Juicy Fruit, which had always been Phil's favorite.

Over the years he'd imagined what he'd say to Phillip if he ever had the chance. Now was his chance, and not one word came to mind. This was not a normal situation by any means, so nothing he'd envisioned saying would be appropriate anyway. And in his imagination, Phillip always forgave him, but from the resentful vibes coming from his old friend and lover, that was not going to happen.

He finally asked, "How does your hand feel?"

Phil sighed heavily and muttered, "I'm sure I'll live."

He wished Phillip hadn't stopped there because he had no idea what else to say.

Finally Phil asked, "How in the hell did this happen anyway?"

A little relieved but also thrown off balance because he didn't know what Phillip meant by *this*, he didn't know how to respond. Was he referring to his accident? Or maybe he was referring to the two of them together in the same car driving to the hospital. If it was the latter, then Cole wondered the same thing. This situation was unreal.

"Keep the towel nice and tight." Cole glanced briefly at Phil's hand.

Phil adjusted the towel, and his hand didn't appear to be bleeding as much now.

Uncomfortable silence lingered between them.

"We'll be there soon. Good thing I still remember where everything is." Cole stopped at a red light and cleared his throat. "Uh, have you lived here all along? I mean, after college?"

Cole winced and wished he hadn't brought up college. The last place they'd seen each other all those years ago was in their dorm room. Phillip had been standing in front of their posters of cars and horses with tears running down his cheeks, and his own eyes had teared up uncontrollably. College was certainly not a time and place he liked thinking of, and Phil... Well, he shouldn't have mentioned college. How could he be so stupid?

The light changed to green, and they crept along in traffic.

Cole focused on the congested road. "I'll get you there as soon as I can. Tom said you'll need stitches."

"I'll still be able to work, don't worry." Phil moved the position of his hand. "Luckily it's my left, but even if it wasn't, this wouldn't slow me down."

Before Cole could respond, Phil continued in a clipped tone. "And in answer to your other question... I dropped out of college a few months after you left. I came back home and followed in my dad's footsteps, and I've been here ever since."

Cole glanced over at Phil. His ex-boyfriend adjusted himself in the seat, and then for the first time on the drive, he turned and looked right at him. They locked gazes. After a couple of seconds, Cole turned and focused on the road ahead, but he could feel Phillip's eyes boring into him. Beads of sweat formed on Cole's forehead. He turned the air conditioner up a notch.

"And that's how I came to be building your kitchen cabinets... Well, yours and your *wife's*."

There was no mistaking Phillip's curt tone, and Cole couldn't blame him one bit. They inched along in stop-and-go traffic, and he glanced over at Phil again. He was still gazing at him with his eyebrows drawn together in a frown and his forehead crinkled.

"Uh, I'm divorced now, so it'll be just me living there, and my daughter when she's with me."

A brief flicker ignited in Phil's beautiful blue eyes. He hoped against hope that it meant Phillip was pleased to hear this news, but his face retained the scowl.

After a minute more, the hospital came into view. Cole entered the driveway closest to the emergency room entrance and located a parking space. "Well, here we are."

He put the car in park, turned off the ignition, and then hurried around to the passenger door. With some difficulty, Phil unhooked the seatbelt. Risking a dirty look or worse, he grasped Phil's right forearm and gently put his arm around his shoulder to help him out the door. He didn't get any resistance, and the strong emotions from being that close to Phillip again gave him goose bumps. He wondered if Phillip felt anything, or if what they'd had was dead and buried by now as far as he was concerned.

If he hadn't known before today, there was no doubt now— Phillip Thompson was the love of his life, and he wanted him back.

CHAPTER SEVEN

PHIL WALKED through the back door of his house feeling like something the cat dragged in. The clock in the kitchen read six-fifteen. This had been one heck of a long day, and tired didn't even begin to describe how he felt. He sat his lunch pail and thermos on the countertop, and the thermos rocked with a loud clink and nearly fell over. All he wanted to do was grab a beer and sit down on the couch, but within a few seconds the cats were at his feet meowing and rubbing on his legs.

"All right, all right. I'll get your dinner." Phil groaned while trying not to trample either cat as he carefully stepped over and around them to get to the cupboard. He reached in, pulled out a can, and looked at the label.

"Mariner's Catch is on the menu tonight, boys."

While he spooned it out, the meowing intensified and didn't stop until he placed their bowls down on the floor.

Happy to have accomplished this task without getting even a drop of stinky fish juice on his bandage, he washed off his other hand and got his beer out of the fridge. He pulled the tab and took it into the living room. Sighing, he sank down onto the couch, drowsiness settling in, but he shook it off and chugged a third of the can and then laid his head back to stare up at the ceiling.

The middle of a dream was all he could think of to describe this afternoon when he'd realized the man from the cat show was standing before him and that it was Cole after all. He should have known no one else would have been hanging around staring at him at the show. His brown-rimmed glasses complemented and accentuated the color of those dark, intense eyes. There was no denying it—Cole was as handsome as ever—the years had been good to him.

Riding with him in the SUV and trying to make conversation had been brutal. He had so much anger inside, but that didn't stop him from wondering all kinds of things about his old friend. Apparently Cole had finished his education. The house he'd designed was proof that he was an architect now like he'd set out to be.

Their ship had sailed fifteen long years ago when Cole, his eyes red-rimmed and glistening with tears, had told him he was leaving California and transferring to a college in New York. He'd said it was the hardest decision he'd ever had to make.

But you did it.

Cole's announcement that day in their dorm room had been so sudden that Phil hadn't been able to fully grasp it. The next few minutes had brought the walls crashing down. Cole had walked out with his luggage, leaving him alone in their quiet, empty room. It was then that he'd realized he had underestimated the impact of the ugly scene with Cole's disgusting old man a few weeks before. That man was a piece of work.

But he would never comprehend what came after all that—the marriage. How many years had Cole's wedded bliss lasted? How old was his daughter?

He took another swig of beer and held up his injured hand. How long would he have to contend with the bandage? The doctor had said the stitches could come out in ten days, but if the wound looked okay, he didn't have to wear the bandage the entire time. Of course he should wear it on the job. His hand throbbed even though he'd taken a pain pill. Maybe the medication was wearing off.

After the doctor had finished treating his injured hand, Cole had driven them back to the house on Shadow Ridge and told him to go home for the day. Cole had immediately disappeared somewhere inside the house, and Phil hadn't seen him again. Not that he wanted to see him again.

He'd wanted to get more work done and to let Dillion know he was okay, so he didn't go right home. The kid had seemed so upset about the mishap and looked relieved to see him back, still apologizing. And of course Tom was glad he'd come back and would be able to continue the job, but he'd also suggested he call it a day. He'd stayed anyway and finished marking the wood. He had wanted to start cutting today, but he'd spent too many hours in the ER. By the time he'd finished marking the wood, Brad and Howard had already gone, so he had decided to go home.

Still having a hard time wrapping his head around the idea that Cole Fisher was back, he finished off his beer.

Batman walked through the room straight over to the cat tree, shot up to the top perch, and began washing his face. Soon after, Robin joined him, settling down on a lower perch. Watching the cats did more to relax him than anything else. They required so little to make them happy. All they needed was one servant attending to their needs and they were set. They had no idea this house wasn't the entire world. He wondered about the cats that were taken from their familiar surroundings to attend the cat shows—like Cole's Siamese. Batman and Robin would freak out. Thinking about the cats reminded him that he should clean their litter box, so he forced himself off the couch and headed to the laundry room.

When the cat box was scooped out and he'd given them fresh water, he decided to fix himself something to eat. The food in the freezer didn't appeal to him, but he had to have something and that was quick and easy, so he grabbed a chicken pot pie to heat in the microwave. Within minutes, it was ready. He poured himself some iced tea, sat down at the table, and ate his food in silence while trying to clear his mind.

After he finished eating, he wasn't tired anymore, but he didn't feel like watching TV. Since he'd gotten his second wind, he grabbed a bottle of water and went outside to work on the cat trees. He only had a few weeks to get another collection ready for the next cat show.

He began dragging his tools and materials out of the garage onto the driveway, hardly slowed down by his bandaged hand. Even after dark, the flood light was bright enough for him to keep on working. With each trip into the garage, he focused on the uncovered Z28 parked in its spot way in the back. He hadn't put the tarp back on because he planned to keep driving it, and why not?

After keeping the car stored away for so long, it had felt great to get back behind the wheel, and Gail had loved riding in it. She thought bringing it out was an excellent idea.

Eve would get a kick out of taking a spin, he was sure of that. Maybe he would call her and ask if she'd like to go horseback riding this weekend at the regional park. What better way to welcome spring? He'd surprise her by picking her up in the car. And he'd make time to wash, wax, and vacuum the car too. A plastic glove would protect his wound. The truck could use a good cleaning too. Just because it was used for work didn't mean he should be driving around in a pigpen.

He began cutting squares of pink and black carpet to size for the perches he'd already saber sawed the other day. The color combination for the custom job wasn't one he'd normally use, but they did look nice once he saw them together. He got into a good groove despite his bandaged hand. The posts between the perches on this tower needed sisal rope because the customer said her cat would prefer it that way. He'd have to wait until his hand wasn't sore to do that part. Using the staple gun for the carpet shouldn't be too hard though.

He finished stapling the carpet to the perches and decided it was time to call it quits. With his hand injured, he didn't want to risk hurting it more and not be able to work on the cupboards out at the job site. He needed that job. Not only that, people were depending on him—Tom... Cole.

His mouth was dry, so he finished off the bottle of water and looked down at what he'd accomplished tonight. Pride swelled up inside him. He worked hard for what he had. So what if it didn't amount to that much? He got by, and he'd earned everything he had.

He looked at the living room window and wondered if Batman and Robin were still on the cat tree. With only a small light on inside the house, he couldn't tell if they were there or not.

He looked forward to this weekend, hoping Eve wanted to go horseback riding, and two weekends after was the next cat show. Maybe he'd get together with Brad soon too. They hadn't exchanged phone numbers, but they'd see each other at work and could make plans. Between all that and the new job, his hours were filled to the brim. He couldn't believe he was working in Cole's house—the place he'd be living in with his daughter. It sounded like he had joint custody. He guessed the ex-wife was in New York.

Phil shook his head. Why was he wasting his time wondering about things that were none of his business? He didn't care about any of that.

His muscles were tensing up, and he realized that he was clenching his jaw—he must have overdone it tonight after having worked a full day. Hopefully tomorrow wouldn't be as screwed-up as today. If he hadn't cut his hand, maybe he wouldn't be so out of sorts tonight. He couldn't put his finger on exactly what was causing this sudden funk that had settled over him.

Cole Fisher showing up didn't have anything to do with this mood. Not. At. All. Sure, he'd been caught off guard seeing him again, but this wasn't something he couldn't rise above. He'd sprung back and gone on fifteen years ago. Why had he let all that sentimental crap into his head the last few days? Cole Fisher hadn't taken anything all those years ago he couldn't live without. After all, it was only love...

Shit. Where had that come from? Love... He hadn't been in love with Cole for many years. That had died eons ago on the day he'd heard about the wedding of Mr. and Mrs. Cole Fisher.

Grabbing his tools, he stomped into the garage to put them away, and went back outside for the cat tree pieces. After storing those, he leaned back against the garage wall to catch his breath and close his eyes.

He hadn't felt a thing sitting next to Cole in the SUV this afternoon. His heart had been pounding because of the pain in his hand. When Cole had brushed that hand to help him with the seatbelt, the strange feeling in the pit of his stomach had been because he hadn't eaten his cookies at lunch and he was hungry. Having Brad hold his hand back at the house to check on his cut had stirred him up more than being near Cole. Phil squeezed his lips together. He was not deceiving himself, not at all.

Exhaustion overwhelmed him, and he sat down on a stack of wood. The events of the day had caught up with him tenfold. All he could do was lean forward and rest his elbows on his knees, his head in his hands. He tried but couldn't forget how he'd felt on that day so many years ago when he'd run into a mutual friend from college who had told him about Cole's wedding. Phil had gone home and gotten physically ill.

Forcing himself to his feet was an effort, but he had to close the garage and check to make sure his truck was locked. Once inside the house, he gave the cats a few treats, grabbed a plastic bag and a rubber band, and went straight to his bedroom. After he pulled back the covers on the bed that he'd haphazardly thrown into place that morning, he stripped off his clothes and ambled into the bathroom for a quick shower. He slipped the bag onto his bandaged hand and secured it with the rubber band before stepping into the stall.

The warm spray worked wonders to relax him. Soaping himself up with one hand wasn't as easy as he thought it would be, but he did the best he could. After rinsing off, he stood with his back to the spray and stared at the tiled wall. He found his balls with his good hand and gave them a little jiggle just to make sure they were rinsed well, but his dick got ideas, so he ran his fingers down the length, bringing it to full attention.

Memories of the first time Cole had touched him came flooding in—the scenic view, the midnight sky above, the look-out point at the lake on the way back to Cole's house, the suddenly spontaneous boy sitting next to him in his Camaro who reached over and unzipped his pants to find the prize inside.

The very best part of the encounter had come at the end of all that—their first kiss—magical and intimate—when Cole had leaned in, and somewhat awkwardly, planted his lips on Phil's with a soft and tender kiss. He could feel those lips now, so clear in his mind that chills ran up and down his spine despite the warmth of the water.

With his eyes tightly closed and the shower spray still running down his back, he stroked himself several times, all the while picturing deep brown eyes and warm, caring hands.

That was all it took to get him groaning and spurring himself on until he shuddered, having a hard time remaining upright, his legs like jelly.

He got out and dried off, but he wasn't sure if he felt better or worse. Suddenly his life had gotten complicated—out of control—and it was because of Cole, damn him. He almost wished he'd go back to New York... almost.

CHAPTER EIGHT

COLE STAYED away from the new house for the rest of the week even though he was anxious to see how Phillip would react when they saw each other again. He hadn't looked pleased that their paths had crossed, but at least he'd been civil. Maybe Phillip needed some time to get used to the idea of Cole being back. That was his hope anyway. He wanted a relationship with Phillip again. Was it even possible? His heart ached at the thought that this might not work out.

He'd touched base with Tom mid-week, so he knew that Phil had been there working along with everyone else—hopefully getting a lot done. Evidently Phil's hand was doing okay.

By midday on this warm and sunny Saturday, he couldn't wait any longer. He said goodbye to Moonbeam and Moonshadow and went out to his SUV to drive to Apple Valley.

His hands shook on the steering wheel as he left the driveway because he was excited to see Phillip. Tom had given him Phil's address and phone number on Monday after he got back from the hospital, and he'd almost called him several times during the week. Not only had he chickened out, he'd nearly had an anxiety attack trying to work up the courage to dial the phone.

The cold sweat and racing heart he'd experienced had been just like the panic attack he'd had on the day he'd told Phillip goodbye at college, and then he'd experienced the same thing when he'd married Meredith.

His wedding day had been rough. In order to make it through the ceremony, he'd kept glancing at his mother in her wheelchair in the front row—dressed to the nines and smiling. He hadn't ruined the wedding, although trying to be a good husband to Meredith had been hell.

He felt like a total fool and that's basically what he was. Three lives were messed up and that was on him, and he desperately wanted to make things right. More than anything, he wanted to see Phillip again, and not just at the job. He dreamed of asking him out and spending time with him, but hell, he didn't even know if Phillip lived alone, or if he was seeing someone. A couple of times, he'd thought about driving by his house to check things out, but he'd stopped himself, refusing to behave like a stalker.

Turning on the radio to a talk station, he hoped that would help him calm down and think about something else on the way to Apple Valley.

A half hour later, he pulled up in front of his new house. The same trucks were there as on Monday, plus one or two more, which pleased him. He got out, shaking a little at the thought of coming face-to-face with his handsome ex-lover—scared but hopeful.

Halfway up the driveway he recognized Tom's son coming from the backyard with his head down and his eyes glued to his smart phone.

"Hey, there," Cole said, to stop the kid from walking right into him.

The boy stopped in his tracks, jerked his head up, and stammered, "Oh, hi, I'm on my break."

His startled expression made Cole smile. "Oh, I see... I don't think we were introduced the other day. I'm Cole Fisher."

"Dillion Anderson," the kid said. "You're the owner of the house?"

"Yes, I am. Thanks for helping out around here."

"You're welcome. I've been helping Phil. He's sanding the wood right now." He stuck his phone in his pocket.

"Is that so... Is he able to work okay with his hand bandaged up?"

"Yeah."

"Uh, what exactly happened the other day when he got cut?"

Dillion's shoulders slumped, and he kicked at the ground with the toe of his boot. Looking down, refusing to make eye contact, he finally spoke in a muffled voice. "I accidently knocked his tool bag over, and everything spilled out on the ground." He stared out into the distance, squinting from the sun. "I started to pick it up, but then my dad called me, so Phil said he'd get it, and that's when he got cut."

Cole could tell how sensitive Dillion was. He seemed like a real nice boy. "Well, accidents happen. I'm sure you're being more careful now."

Dillion looked at Cole, smiling ever so slightly. "I've got to call my girlfriend before my break ends." He pulled his phone out of his pocket.

"Oh, yeah, go on ahead," Cole said. "Don't let me keep you."

Dillion walked farther down the driveway, and Cole continued toward the backyard. When he reached the gate, he heard two male voices talking and laughing—one was Phillip's. He didn't open the gate, just stood there in the shadows peeking over to see who Phil was talking to, and he recognized the electrician. No one else had a head of hair like that.

He heard Phil say, "Okay, I'll meet you there at six-thirty."

"Great, see ya then," the ponytailed guy said before going into the house.

His stomach dropped. Were they dating? Had they met here on the job, or before? Turning around and going to find Tom might be the best option, but he thought better of it. He was not going to let what he'd overheard discourage him, and he had to speak to Phil now. Dillion would be back soon, and if he wanted a private conversation, there was just a small opening, and he was going to take it. He steeled himself, opened the gate and walked through.

Phil was using the electric sander, but he shut it off and stood there watching Cole approach. Cole sent his gaze straight to those blue eyes. He wanted to see if he could still read them after all these years. How did Phillip feel seeing him again? Phil's raised eyebrows helped give Cole confidence, especially when he got closer and noticed his dilated pupils.

When Phil's lips parted slightly and he briefly scanned him up and down, Cole took that as a good indication that he liked what he saw. That was encouraging, but then he picked up a piece of sandpaper and began sanding by hand.

Still as stubborn as ever.

Cole walked to within a few feet of him, his heart beating fast. His temperature rose a degree or two, and he wished he could reach out and touch him. Instead, he dug a stick of gum out of his pants pocket and held it out toward Phillip, who wouldn't even look at him for several long seconds. Finally he did. He saw the gum and smiled, and God, he looked good.

"Is Juicy Fruit still your favorite?" Cole asked.

Phil took the gum and put it in his pocket. "I guess so. I never really thought much about what my favorite gum is."

Cole lowered his head. He didn't believe that and wished Phillip would stop being difficult, but he didn't seem to want to give an inch.

He looked at Phil again. "How's the hand doing?"

"Never been better." Phil smiled again and didn't seem as distant. He even took the gum out of his pocket, took the wrapper off, stuck it in his mouth, and started chewing.

"Well, uh, I just came by to check up on... things. See how everyone's doing. I saw Dillion out front. Seems like a nice kid."

"Yeah, and he's a good helper. I wasn't too sure about him at first, but he's doing just fine."

"Seems like you're coming along well on the cupboards." He looked at the pieces of wood stacked up next to the sander. "You do good work just like your dad. How is he anyway?"

Phil set the sandpaper down, took a long drink from his water bottle, and then sighed. "My dad passed away two years ago."

Cole was taken completely by surprise, and a wave of nausea washed over him.

"Hey, you don't look so good. You're white as a sheet." Phil touched Cole's arm. "Do you need to sit down? Let me get you some water."

"I'm all right," Cole said, and then without thinking, he pulled Phil into a hug. "I'm so sorry, Phillip," he whispered. And he was sorry that Phil had lost his dad, but way beyond that, he was sorry his choices had made it impossible for him to have been with Phillip through all life's hard times and happy ones too. There was so much he wanted to say, but the words couldn't squeeze through the big lump in his throat, and he wouldn't know where to begin anyway.

Phil didn't resist his hug and wrapped his arms around Cole.

Cole choked back tears and drew strength from his old friend. Their embrace only lasted for a few seconds, and then Phil pulled away. A sudden chill passed through Cole's body, and he took a step back, wiping at his eyes.

"What happened to him?" he managed to ask.

"Heart attack." Phil stared off into the distance, blinking hard, his eyes glistening.

"Is your mom..."

Phil glanced back at Cole again. "She's fine. She lives in Santa Barbara with her older sister now."

Cole sighed in relief. "Well, I'm sure sorry about your dad. He was a good man."

"Thanks..." Phil's face darkened then. "I heard your father died too. I saw it in the newspaper some years back."

"Yeah, well, no great loss like your dad," he said, and he meant every word.

Phillip's jaw clenched and his lips narrowed. Cole knew exactly how he felt without Phil saying anything, and he didn't blame him one little bit.

"I noticed in your old man's obituary that your mom had passed on," Phil said.

Cole swallowed hard. "Yeah, she put up a good fight, but the cancer got her in the end."

Talking about his parents, especially with Phillip, made him uncomfortable. They were the reason everything had fallen apart for him and Phil. "Uh, anyway... I should go in and talk with Tom. I've kept you from your work long enough."

"Okay, sure." Phil picked up the electric sander and positioned it over a piece of wood.

Cole hesitated, his hands sweating.

Phil met his gaze, scrutinizing him with those blue eyes that Cole had known so well. His ex was waiting for him to either go inside or talk, so he had to decide which it was going to be.

Gathering his courage, he cleared his throat. "Do you think we could go out together sometime?"

His throat was so dry his words had to fight their way out. He wished he'd put a piece of gum in his mouth.

Phil stared at him for several seconds. Finally he said, "I don't think that's a good idea."

Cole's chest tightened. "Why not? Are you in a relationship?" It killed him to ask, but he needed to know.

"We had our chance and it didn't work out. There's no use pretending we can pick up where we left off. We're different people now." The breeze ruffled Phil's hair, and he ran his hand through it.

Well, he hadn't said he had someone else. The electrician seemed to be just someone to pass time with, or he'd have used the guy for his excuse, but he hadn't. At least that was something. A small ray of hope lit up inside him.

Cole nodded. "Okay, I won't push, but I reserve the right to revisit the subject again in the future."

He forced a smile before turning and walking over to the kitchen door. He paused in the shade and watched Phil use the sander. Phil's well-toned and muscular arms made his heart flutter again. Damn, it had felt so good to hold Phillip in his arms. And surprisingly, he wasn't too discouraged when Phil hadn't agreed to go out with him. There'd be time to sway him in his direction—away from the pony-tailed guy.

With a determined smile, he opened the door and stepped inside.

CHAPTER NINE

PHIL WALKED into the Breezeway Pub—the only gay bar within sixty miles—at six-forty. He'd hurried home from work to change clothes and feed the cats, all the while considering canceling the date. He liked Brad, though, and didn't want to be a wet blanket. Lord knows, he needed some relaxation after the week he'd had. It remained to be seen how much relaxation he'd be able to get with the buzzing in his brain. Ever since Cole had shown up earlier today, his mind had been whirling. Too many long-buried emotions had bubbled up after their conversation and that damn hug. He tamped down his thoughts for about the tenth time.

He scanned the faces in the dimly lit, crowded room. He didn't see a man with a long ponytail among those gathered for a Saturday night of merriment, but Brad had to be there somewhere since his truck was in the parking lot. Finally, a long-haired guy sitting at the bar turned to look toward the door, and Phil recognized Brad. He looked different with his hair loose. Phil took a deep breath, put on a smile, and headed over. When he got closer, Brad flashed his dimples.

"Hey, Phil," Brad said in his relaxed manner, lifting himself off the bar stool and patting him on the shoulder. He acted as if they'd been out hundreds of times before.

Phil sat down on the bar stool next to him, wishing he already had a drink. Thankfully, the bartender came right over, and he ordered the same kind of beer that Brad had.

"How ya doin'?" Brad scooped a handful of peanuts from the bowl sitting in front of him. He slid it closer to Phil. "Hey, you took your bandage off. Let me see how your hand looks."

Phil took a few peanuts, trying not to be annoyed by Brad examining his stitches. He wasn't having much of a reaction to the guy basically holding his hand.

Shortly, the bartender set his beer down. Glad to have his hand back, he picked up his beer and took a long drink.

After swallowing, he joked, "You're not a doctor, are you?"

Brad laughed. "I wish. Well, not really. I'd take the money, but that's not really the kind of job I'm cut out for."

"Me neither," Phil said.

"We can grab a table now if you want or wait till we're done with these." He lifted his mug and said with a wink, "To a great Saturday night." They clinked their glasses.

Phil glanced around at the growing crowd. "Maybe we'd better get a table now seeing as how it's filling up in here."

"Sure, good idea." Brad stood and led the way across the crowded room to an empty booth. They sat across from one another, and when Phil stretched out his legs, his foot bumped Brad's. His face heated.

Brad smiled and took a drink before leaning in to speak. "I've seen you in here before."

"Oh, yeah?" Phil said, surprised, mainly because he didn't remember ever seeing Brad there, but now he knew why he had latched on to him that first day at work like he had.

"Nice place, especially for the area. We're lucky to have this." Brad glanced around them.

Phil drank some more of his beer. The waitress approached and asked if they wanted anything to eat. They both ordered fish and chips and another beer.

When she'd gone, Brad rested his forearms on the table and leaned in again. "So, you said before that you'd gone to college for a while—L.A., wasn't it?"

Phil was impressed that Brad had actually been listening to him the first day they'd met. "Yeah, University of Southern California."

"What was your major?" Brad asked, seeming genuinely interested.

"Theater design," Phil answered. "But, like I said before, I didn't really get too far."

"College wasn't your thing?"

Phil gave a half-hearted shrug. "I guess you could say that."

"Well, I never went to college. I'm happy doing what I do. Can't complain, especially with all the building going on around here. You must get a lot of work too. It's funny our paths haven't crossed before now."

The waitress came and set their beers down. "Food will be right out," she said before hurrying off.

Sitting back in his seat, Brad rested against the seatback looking slightly uncomfortable. For the first time since they'd met, he seemed out of words.

Brad glanced toward the bar. "I wish we had some of those peanuts." He folded his arms across his chest and looked around the room but didn't seem to focus on anything in particular. "I'm getting hungry. Hope the food comes before long," he said impatiently.

"Well, she said it would be out soon," Phil said. "Are you okay?"

"Uh, yeah, sure." He paused and took a drink. His Adam's apple bobbed up and down as he swallowed.

Phil wondered what was going on.

Brad cleared his throat. "Phil, there's something I want to ask you."

"Okay, go ahead." Phil had a feeling he was going to say something about them hooking up later.

"Mr. Fisher, the owner of the house..." He paused and then met Phil's gaze. "How well do you know him? I mean, I know he drove you to the hospital the other day."

Phil was momentarily speechless. He didn't want to answer, but he had to. "Uh, why?" He ran his hand over his face. "What makes you ask?"

"I saw you talking to him this afternoon... and you guys were hugging. Looked a bit... uh, intimate."

Phil lowered his gaze to the tabletop, wishing he could hide underneath. It would have been much easier if Brad had propositioned him. Phil had wanted to push what happened with Cole this afternoon out of his mind. He had to face it and tell Brad something.

After taking a deep breath, he let it out. "We go back a long time... We dated in school."

Brad pressed his lips together, nodded, and said, "So, I have competition then?"

Phil didn't have to answer because the waitress appeared next to the table, setting the plates of fish and chips in front of them.

"Ketchup?" she asked. "Please," Phil answered.

"Let me know if you need anything else." She set the bottle between them and moved on to another table.

Phil squeezed ketchup on his fries, and Brad finally came out of his apparent trance and put his napkin on his lap.

Phil didn't like this other side of Brad—quiet and unsure of himself. He didn't like being responsible for the change in his date. After all, the guy had feelings.

Phil sighed and said, "Cole Fisher and I don't have a relationship. We hadn't seen each other in years. I can see why you'd think something was going on, but he'd just found out my dad had died. That's all that hug was about, so no, you don't have competition."

"Your dad died?" Brad asked with wide eyes.

"It was years ago, but Cole knew him so..."

Brad nodded. "Okay, I get it." He seemed to relax than and even smiled enough to show his dimples.

Phil smiled too, determined not to let Cole stop him from moving forward. "You know, the food you ordered doesn't go with your image," he joked.

Brad picked up his fork and drew his brows together. "My image?"

Phil grinned and put a french fry in his mouth. He chewed, swallowed, and took a drink of beer, enjoying the blank look on Brad's face. "I thought you were a health food nut."

Brad moved the food around on his plate. "It's fish. What's healthier than fish?" The corners of his lips turned up.

"Uh, maybe fish that's not fried." Phil smirked.

"Ah, so you do know something about health."

"Enough to know that fried food isn't the healthiest way to go."

"If you know that, why are you eating it?" Brad's fork dangled in his fingers.

"Same reason you are I guess."

Brad grabbed the ketchup and squeezed a generous amount onto his plate.

They ate their food with just a word here and there about the baseball game on the TV. When they were finished and the waitress had cleared their dishes, Brad asked, "Do you play pool?"

"I play sometimes."

"Maybe we can have a game or two. As long as you won't use your hurt hand as an excuse for why you lose." He winked.

"Sure. Sounds good," Phil said, glad Brad was back to his old self and that he'd suggested pool rather than hitting the dance floor. He was determined to live in the moment and forget the past, at least for tonight.

Phil rolled out of bed, careful not to disturb the cats. They weren't used to getting up this early. He quietly threw on his old clothes and headed to the kitchen for some coffee. He'd had a nice evening with Brad, which had ended early, before midnight, and now he was looking forward to picking up Eve in the Camaro for their horseback ride. The cabinet making job didn't leave much free time, so he had to squeeze everything in the best he could, and he wanted to wash the car before picking up Eve.

He worked steadily for an hour and had the car shining. Satisfied with the results, he headed back inside. The cats were up waiting for their food, and he took care of them first.

After a quick shower, he sat down to have his cereal. He thought about what it had been like to drive the car again. Taking Gail out in it the other day was the first step in erasing the unhappiness he associated with the car, and today Eve would get to ride in it and help him create more happy memories. He'd been foolish to have hidden the car away all these years, letting his bad feelings fester. Those feelings needed to be put behind him. The car had nothing to do with him and Cole—not really, and he had to make new memories.

He finished eating, put his bowl in the sink, and went outside to leave.

Chuck was standing by the car, and he whistled while giving it the once-over. "Where'd this come from?"

"From the past," Phil answered, ignoring the brief tightening in his chest.

Chuck gave him a long stare before asking, "Have you had this in the garage since you moved in?"

"Yeah. I had a tarp over it, but I finally decided to bring it out."

"I guess so!" Chuck said. "A car like this should be seen. What year is it?"

Phil rubbed the back of his neck. "It's a '96. I decided to start driving it again, and I was just leaving. Is there anything you need before I go?"

"Yeah, well, I wanted to ask if I can use your pitchfork. I'm spring cleaning, and I have to get some tumbleweeds and leaves gathered up and thrown in the trash."

"Sure, let me find it." Phil went into the garage, grabbed the garden tool, and then came out and handed it to Chuck.

"Thanks, I'd sure rather go riding in this car than work in the yard. When's the next cat show? I'll help you load up the truck and trailer whenever you need me."

"Thanks, Chuck. It's in two weeks. I'm going to work on the cat trees this evening."

"Okay. Well, you have fun in your car. I'll see you later."

"Have a nice day." Phil closed the garage and got into the car. He smiled at Chuck, who watched him back out of the driveway.

Eve opened the apartment door. "Uncle Phil, where did you come from?"

"Well, it wasn't from outer space if that's what you're thinking."

His niece laughed, and Gail called from inside the apartment, "Aren't you going to let your uncle in?"

Stepping aside so Phil could enter, Eve said, "I've been looking out the window for the last fifteen minutes. You must have come when I was looking at Mom's painting."

"Hi, baby brother," Gail said, not taking her eyes off the canvas in front of her.

Eve peeked out the window. "I don't even see your truck. Where did you park?"

Phil and Gail joined her at the window. "I didn't come in my truck. We're going in my car today," he said.

"What car? Did you get a new car?" Eve's gaze widened.

"It's not a new car, but you've never ridden in it," Phil said.

Standing behind Eve, Gail put her hands on her daughter's shoulders and then pointed outside the window. "See that red sports car? Your Uncle Phil got that car when he was just a couple years older than you are."

"That's your car?" Eve peered up at Phil.

"Yeah, sure is. Your mom helped me buy it way back when. Would you like to ride in it?"

"Yeah!"

"Uncle Phil took me for a ride the other day. I didn't tell you because I wanted you to be surprised." Gail rubbed Eve's shoulder.

"Well, I am. It's awesome! Is that what's been under that dusty old tarp in your garage?"

"Yeah, but don't worry. I spent all morning washing it, so you won't get any dust on you."

"Dirt doesn't bother me. We're going horseback riding aren't we? I've gotten plenty of dust on me from riding in your old truck." Eve tried to look innocent, but her eyes danced with mischief.

"You always want to give me a bad time, don't you?" Phil tugged on Eve's ponytail and kissed the top of her head.

Gail laughed and picked up Eve's backpack. "Here, don't forget your stuff. Your picnic lunch is in here for after your ride."

"Thanks," Phil said. Ready to go?" he asked Eve.

His niece rolled her eyes. "I've been ready for a half hour, Uncle Phil."

"Have a nice, quiet day," Phil said to Gail, kissing her cheek.

"Bye, Mom." Eve dashed out the door, and Phil followed her.

CHAPTER TEN

COLE GOT out of his SUV and took a deep breath. He'd wanted to come out to the park ever since moving back to the area, and he needed a distraction today, so here he was. Ever since yesterday, he'd been thinking about Phillip and the electrician going on a date, and it unsettled him. He'd have given anything to have spent the evening with Phillip last night.

The park appeared well kept up, just like he remembered, and being back was exhilarating, especially when he thought about bringing Dana here. The entrance fee was double what it had been back when he was in high school, but that was a sign of the times. Judging from the number of cars there, people didn't seem to mind the cost.

He smiled to himself remembering the nights Phillip had driven them out here in his red Camaro after closing time. Overnight campers were allowed in with a pass, and their friend who had worked at the gate had always let them in without one. He started walking toward the corrals where they'd parked on those dark, warm nights to talk and make out—and more. He caught a whiff of honeysuckle and noticed the lamas, camels, and horses out in the meadow. His emotions almost overwhelmed him, and he had to pause and compose himself.

After admiring the horses at the corral for about ten minutes and imagining bringing Dana here to ride, he turned away and headed toward the lake on the other side of the park where most of the people were enjoying the mild day. He approached the parking lot and a bright candy apple red sports car parked on the far side of the lot, opposite from where he'd parked his SUV, drew his attention.

As he got closer to the car, the sun hit the paint and brought out its shine. He let out a gasp at the beautiful vintage Camaro so much like Phillip's that it took him back in time.

He couldn't help but be drawn straight to the classic red car. Someone had taken great care of it. He swept his eyes over every inch and couldn't believe what he was seeing. Everything was exactly like Phillip's car. The wheels were the same, it was a Z28. He wasn't an expert on cars, but this one looked like it could be a mid-nineties model. Peeking inside, he noticed that the seats looked exactly like the ones in Phillip's old car. He stood rooted to the ground for a moment, then ran his hand through his hair and slowly moved to the back to check the license plate. The numbers and letters seemed familiar, but he couldn't be one hundred percent sure. What was the chance that Phillip's car would be here?

This was unreal—maybe he was dreaming, or his imagination was running away with him. He bent down again to peer through the window for a better look inside. After scrutinizing the front and back seats, he decided this was the car. Whoever owned it had taken great care to keep it in mint condition. Had Phillip kept the car all these years?

Just then he heard a young girl's excited voice blurt out, "Someone's trying to break into the car."

He jerked back, glanced in the direction of the voice, and widened his eyes. Phillip and the girl from the cat show were coming his way. They slowed their pace, and she stretched up to say something near Phil's ear, and then he said something back to her.

He jammed his hands into his pockets, stepped back another couple of feet from the car and smiled at the approaching pair. Phil wore a blue baseball cap, and his dark glasses hid his eyes, so Cole couldn't get a read on his emotions. He couldn't think of anything to say, so he hoped Phillip would say something.

They stopped a few feet from him, and Phil said, "Hey, Cole."

"Uh, hi. I thought this was your car." Cole felt foolish and wished he could think of something intelligent to say.

"Cole, this is my niece, Eve. Eve, this is my old friend, Cole."

"Hi, Cole," Eve said with a big smile.

"Pleased to meet you. You must be Gail's daughter."

"Yes, I am," Eve answered, looking up at Cole the whole time, still smiling. "We went horseback riding today and then we had a picnic, and I got to ride in Uncle Phil's Camaro."

He chuckled. "That sounds like the perfect way to spend a Sunday." He gazed at the Camaro again. "That's why I was looking at it. I was trying to decide if this was the same car."

Phil remained quiet, and Cole wished he could see his eyes—damn the dark glasses. He was totally uncomfortable not being able to tell what he was thinking.

Clearing his throat, he looked down at Eve, who seemed friendly, and said, "When my daughter arrives for the summer, I hope to bring her out here. She's about your age. Her name's Dana."

"How old is she?" Eve asked.

"Twelve years old."

"She doesn't live here?"

"She lives in New York, but she's coming for the whole summer. Maybe you can meet her while she's here." He shifted his weight nervously from one foot to the other.

"I'd like that."

"Well, let's not get carried away. We'll have to see." Phil placed Eve's cowgirl hat, which had been hanging down her back, on her head. "Now, we really need to get you home. Your mom's waiting." He put his hand on Eve's shoulder, steering her in the direction of the passenger door.

Eve stopped in front of the door and looked up at him. "Uncle Phil, maybe your friend would like a ride in the car."

"I'm sure he doesn't have time," Phil said firmly.

Eve pursed her lips. "He could ride with us when you take me home, and then you can bring him back up here to get his car." She then turned to Cole. "Do you have your car here? Are you in a hurry to leave?"

"I'm parked over that way." He indicated the direction with a nod of his head. "I'm just kinda kicking back today and taking things as they come."

Phil remained quiet, and Eve kept at him. "Well, I just thought it might be a good idea." She sent Phil a pointed look. "He said he has time. But if you don't... I guess it was a bad idea."

Cole had to try hard to hold in a laugh.

"It's not that I don't have time." Phil let out a big sigh and gave up a tight smile. Looking at Cole, he said, "If you'd like to ride along with us, get in."

There was no way for Cole to hide his grin as he stepped toward the car. Eve, wearing a mischievous smile, quickly moved to open the passenger door. "Why don't you ride up here. I'll take the back."

"He can ride in the back seat," Phil said sternly, and the smile that had played on his lips a moment ago was gone.

"That's cool," Cole said. "The back is fine with me. I don't want to take your seat, Eve."

Eve's chin tilted downward, and her smile disappeared, but she didn't argue. Once everyone was inside and buckled in, Phil backed out of the parking spot and headed out, stopping briefly at the gate to pick up a return pass.

All three were quiet—too quiet, so Cole cleared his throat and tried to get a conversation going, though he doubted Phillip would converse with him. "Do you go horseback riding often?"

Eve turned slightly in her seat to look at him. "This is the first time this spring. We usually go two or three times during the spring and summer. I had a horse named Thunder today. He was a chestnut. Uncle Phil's was a buckskin." She turned to Phil. "What was his name, Uncle Phil?"

"Buckshot," he said, barely loud enough to hear.

"Oh, yeah, I knew it was something strange." Eve let out a little giggle.

Eve's enthusiasm more than made up for Phil's lack of it. Cole didn't know if she was always like this, or maybe she was trying to get her uncle to lighten up.

"Dana has never ridden. I'm hoping to introduce her to riding while she's here."

"She's never ridden before?" Eve said, sounding surprised.

"Being from the city, she's into other activities—dance, music—things like that. I've been on a horse though. Your uncle and I used to go riding a lot back in high school, remember Phil?"

"Oh, yeah," Phil replied with a deep sigh.

The bad vibe he received made him change the subject fast. "What grade will you be in next year, Eve?"

"I'll be a freshman in high school. What grade will Dana be in?"

"She'll be entering her last year of middle school. She's mature for her age. I think you'd like each other."

"We're almost there," Phil said.

Cole wondered if he'd be able to pull more words out of him on the ride back to the park with just the two of them in the car.

Soon, they pulled in a parking space in front of Eve's building. Phil kept the motor running and made sure Eve had all her gear. "Let your mom know why I didn't come up," he said.

Before she opened the door, she glanced toward the back seat. "Are you going to sit up here now, Cole?"

For a moment he was unsure what to do. He had the feeling Phillip didn't want him in the front seat, but sitting in the back, like Phil was his chauffer, seemed really stupid, so he got out, said goodbye to Eve, and slid into the shotgun seat.

After Eve was safely inside the apartment, Phil backed the car up and shot out of the lot like he used to drive fifteen years ago.

Cole grabbed for the seatbelt and secured it around himself. "Take it easy, will you? I'd like to live to see tomorrow."

"Don't tell me you've turned into a pansy." Phil gave the car more gas.

Luckily, they caught up to some traffic, and Phil had no choice but to slow down and drive like a grown man. "Traffic will be heavier on the way back. People are on their way home this late in the afternoon," he said.

Cole breathed a sigh of relief, and when his heart rate leveled out, he smiled and said, "This is still an amazing car."

That earned him a smile that took him back in time, and there was nowhere he'd rather be right now than in this car sitting next to Phillip Thompson. He wanted this day to go on forever, and he was glad for the slower traffic.

"Your niece is something special," he said.

"Yeah, she's pretty much perfect." Phil's pride in her was evident in his smile.

"How's Gail doing?"

"She's okay. She works as an admissions coordinator in a nursing home here in Apple Valley, and she's an artist in her spare time. She's working toward getting a showing with a gallery. Her paintings are beautiful."

Cole nodded. "That's good. Does she have a nice husband?"

"She's not married—never was—the bum left her when he found out she was pregnant. Never saw him again. Gail did not deserve that, and neither did Eve." Phil let out a pronounced sigh.

Cole drew in a long breath. "Damn, I'm sorry to hear that. No wonder you stepped into the father figure role. Looks like you do a great job."

"How would you know?" Phil asked, sounding resentful.

"Uh, well, I don't know, but from what I saw today and at the cat show the other weekend..."

"Oh, yeah. That was pretty crazy." Phil took a brief look at Cole and then focused on traffic. "Did you know that was me there?"

"No, but I got a real odd feeling. It looked a little like you, but the facial hair threw me off."

"The glasses threw me off." Phil glanced Cole's way again, and they both smiled. "They suit you."

"The beard suits you." Heat crept up Cole's neck, and he avoided staring at his ex. An electric current rushed through him. Sitting inches apart in this car where so much love had been shared made him dizzy with excitement.

After an awkward silence, Phil asked, "Is the hurry to get your house finished because your daughter is coming?"

Cole swallowed hard. "Yes, I'd like to move her in there rather than have to bring her to the house I'm renting in Oak Hills."

"Oak Hills? Why way up there?" Phil stopped at a red light.

"Uh, long story." Cole smiled nervously.

"So, you and your Siamese cat are living in Oak Hills."

"Me and my two Siamese cats."

"I have two cats too."

Cole raised his eyebrows. "Wow, you do? Do you show them?"

"No, they're mixed breed—got them from the pound." Phil started driving again when the light changed, their car sandwiched in the lanes of traffic.

"I didn't want Moonshadow and Moonbeam ruining the rented furniture, so I got them a cat tree on the second day of the cat show."

Phil glanced at Cole. "You could have gotten one that Eve and I were selling."

"I got a different style—the more sculptured and sleek ones. You've probably seen them."

Phil kind of snorted and then smiled. "How's that working for them?"

"Uh, so far not so good, but once they warm up to it, I think they'll learn to love it."

"Yeah," Phil said. "My cats, Batman and Robin, have one that I made. They're on it every day."

"Well, your trees looked a little big to me. I needed to save space."

"Maybe once you're in your new house, you can get one they'll use." Phil gave Cole a sideways glance.

Cole's hands started sweating, and he cleared his throat. "Hey, you want to stop off and get something to drink? I'm buying."

"I think we should get back to the park, unless you're dying of thirst or something."

"I could use a Coke. Plus, I just thought we could talk." He wiped his hands on his pants.

"We're talking."

"Exactly. I thought we were having a good conversation, getting to know each other again."

Phil switched lanes and turned off the main drag, unexpectedly entering a fast food drive-through line. "Look, this isn't like we're on a date or anything. We'll get a drink to go," he said, sounding irritated and pulling ahead close to the next car's bumper.

"You had that good of a time last night with Brad, huh?"

"What?" Phil turned slowly and looked right at Cole. "That is none of your damn business."

"Okay. I'm sorry. I shouldn't have said anything." He looked away, clenching his jaw.

"Damn right."

They waited in silence until Phil pulled up to the speaker. He turned to Cole. "A Coke then... Large?"

"That'll do," Cole said, turning his head toward Phil again.

Phil answered the voice from the speaker asking for their order. "We'll have two large Cokes—nothing else, no sandwiches, no fries, just the drinks."

Cole thought he must be responsible for bringing out the old curmudgeon in Phillip, and he felt sorry for the gal on the other side of the speaker. An uncomfortable silence filled the car as they waited for their turn at the window. With each passing minute Cole felt the tension increase.

Relieved when their turn came, he took money from his wallet and passed it to Phil so he could pay.

"Thanks," Phil grunted.

"You're welcome." He stuffed his wallet back in his pocket and wished their pleasant conversation from earlier had continued.

Once Phil returned Cole's change to him, they stuck their straws into the lids of their drinks. Phil pointed the car in the direction of the park again and turned on the radio. The traffic had thinned out some, and soon they approached the main gate and showed their return pass. Cole indicated where he was parked, and Phil pulled into an open space three cars away. Cole had been half expecting him to stop near his SUV, let him out, and then take off, so when Phil turned off the radio, he welcomed the chance to talk some more.

"It was good seeing you, meeting your niece, and getting to ride in the Camaro again." Cole put his cup into the drink holder next to Phil's. He wasn't in any hurry to leave, and he wanted to talk. Phil had lost the annoyed look from earlier and was leaned back in his seat and seemed relaxed. He took that as an indication he might have some success if he tried again.

Phil killed the engine, took off his sunglasses, and looked him in the eye. "I'll come right to the point. We had our chance and we couldn't make it work so..."

Surprised by Phil's statement, Cole said firmly, "I think we'd still be together if I hadn't transferred to New York."

Phil clenched his jaw, and his whole body appeared tense. The deep sadness in his eyes ripped at Cole's heart. He wasn't expecting the seething anger that came next.

"You telling me this just makes everything worse! Can't you see that?" Phil spit out.

The back of his throat tightened. "I'm sorry. I don't know what to say..."

"How about goodbye! I wouldn't have even had you in this car if Eve hadn't pushed for it. She knows who you are, and she thought she was doing a good thing, but it's just made everything worse." Phil's fingers were curled around the steering wheel so tight they were turning white. "At least we can be civil to each other at work and pretend we're old friends, but we are no longer friends, Cole, and it's time for you to get out of the car."

The last thing Cole wanted was to get out of the car. He couldn't let their afternoon end this way. "Phillip, listen... let me apologize for wrecking our lives. It's all on me, and I just wish I could make it up to you somehow."

"Well, you can't. It's way too late."

Desperation rose up and seized him. "My folks are both gone now. I'm divorced." He gestured wildly with his hands, trying to convince Phil to see things his way. "I don't live in the closet anymore. You're free too as far as I can tell."

Phil closed his eyes, looked down, and shook his head. "For a smart man you aren't very smart at all. It's impossible to erase fifteen years, Cole. I'm not the man I was, and neither are you. You hurt me so bad..."

"If we could just spend some time together... Give this a chance, Phillip, please." He almost reached out and touched him, but resisted the urge, sure of the negative reaction he'd get.

Phil stared out the windshield. At least he wasn't insisting Cole get out of the car anymore.

"You know what started the string of events back then that led us down this path," Cole said quietly.

"You mean the day your old man caught us in bed in our dorm room?" Phil snapped.

"I don't like to think about that day." Cole squeezed his forehead with his thumb and middle finger. After a few beats, he took his hand away. "I was thinking our breakup had more to do with my mom's cancer. You know I only went along with what my father wanted because I didn't want to upset her—the doctors said she needed to avoid stress. They were moving to New York to be close to the best doctors and hospitals, and she didn't need to have my situation piled on top of all that."

Phil gaped at him. "Your situation? You mean that you're gay and that we were in love. Your old man used our relationship to control you. If he hadn't found out about us, he would never have insisted you transfer and move to New York with them."

"Maybe he still would have wanted me there. Mom needed me. You know that."

"Yeah... I know." Phil rubbed the back of his neck and closed his eyes for a moment. When he opened them again, he spoke in a strained voice. "What I don't know is where your *marriage* came in. What purpose did that serve?" he asked, his words almost catching in his throat.

Cole's guilt weighed heavily on his shoulders whenever he thought of Meredith—and now it was almost more than he could take seeing firsthand how bad he'd broken Phillip's heart. Tears threatened to fall, and it took several long moments before he could attempt to speak the truth.

"My dad set me up with Meredith. He wanted Mom to see me married with a family. He thought that would help her get through the treatments. Those were hell, Phil, worse than the cancer."

"So you agreed to an arranged marriage?" Phil asked, the shock in his voice coming through loud and clear. He stared wide-eyed at Cole like he was seeing a crazy person.

"No, it wasn't exactly like that... not an arranged marriage. He introduced us and encouraged the relationship."

"I don't need to hear the gory details," Phil said. "The whole thing just sucks."

"I know," was all Cole could say.

"Why the hell did you stay married to her for all those years? You couldn't have been happy."

Cole looked into Phil's eyes. "I wasn't happy until Dana was born. She's everything to me, Phillip. I know if you can't understand anything else, you can understand that."

Cole hated the pity in Phillip's gaze, but then those blue eyes lost their warmth and took on an icy stare.

The muscles in Phil's neck became visible as his anger rose. "Did your old man threaten to cut you out of your inheritance if you didn't go along with what he wanted?"

"No, that was never mentioned! Shit, Phil, I was their only kid. That was not a factor, and I can't believe you'd think that of me."

"Okay, whatever you say."

Cole lifted both eyebrows. "You don't believe me?"

Phil rested his head on the headrest and stared blankly above.

Cole seethed inside, and he closed his hands into tight fists. How could Phil even wonder for a moment that this had been about money?

Finally, Phil lifted his head and spoke. "I believe you, Cole, but that doesn't help me feel any better about what happened—about you actually marrying that woman."

"But all that's in the past, don't you see?"

After a few beats, Phil looked at him, his face serious and his eyes misty. "I'm not letting you back into my life again. I intend to do my best on your kitchen cabinets and get them done as fast as possible, but as far as having any kind of personal relationship, that's not in the future for us now or ever. It's time for you to go."

There was no use trying to change Phil's mind, so Cole didn't say another word. Too tired to argue with someone as stubborn as Phillip, he opened the door, got out, and headed to his SUV. He had to guess at the direction because his eyes were so full of tears he could hardly see.

The Camaro's engine roared to life, and his stomach clenched at the squeal of tires on the asphalt. He didn't look as the car sped away.

CHAPTER ELEVEN

THE PARKING lot at the Pasadena Convention Center was filling up fast when Phil and Eve arrived for their day at the cat show. After parking by the back entrance, they got out, and Phil began untying the cat trees in the trailer.

"If you can't find Michael right away, just text him, and text your mom too, so she'll know we're here," he told Eve before she hurried toward the entrance to check them in.

Phil yawned and rubbed a hand over his face. He needed coffee and would seek some out once he got the trees set up inside. Ever since he'd sent Cole on his way two weeks ago, he hadn't slept well. He'd made that decision with his head and not his heart, and he'd felt like shit ever since. If his heart really wished he'd given in and started something up with Cole, it was as dumb as a bag of hammers.

He'd only seen Cole at work a couple times during the past two weeks, and they'd said a polite hello but nothing more. Cole might have been there other days and stayed out of his line of sight, or he was satisfied with the progress they were making, and he didn't feel the need to check up on them that often. Whichever it was, Phil was glad. Seeing him was too painful.

On the drive today, he'd had to try to convince Eve that dating

Cole would be a big mistake. Gail had accepted his decision a lot better than Eve had when she'd called him the night of the horseback ride. He thought he could get Eve to stop badgering him by telling her he was seeing someone else. Normally she'd have been glad to hear that kind of news, but she'd really taken a liking to Cole, and she was stubborn as a mule and had her own ideas about what was best for him. Maybe she sensed that he wasn't very invested in the relationship with Brad.

By the time Eve came back with Michael, Phil had all the ropes untied. He was sure glad for Michael's help, especially today.

"Phil, what happened to your hand?" Michael asked.

Phil glanced at his bandaged hand. "Just a mishap at work. I got the stitches out on Monday, but I'm wearing the bandage for a while longer."

"Wow, stitches. That must have hurt. I can call Gary to come help us so you won't have to do as much. He's here today."

Phil shook his head. "No, I'm fine. He's probably busy inside with your stuff, and I've been working every day, so this is a piece of cake."

"I'll help," Eve said.

"I don't want you lifting anything too heavy." Phil started removing one of the cat trees.

"Don't worry about me." She flexed her muscles.

"You could hurt your back, and your mom would kill me."

Eve rolled her eyes. "Leave Mom to me."

Between the three of them, they had all the cat trees inside in short order. Michael helped arrange them in their section before he left to tend to his own merchandise.

Eve looked over all the cat trees. "Where's the pink and black special-order tower?"

"I sent it to the customer by UPS a few days ago. She couldn't come to Pasadena to pick it up," Phil said, as he arranged the little flags on some of the towers. "If you'll take over here, I've got to go move the truck to a regular parking space and then get myself some coffee. What do you want, honey?"

"I'll take coffee too," she said with a big grin.

He regarded her with a skeptical eye.

She giggled. "Gotcha, Uncle Phil. I'll have a Dr. Pepper."

Smiling, he shook his head. "Okay, coming right up after I move the truck."

After finding a parking space as close as possible, he went back inside. On his way to get the drinks, he glanced around for Michael's section and caught a glimpse of him and Gary standing behind their tables piled high with bags of cat food. At some point today, Eve would want to get samples for Batman and Robin. He wondered if Betty was there with her T-shirts, so he took a short detour and saw her from a distance arranging them on a portable garment rack. Once his cat show friends were accounted for, he headed to the food area and stood in a short line to get the drinks.

Would Cole be here today with his cat? Dammit, why did he have to think of him? He'd steer clear of the show ring and the show cat aisles because he didn't want to see him. Considering how they'd parted the day at the park, Cole would want to avoid him too, and he was sure he wouldn't come over to the vender area.

With coffee in one hand and Dr. Pepper in the other, he moved carefully around the crowd that had increased significantly in the hour and a half since he and Eve had arrived. Once back at their vendor space, he gave Eve her drink, and he couldn't wait to have a sip of his coffee. He sat down in a chair that Eve must have brought from somewhere, and he noticed a second one adjacent to his.

"Thanks for finding the chairs," he said.

"Betty came by with one and told me where they were, so I got another. I thought you'd like to sit down."

"You thought right." He took a bigger sip of the hot coffee.

"Are you okay, Uncle Phil?"

"Sure. I just needed a little caffeine." He smiled, looked around the auditorium, and took in all the vendors.

"The funny cat trees are set up over there," Eve said, indicating where she'd seen them across the room.

Smiling, he thought about Cole having bought one, and he questioned his ex's taste in cat furniture. Why did Cole have to keep popping into his head?

Phil and Eve stayed busy all morning, showing towers and answering questions. Every time he thought about taking time out for lunch, someone else wandered in, but he finally decided they'd need to eat anyway.

"Do you want to go get us something to eat while I stay here?" he asked Eve. "Looks like we're going to have to work through lunch."

"Okay. What would you like? Your wish is my command." She got up from her chair.

Phil pulled some bills from his wallet and handed them to her. "I feel like pepperoni pizza today."

She clutched the bills in her hand. "Okay, and what do you want to drink, more coffee?"

"No, I'll have a Coke. Can you carry it all?"

"Sure, no problem."

A woman came up and began asking questions about the colors on the trees, obviously quite interested in a custom-made tower.

Eve mouthed the words, "Be back soon," and dashed off toward the food vendors.

After answering all the woman's questions, Phil wrote down her order. She left, and he realized that he didn't know what time Eve had gone to buy the food. With a lull in customer activity, he was really starting to get hungry. He figured everyone was having lunch, and he hoped the downtime would hold long enough to give him and Eve time to eat in peace.

He leaned against a tall cat tower and gazed toward the front doors. Finally, he heard Eve's voice behind him. "Look who I found, Uncle Phil."

He turned, shocked to see Cole standing next to her. His ex-lover displayed a shy smile, something Phil had seldom seen the whole time he'd known him. Cole held on to a cardboard beverage holder containing three drinks, and Eve had three individual pizza boxes in her hands with napkins and straws situated on top.

Phil stepped forward and grabbed the boxes as Eve whispered, "He was in the pizza line, and I thought I should ask him to eat with us."

Her *cat that ate the canary smile* wasn't lost on him. He sighed. What could he do at this point?

"Hey, Cole," he said. "Maybe I can get another chair." He set the pizzas on one of the chairs, and Cole set the drinks on the other.

"I'll go get one," Eve said, and then darted away before either of them could react.

"She never runs out of energy," Phil said.

"Makes me miss Dana even more." Cole shoved his hands into his pockets. "I hope you don't mind my crashing the party here." He gazed to the top of the cat tower he was standing next to.

"It's fine." Phil glanced in the direction Eve had gone.

She was hauling the extra chair their way, so he hurried over to help her. Once he got it to their space, he unfolded it and set it in front of Cole.

"Have a seat."

Cole sat down, and Eve picked up the pizzas and sat down too.

Phil held up the beverage holder. "What do we have? Coke for you, Cole?

"Yeah, I have Coke."

"Two Cokes and a Dr. Pepper," Eve said. "The Dr. Pepper has a DP written on the cup."

"So it does. That's helpful." Phil passed them out and sat down.

Eve handed out the pizzas, straws, and napkins. "We all have pepperoni."

"That simplifies things too," Phil said.

They opened their boxes, balancing them on their laps.

Cole continued to stare at the cat towers while they ate, and Phil wondered why.

Eve must have noticed too, because she said, "Uncle Phil builds these in his garage. He even takes custom orders for color, type of carpet, and you can get sisal rope or carpet on the uprights."

"They're very nice," Cole said.

"The cats love them. Those *refined* towers over there," she nodded her head toward them, made a gesture with her wrist, and wrinkled her nose, "are very, shall we say, formal, compared to ours."

Phil couldn't hold in a chuckle and nearly spit Coke out of his straw.

Eve gave him an innocent look. "I'm just telling him which towers the cats prefer."

"I know, honey, and you're right. Cats love ours." He looked straight at Cole and smiled, realizing how Cole's presence had given him more of a pick-me-up than ten cups of coffee. This bothered him because he'd convinced himself that Cole was his past, and he didn't want him in his life, but he couldn't ignore how good this felt. He also couldn't ignore the fact that Cole had always been the most handsome and sexy guy he'd ever seen.

Pulling himself out of his thoughts, he sent his gaze to Eve. "Uh, Eve, I hope you've never made comments to the customers about those other cat towers like you just did to Cole."

She rolled her eyes. "Uncle Phil, I'm among friends here. I wouldn't go saying that to customers—even if it's true."

"Good to hear." He glanced at Cole and noticed his amused

smile, glad he didn't seem insulted by Eve's comment. She didn't know he'd actually bought one of those towers, and he wasn't going to tell her and embarrass him.

They'd just finished their food, and a husky voice came over the loudspeaker.

Please close all exits. We have a cat on the loose... Please close all exits!

Cole stood up and set his empty pizza box and paper cup on the chair. "I really shouldn't have left Moonshadow alone for this long. I'm going back to check on him, and we're due in the show ring soon."

"You don't think it's him that got out, do you?" Eve asked.

"No, but I'd feel better seeing him safe in his cage anyway. Thanks for the company." He started walking away.

Phil got up and caught up with him. "I'll go with you. Eve can stay with the towers for a few."

"Okay, if you want," Cole said, not slowing down.

They weaved through the crowd toward the show cat isles, and Cole quickened his steps.

To help calm his worried ex, Phil said, "There are hundreds of cats in here. It can't be yours that's missing."

The booming voice came over the sound system and delivered the same announcement, which only appeared to make Cole more uneasy. Seeing Cole that way, unnerved Phil, and his chest tightened. He could tell Cole felt the same about his cat as he did about Batman and Robin.

They reached the cage decorated with leopard material and various ribbons hanging on the outside. Only the black bowls and black litter box were inside. Phil's stomach dropped, and Cole cursed. Phil conjured up a picture of his own cats napping safe at home on their cat tower. Cole's poor cat had to be terrified.

He put his hand on Cole's shoulder. "We'll find him, don't worry. The exterior doors are closed. He's here somewhere."

Cole turned to the man at the next cage and asked, "How did he get out?"

"I'm so sorry, but my son opened the cage door. He knows he did wrong and he's sorry."

A little boy with a head of curly red hair sat on a stool sniffling. He looked about six years old, and Phil felt sorry for him, but he also felt bad for Cole, who was questioning the boy's dad about which way Moonshadow had gone and a whole host of other questions. Other cat people had gathered and were talking a mile a minute.

Phil stepped away and sent a text to Eve to let her know what was happening. He wanted to go look for the cat, but the auditorium was huge, and he had no idea where to start.

He turned his attention to Cole again, who was pacing back and forth looking helpless. He felt helpless himself. Cole stopped in his tracks when the announcer came over the loudspeaker again.

The Siamese cat has been found and will soon be reunited with his human.

Everyone cheered at the good news, and suddenly he was hugging Cole. As soon as he came to his senses, he backed away as if he'd touched fire, but what the heck, Moonshadow was found, and if that wasn't cause for a hug, nothing was. With all the stress and confusion, Cole probably wouldn't even remember the embrace.

Then he noticed Eve standing nearby, her lips curved into a smile and her eyes twinkling. Did she have a content expression because the cat had been found, or had she seen him hug Cole, or maybe both? He'd need to explain to her that the hug meant nothing. Getting her hopes up that anything could happen between them would only disappoint her, because it couldn't—it wouldn't. Nothing had changed since the day at the park.

Sometimes you just have to move on.

CHAPTER TWELVE

"EVERYTHING IS fine now, sweetie, believe me. Moonshadow told Moonbeam all about his adventure when we got home," Cole said into the phone.

"You need me there to help you with the cats, Father."

"I know, and the time will come soon. I've been getting ideas for things we can do while you're here. You're going to have a summer to remember."

Dana didn't say anything, and he heard muffled whispering on the other end of the line. "Dana, are you talking to your mother? Dana?"

"Mother wants to talk to you," Dana said after a few seconds of silence. Then her words came out so faint he could barely make them out. "She's in a bad mood—be careful."

"I love you, sweetie." He stood up from the couch with the phone pressed to his ear and waited to hear what Meredith wanted.

"How's the house—almost done?" Meredith asked gruffly.

"Soon, and once it's ready, I'll be moved in fast."

"Don't you have to shop for furniture?"

"I have everything chosen. Just waiting to give them the word on when to bring it. I found the perfect bedroom set for Dana."

Meredith snorted and then laughed. "How would you know

what the perfect bedroom set is for our daughter?"

"What's that supposed to mean?" He paced a little and hoped the conversation would be short.

"Nothing. Okay, you bought furniture. Now can I send the stuff you left here?"

"Uh, no, hold off on that for a little longer."

"I thought you said you were nearly in the house. Why can't I send it?"

Moonbeam walked into the room, so he sat back down on the couch, giving the cat a lap to jump onto. The cats provided a sense of calm, something he sorely needed whenever he spoke to his ex-wife.

"Cole, it's only a few weeks until Dana is supposed to arrive there. Do we need to adjust the date?"

"No!" he growled out harsher than he'd intended.

"I'll call you in a week, and maybe by then I can mail the stuff. I'm packing the boxes now so they'll be ready."

"Whatever you want. I'm sorry it's in your way."

"I told you before that I'm rearranging my office, and it involves a lot of work. Having more responsibilities at my job requires I have more space. I'm willing to pack your stuff, what more do you want!"

He sighed, concentrated on scratching Moonbeam's ears and noticed he needed to give the cat a good brushing session. Probably Moonshadow too. This house would be full of cat hair when he moved out. He'd have to clean thoroughly before he left or hire someone to do it.

"One more thing we should touch on and that's meals while Dana is there. I don't want her eating a lot of fast food. Restaurant food is okay as long as it's good quality. I don't want her coming back this fall having put on weight. Will you be hiring someone to cook?"

"I'm perfectly able to fix Dana's meals, and Meredith, kids her age do eat fast food. There's nothing wrong with that. I plan for her to be quite active while she's here anyway. I've got a big yard, a pool, and I'm putting up a basketball hoop..."

Meredith snickered. "Sounds exciting, but I can't see how a basketball hoop will help Dana stay in shape. She won't be interested in the least."

"We'll see."

He strained to hear what Meredith said next, something like

this will be a hoot, and he wasn't amused. At least she wasn't trying to weasel out of allowing Dana to visit.

Once he was finally off the phone, he rested his head against the couch, wishing he could have talked with Dana longer. He looked over at the cat tree and hoped Moonshadow would be on one of the perches, but there was no sign of him. He'd had the thing for weeks and neither cat had used it that he could tell. Maybe he would have to buy one of Phillip's trees after he moved into the new house.

He needed to get out to the house more and make sure the men were working as fast as they could. Phillip's cold and aloof attitude toward him when he'd visited the house the last couple weeks had been hard to take, and he'd received dirty looks from the electrician. Was Phil really serious about the guy? Brad seemed into Phil, and Cole couldn't blame him. Phil was sure a looker.

Phil had been friendly at the cat show. Would he treat Cole differently now? When the cupboards were finished and Phil moved on to another job, would they ever see each other again? If he couldn't get Phillip to reconsider rekindling their relationship, there'd be no reason to see each other—Unless Eve and Dana became friends, and if that happened, then their paths would probably cross.

Getting the girls together would be great because he really liked Eve. She'd be a good influence on Dana. He and Eve had exchanged phone numbers yesterday while talking in the pizza line, and he was glad. He hadn't seen any young girls around his new neighborhood. Would Phillip be okay with Eve meeting Dana? He'd been noncommittal the other day at the park when the subject had come up. And of course Eve's mom would have a say in it as well.

He took off his glasses and rubbed his eyes. He'd really had a nice time with Phillip and Eve yesterday...up until Moonshadow escaped the cage. Luckily that ended well. If only he and Phillip could end well too.

After having a pleasant lunch with Phillip at the cat show, maybe they'd be more relaxed around each other. Phillip had also initiated that hug after Moonshadow had been found. Getting his cat back safe and sound and receiving that hug had put him in high spirits for the rest of the day.

Thinking positive about his relationship with Phillip was the only thing to do. Despite the dismal conversation with him at the park, things had gone well at the cat show. They had the cats in common, the girls too, and their past. All that could be built upon, but he'd hurt Phillip so deeply.

Earning back his trust would take time, and he needed to be patient. He'd already waited fifteen years, and he was sure he had it in him to wait as long as it took. Phillip Thompson was worth it.

CHAPTER THIRTEEN

AS HE headed home from work, Phil wondered what Batman and Robin thought about having visitors in the house today. They'd been apprehensive last night when he'd brought his mom and aunt home from the bus station. He hoped the cats had warmed up to them today and kept them company since he couldn't stay home. Taking time off work wasn't an option.

He'd thrown himself into his work for the past few weeks, determined to get the job done. After his hand had fully healed, he'd worked unhindered staining the cabinets. Working with plumbers in the kitchen for the past week hadn't always been smooth sailing. Dillion had been a big help hanging the cabinets though—he was a lot stronger than he looked despite his slight build, and Phil had been grateful for that.

He pulled into the driveway and got out of his truck. The back door swung open and his mom stood there smiling. That was something he hadn't seen very often at his door. He smiled back, walked up to her, and he gave her a hug and a kiss. They went inside, and she poured them a glass of iced tea.

He sat down at the table with her. "Where's Aunt Ruth?"

"She's taking a nap so she'll be ready for tonight."

"I'm glad you two could come. It means a lot to Eve." He drank some tea.

"I wouldn't miss seeing my granddaughter graduate from junior high. She's such a sweet girl. Gail has done a wonderful job raising her."

"Yes, she has."

"And you have too." His mom patted his hand. "They count on you, and you've always been there for them."

"Thanks, Mom."

"Did you get a lot done at work today?" She took her hand away and sipped her tea.

"All that's left now is putting the hardware on, so the pressure is basically off. At least my part is almost done, so the floor man can get in there."

"What a coincidence that you found yourself working on Cole's house. I couldn't believe it when you first told me."

"Yeah, I couldn't either, but I made it through, and now I'm almost done, so that's that."

She lifted one eyebrow. "The two of you won't be seeing each other after this?"

"We're different people now, Mom. He was married for years, has a daughter..."

"Yes, that's true, but did that change him into a different person, or are you not able to forgive him?" She reached over and put her hand on his. "Maybe you need to think about seeing someone... a counselor to help you get past this."

He sighed. "Mom, why are we getting into such a deep subject? Why don't we just enjoy this time together and have a great evening at Eve's graduation? I think that's best for all of us."

His mother got up from the table and took her glass to the sink. "I'm going to go put on my dress and see if Ruth is awake. We'll need to leave before too long, won't we?"

He checked the clock. "In an hour or so. I'll go shower—doesn't take me long. I'll feed the cats before we go, unless you and Aunt Ruth overfed them today."

His mom laughed softly. "We didn't do anything but pet them and play with them a little—no extra food."

He smiled. "Okay, I'll take your word for it."

"They're the sweetest little cats," she said, more to herself than to Phil.

He watched her leave the kitchen and then he finished off his tea. What his mom had said about a counselor had hit him totally out of the blue. He couldn't believe she thought he needed counseling. That was bizarre.

He set his glass on the table, and work crept into his mind. Cole hadn't been at the house much these past weeks. Even when he'd stopped in to check on the progress, he hadn't had much to say. Although, with Dillion around and the plumbers in the kitchen, things had been noisy and hectic—not conducive for conversation. That was for the best though. His duty had been to do a good job for the boss, and he'd done that. End of story.

Phil spotted Gail in the crowd that was gathering in the lobby of the school's auditorium. He guided his mom and aunt over to her, and they greeted each other with hugs.

"We can go sit down whenever we want," Gail said to their mom and Aunt Ruth. "And I need to speak with you," she whispered to Phil.

"Maybe it'll be quieter in our seats. Let's go sit down." He took his mom's arm and escorted her while Gail helped Aunt Ruth push through the thick crowd of excited family members all talking at once.

When they finally figured out where to sit and Phil helped them down the row, the two older ladies took their seats without hesitation.

"I felt like using my cane to help clear a path through all those people," Aunt Ruth joked. "And you could have used yours too, Elizabeth."

"Thank goodness no one had to resort to beating off the crowds." Phil helped his mom set her cane by the chair and find a spot to hang her purse on the seatback. "Are you comfortable, Aunt Ruth?" he asked.

"Yes, I'm doing okay now," she answered.

He glanced around for Gail. She stood a few rows away talking with some women, probably other mothers. He sat down next to his mom.

"Looks like we've got a good view of the stage," he said.

"Yes, I think we'll be able to see just fine from here."

"I hope the microphone works well. My hearing isn't what it used to be," Aunt Ruth said.

"Oh, I'm sure it will be in good working order," Phil's mom said.

Phil checked his watch. "We don't have long to wait."

The seats filled up as the minutes ticked by, and he'd lost sight of his sister amongst all the people. When was Gail going to come and sit down and tell him what she wanted to say?

As he looked around for her, he saw a guy who looked a lot like Cole standing at the entrance to the auditorium. Blinking a couple times, he tried to decide if his eyes were playing tricks on him. This man wasn't wearing glasses, and he was dressed in black slacks, a white dress shirt, and a black and purple-striped tie.

California casual attire was more comfortable for him, so he hadn't bothered with a tie, but now he wished he had because most of the men wore them. He had a couple ties, neither of them in such a bright color as purple. At least he'd worn dress pants and a dress shirt—not his usual Levi's and T-shirt. He'd even put on dress shoes, which sure didn't feel very comfortable.

He kept his eye on the man at the door, waiting until the guy turned his head. After a few more moments, he did, and Phil sucked in a breath. What the heck was Cole doing here? He sure looked good all dressed up. Cole had always had a sense of style and knew what to wear to different functions. Maybe he'd chosen a purple tie because of the school colors. He bet Cole had on some real nice shoes.

Gail navigated her way down the narrow row, diverting his attention from Cole. She had some difficulty passing the people already seated, but she finally reached the empty chair beside him. Instead of sitting down, she put her hand on his shoulder and leaned down to speak into his ear.

"Phil, Cole's going to be here tonight. Eve invited him. I was so shocked, and there wasn't anything I could do because she told me after she'd called him and extended the invitation. I don't know what's gotten into her."

"Yeah, I just noticed he's over at the entrance," he said, motioning toward Cole.

"So, he's here. I'm sorry. I know you said you didn't want to see him other than at work."

"Calm down. It's okay. What's done is done. This is Eve's graduation, and if she wants him here, that's all right with me."

Gail sighed loudly. "Thank you. One less problem to deal with then. I should bring him over. I'm not sure if there's a chair for him, but we'll figure something out." She struggled past the seated people, reached the aisle, and took off toward Cole.

Phil's mom turned to him. "What's going on?"

"Eve invited someone, and Gail's going to bring him over. It's Cole, so try not to faint."

Her eyes widened. "Cole? Well, how nice, I guess. Why would she invite him? I'm confused."

"She's met him a couple times and she likes him. His daughter is coming for the summer, and he told her he'd like them to meet, so maybe that's why she took a liking to him."

Phil's mom turned to Ruth and began filling her in. Aunt Ruth had met Cole once before, years ago, but he didn't know if they would remember each other. He looked down the row trying to determine if there was any way to make room for him. He stood up to see if there were enough chairs for people to move down one seat, and once he got everyone's attention, he was able to make that happen.

A minute later, Gail and Cole arrived at the end of the row. They seemed relaxed around each other, making conversation and laughing a little.

Phil stood and motioned to them. "There're two chairs here," he said loud enough for them to hear.

Gail nudged Cole to go first. Why did she decide that he and Cole should sit together? He didn't want to make a big deal over it and cause a scene at Eve's graduation so he'd adapt.

"Hey, Cole," he said, once he'd reached the chair beside him.

"Fancy meeting you here." Cole smiled at him.

"I almost didn't recognize you without your glasses." Phil stared into Cole's eyes. Heat prickled his cheeks, and he quickly averted his gaze.

"Sometimes I wear contacts," Cole answered.

Once they were seated, Phil's mother leaned forward and peered past him at Cole.

"Cole, you remember my mom, don't you?"

"I sure do. Good evening ma'am. It's nice to see you." Cole reached across Phil to give her hand a squeeze.

Phil tried hard not to let on how his body, especially below the waist, was reacting to Cole's arm brushing across him. His face grew hotter, and his stomach fluttered. His mom smiled at Cole. Ruth leaned in and looked their way.

"Aunt Ruth, this is Cole Fisher, my old school friend."

"Hello," Ruth said with a thin smile. Phil didn't think she recognized him.

"Nice to see you," Cole said to her.

"Do you remember meeting my aunt way back when?" Phil asked Cole as they leaned back in their chairs.

"Sure I remember," Cole answered. "I'm glad to see your whole family could be here."

"Yeah, Mom and Aunt Ruth are staying with me for a couple days."

His mom patted him on the arm. He got the feeling she was happy that Cole had joined them.

"That's real nice," Cole said.

An uncomfortable silence settled over them, but within seconds the lights brightened, and a gentleman walked onto the stage. Phil was grateful the ceremony was about to begin because after exchanging pleasantries, he had no idea what to say. Cole being there had taken him by surprise, and he wasn't sure how to handle it. All he was sure of was that the more he was around Cole the more affection he felt for the man. His heart needed to wise up.

After a brief introduction and welcome to the event, everyone stood, and the kids marched in and stood in front of their seats at the back and each side of the stage. Gail must have known where Eve would be because she was taking a ton of pictures. Phil had a hard time locating Eve, but he finally caught sight of her in her purple cap and gown. She looked very grown-up. He leaned down and whispered her location to his mom. Judging from the big smile on Cole's face, he must have seen her too.

After the students took their seats, the audience sat down. By the time several speakers took the stage and gave speeches, Phil was getting tired and couldn't help squirming in his hard chair. He glanced to his right. His mother looked tired too, but a quick peek to his left revealed that Cole was wide awake and totally into the ceremony.

The adult speakers were finally done, and the salutatorian and valedictorian spoke at the podium. Then, the graduates sang the school song. Finally, the vice-principal started calling students' names and the principal began handing out the diplomas. Phil found it excruciatingly slow waiting to hear Eve's name. There must have been 300 students. Cole still looked happy and alert, maybe thinking ahead to when his daughter would also graduate.

At last, he heard *Eve Elizabeth Thompson*, and he, Cole, and Gail stood up. Phil helped his mom up, and Aunt Ruth struggled to her feet as well. They all clapped loudly, and Cole gave a commanding whistle with his fingers in his mouth. Phil had never perfected that skill, so maybe Cole had served a good purpose after all because Eve turned her head in their direction. She smiled widely while holding up her diploma, allowing her mom the opportunity for some more great photos.

The ceremony concluded with the closing remarks, and he suddenly wondered if Gail had invited Cole to join them for dinner. He wished he didn't care, but he wanted him there. In the noise and confusion of leaving their seats, he couldn't get his sister's attention. He quickly asked Cole to help his mom and aunt while he caught up to Gail. Before they reached the students in the reception area, he tapped her arm and whispered in her ear.

"Is Cole coming to the restaurant?"

"Eve invited him," she said, sounding apprehensive.

He let out a breath. "That's okay, don't worry about it."

Gail kissed his cheek. "Thank you." She hurried away to find Eve among the rest of the students.

Cole appeared next to him with his mom and aunt on each arm. Phil felt a bit guilty for rushing away and leaving Cole to tend to them.

"Thanks, buddy." He nodded toward the two ladies. Phil hadn't called anyone *buddy* in fifteen years, and he didn't know how that slipped out.

Cole stared at him as if he didn't even realize he was being crowded and bumped into by friends and relatives of the graduates—like everyone else was invisible, and they were the only two people in the room. The look was so intense that Phil had to turn away.

Phil took his mom's arm and steered her toward the large group of kids wearing caps and gowns. Cole followed behind with Ruth on his arm. Phil caught sight of Gail's auburn curls, and he guided his mother over to her, but he didn't see Eve anywhere.

"Hey, where's Eve?" he asked.

"Lovely graduation," their mom said.

"Eve's over there." Gail pointed to Eve crying and huddling with another girl.

Phil narrowed his eyes. "What's going on?"

"Eve's been on an emotional roller coaster lately," Gail said, looking a bit flustered. "Remember, I mentioned that her BFF will be moving soon? She's having a harder time adjusting than I thought."

"What a shame," Aunt Ruth said.

"I'll go get her." Gail walked over to join the girls.

Phil glanced at Cole. "I guess you heard that. Just a bit of teenage drama."

"No problem. I've been through plenty of that, and my daughter's not even a teen yet." He chuckled softly.

"How old is your daughter?" Ruth asked.

"Dana is twelve. She'll be with me for the summer."

"I see. That's nice."

"Twelve years old is a sweet age," Phil's mom added.

Phil didn't like how the conversation irritated him—a reminder of Cole's marriage, which always irked him. Waiting awkwardly, he wished Gail would come back with Eve, and they could all leave for the restaurant.

Taking longer than he'd have liked, Gail led Eve back to their little group. Eve's eyes were a bit red, but all things considered, she'd pulled herself together well. She proceeded to give each of them a hug, murmuring a few words in each of their ears.

Before she threw her arms around him, she smiled and said, "The show must go on."

He kissed her head and hugged her tightly, proud of her inner strength.

She hugged Cole last. Phil thought he heard "thanks for coming." He was surprised at how comfortable she seemed with Cole, a guy she'd only met a couple times. He'd been sure she'd invited Cole because of him, but her friendly interaction with him seemed to indicate they had somehow formed a friendship all their own.

They all walked out together, and Cole smiled and said, "See you at the restaurant." He turned and headed toward the parking lot.

Phil escorted his mom and aunt to the Camaro while Gail and Eve headed to their car.

Phil pulled into the parking lot of The Red Lobster and Cole was already there standing by his SUV. After Phil parked, Cole hurried to the passenger side of the Camaro and opened the door for Ruth and Elizabeth. Phil rushed around the car, and together they helped Aunt Ruth out first.

Phil's mom groaned a little as she struggled to get out of the back seat, but she smiled when she was finally outside the car. "We almost needed a crane to get me out," she joked.

"I didn't think you'd even be able to get up into my truck, so I thought you'd do better in the car." Phil grabbed his mom's cane from the back seat and handed it to her.

"It's a lovely car." Aunt Ruth rearranged her purse.

"Yes, it is very pretty." Phil's mom patted him on the shoulder. "I remember the day Phil got it. He was so excited."

"You must have had fun in a car like this back in the day," Aunt Ruth said.

Phil chanced a glance at Cole, who looked like he was holding in a smile. Was the talk about the car bringing back some of the same memories for Cole as it was for him?

They all walked slowly up to the restaurant's entrance. Phil was glad for the help with the ladies, but he wasn't sure how he felt about Cole being included in their evening. One minute he was okay with it and the next he wasn't, but he didn't have a choice, so he was trying to make the best of the situation.

"Shall we go in to wait?" he asked his mother.

"Yes, maybe we can sit down inside," she answered.

"That sounds like a good idea." Ruth's cane tapped with each step she took.

Once in the foyer, the women found enough room to sit down on a bench, and Phil walked over to the hostess podium.

"Reservation for Thompson," he said to the young lady. "The other two people in our party will be here shortly, so we'll wait out here before being seated."

The hostess nodded and smiled in agreement.

He rejoined the others. Cole stood near the bench, a slight smile lifting the corners of his mouth. Phil took a deep breath. Cole was so handsome dressed up like he was, and Phil tried hard to wipe the image of Cole taking off those nice clothes before bed. Did Cole still sleep naked? He closed his eyes briefly before opening them and willing himself to think of something that wouldn't end up getting him into trouble.

Then Cole stepped up close, and while tugging on the front of Phil's tieless shirt and grinning, he said softly, "I guess you never learned how to tie a necktie—still need me to do it for you just like back in school?"

Phil drew his brows together. The statement rubbed him the wrong way. He didn't appreciate Cole poking fun at him, and he glanced around to see if anyone had heard. Still frowning, he stared at Cole.

Cole's grin disappeared, and he stepped back. "Sorry, that was a dumb joke."

Just then, the door opened, and Gail and Eve appeared, diverting a potential unpleasant reaction on Phil's part. He hurried to hold the door and greet them, and then the hostess led them to their table.

During dinner, he let go of his annoyance, and once again he began enjoying Cole's company. Eve had wangled the seating arrangement, putting Cole next to him. Maybe she'd be an event planner someday.

"The food is delicious here," Ruth said, and Phil's mom agreed.

"The service is good too." Gail looked at Phil, and she added, "Good choice on the restaurant."

"Are you having a good time?" Phil asked Eve, who sat across from him and Cole.

A wide grin spread across her face. "How could I not—it's the beginning of summer vacation!"

"Do you have a lot of fun plans for the summer?" Cole asked.

"I will, but I haven't made any yet. My best friend is leaving..." She glanced down, blinked hard a few times, but then she raised her gaze and gave Cole a big smile. "I'm looking forward to meeting Dana."

"I think that's going to work out real good." Cole wiped his mouth with his napkin.

Phil wasn't sure about the prospect of the girls meeting. After all, Dana was a couple years younger than Eve. Cole had said Dana was mature for her age, but so was Eve. Well, whatever—they'd work it out. All he knew at the moment was he felt pretty good. Food always had that effect on him, and his wood-grilled shrimp and sirloin tasted delicious.

Cole had been fairly quiet during dinner, probably regretting opening his big mouth and putting his foot in it earlier. He'd always been a jokester though, and Phil didn't think he meant to be mean-spirited. Maybe he'd overreacted to Cole's comment. He still wished he'd worn a tie.

After the ladies had their leftovers put into little boxes and the dessert plates were cleared, the waitress brought the check. Before she could put the folder in Phil's outstretched hand, Cole swooped in to grab the check. Phil was momentarily stunned, but he wasn't about to let moneybags pay the tab when he'd been invited to join them, and he could not believe how bold Cole was acting—treating him like he wasn't able to pay for his family's celebration. He took hold of the folder and yanked it right out of Cole's hand. Cole didn't quibble, which was good because he was prepared to make a scene if he had.

Everyone gathered their things and walked out to the foyer. The women handed their boxes to the men and made a beeline to the ladies' room. Did Cole feel as uncomfortable as he did as they stood there together holding on to the doggie bags?

"I guess you'll be heading back to Oak Hills now," he said.

"Yes, but I'll wait and say good-bye to everyone." Cole adjusted the boxes in his hands.

"Sure." Phil shifted his weight nervously from foot to foot. Evidently Cole wasn't in a big hurry to leave, so maybe he was the only one who was edgy.

"Are you trying to get rid of me?" A muscle in Cole's jaw twitched.

Was that a serious question or was he joking with him? "Why would I want to get rid of you?" he asked, not even trying to disguise the sarcasm in his tone.

Cole focused on the floor as if there was something very interesting down there. Phil almost wished his words hadn't come out so harsh. He was just so damned confused. One minute he was glad Cole was there and the next...

Cole finally looked up and locked eyes with him. "If I made you uncomfortable by being here tonight, I'm sorry. I should have left after the graduation."

"Look, this was Eve's night and she invited you, so I tried to make the best of the situation. I guess I didn't always succeed, but I did try."

"I was hoping..." Cole let whatever he'd been going to say remain a mystery.

Phil sighed. "Look, this wasn't a date or even close. You came for Eve and helped make her graduation special—that's it. The evening is over now and it's time for you to leave."

Cole looked down at the floor and then back at Phil. "You didn't bring Brad or anyone else."

"What the hell does that have to do with anything?" Phil spit out.

"I'm sorry. I shouldn't have said that." Cole drew in a long breath.

"I'll say this again—I have no interest in giving us another shot, so don't get any ideas just because we spent this time together with my family."

The ladies' room door opened, and the women filed out talking and laughing. Thankfully, none of them seemed to notice any tension between the two of them. A headache started building in his temples, and all Phil wanted was to get his mom and aunt home.

They stepped outside, and he watched each of the ladies in his life say goodbye to Cole. When that was done, Cole glanced Phil's way and gave a slight nod, said, "Thanks for dinner," and then he walked quickly into the parking lot toward his SUV.

Even though he had said this was what he wanted, for Cole to leave, his emotions were all over the map, and he had to try hard to compose himself.

He'd been doing fine until Cole had blown into town, and he wished his ex had never set foot back in Apple Valley. With that man around, his uncomplicated life was becoming a thing of the past. He sighed and looked up at the stars. Uncomplicated was good, but maybe uncomplicated was just another word for boring.

CHAPTER FOURTEEN

WITH MAY almost in the rearview mirror, Cole had been checking in at the house nearly every day since Eve's graduation, and he was pleased that almost everything was finished. Today, like each of the past ten days, he sped along the freeway toward his new house. His SUV seemed to know the way without him having to steer it along.

Brad had been the first of the original workers to move on, and he had been glad to see him go—not that he was jealous—he was sure that Phillip wasn't serious about him. There was something about Brad that hadn't impressed him since day one. He wasn't very cordial, bordering on rude, as far as he was concerned. Tom had said he was excellent at his job and that's all Cole had needed. Though, he did have to wonder why Phillip had taken up with the guy. Brad was nice-looking despite the long mane, and evidently, he had more to talk about with Phillip than with him. Maybe bosses made him uncomfortable.

He turned up the air conditioner a notch. Today would probably be Phillip's last day, and Howard would finish the kitchen floor within a day or two. Then only the wall covering professionals stood in his way. They'd require another week to finish, and the Memorial Day holiday would slow them down by a few days. He was optimistic though, and if nothing went wrong, he'd have the house ready for Dana's arrival. She had her plane ticket, dated June fifteenth, which was just over three weeks away.

Meredith was worried about Dana flying alone, and he had the distinct impression she wanted him to suggest that she accompany their daughter, but that wasn't going to happen. Luckily, taking the time away from work would be a big burden on Meredith, so she hadn't pushed. Dana didn't seem to have any qualms about flying alone anyway.

After rounding the bend leading into the valley, the glare hit his eyes, and he lowered the sunshade. This place already felt like home, and once Dana arrived it *would* be home.

Excitement filled him at the thought of their new house filled with the furniture he'd selected. He'd chosen different furnishings from what he'd been used to, but he was no longer a big city dweller, and his new home in the California desert called for something completely different. He couldn't wait for Dana to see it all—and for Moonshadow and Moonbeam to see their new home too.

Having this project come together now to occupy his every waking moment was what he needed to help rid his thoughts of Phillip's stinging words on the night of the graduation. His optimism had taken a big hit that night, and he still hadn't recovered. He'd need all the strength he had to keep trying. Every time they had made a step forward they'd take two back. He didn't want to give up, but he didn't want to hurt Phillip anymore either—his pain was so evident. He'd stayed out of Phil's way at the house, and they hadn't spoken since that night.

Sighing, he tried to push thoughts of Phillip Thompson out of his mind. Thinking of their damaged relationship hurt way too much. He wished they could retrace their steps and go back to how they once were, but that seemed impossible after what he'd done to them.

When he reached the house, Phillip's truck was parked in the driveway for probably the last time. Tom had said all Phil had left to do was finish putting the hardware on the cupboards. They were beautiful—better than he could have imagined. He was impressed with Phillip's ability, but his dad had been a fantastic carpenter too, and obviously Phil had inherited the talent. Of course it helped that his dad had taught him all he knew. He took a deep breath and closed his eyes. One step closer to having the kitchen done, and that was a good thing, but Phillip not being around anymore depressed him.

He headed into the house, stopping for a moment to admire the hardwood floor in the entryway and in the formal living room. The sound of a drill came from the kitchen, and he assumed it was Phillip working. He entered the family room, happy to see the painters were more than half finished. The room took on some personality now that the walls had some color. The warm earth tones gave the space a relaxing, homey feel. He especially liked the Saddle Tan paint on the accent wall. The painters must be on lunch break because they were nowhere to be seen, but they'd left their ladders, drop cloths, and paint cans. Standing there facing the stone fireplace, he imagined his oversized handcrafted wooden clock hanging above, and how it would dress up the room even more. He had plans to decorate the rustic mantle with pictures of Dana and the bronze galloping horse statues that had called his name in the store.

He decided to go upstairs to check on the progress in the bedrooms. When he stepped out of the family room Dillion stood in the entryway with his phone in his hand. Not wanting to interrupt if he was about to make a call or send a text, he didn't go any farther, but Dillion kept standing there staring at the phone. Cole waited a little longer, and then he took a step toward the boy and cleared his throat to get his attention. When that didn't work, he spoke up.

"Hi, Dillion."

The boy must have been deep in thought because he nearly jumped out of his skin, gaped at him momentarily and stuck his phone in his pocket.

"Uh, sorry, I didn't mean to startle you," Cole said.

"That's okay, Mr. Fisher. I was just trying to make up my mind about something."

"Sounds serious. Anything I can do to help?"

Dillion's eyelids drooped, and he wouldn't make eye contact.

"I'm sorry if I interrupted you. I was just having a look around. Are you okay?" Cole took a step toward him.

Dillion rubbed his hand on his temples as if the weight of the world was crashing down on him.

"I'm a pretty good listener." He briefly squeezed Dillion's shoulder.

"I think my girlfriend and I are breaking up," Dillion finally said, looking up at him.

"Oh, well, no wonder you look upset. What do you mean you *think?*"

"She said we should take the summer off from dating. I don't want to. I was thinking of calling her to try to change her mind, but I've already told her I don't like the idea, and she still says we should."

"Did she give a reason?"

"She said we're too young to know if we're really meant for each other. She says we need to date others before we can make up our minds. I know she's the one for me. I don't want anyone else." Dillion's eyes welled up with tears.

"So, you didn't have a fight or anything before she came to this conclusion?"

"No, nothing like that. I think other people were the reason she started thinking this way because we were happy. We have a blast together, and I don't want it to end." He lowered his gaze to the floor.

"Well, maybe it won't. Maybe she'll miss you and want to come back. Maybe you have to give her this time."

"Can I ask you a question, Mr. Fisher?"

"Of course, anything."

He glanced up at Cole, and with tears shimmering in his eyes, he asked, "Do you think kids my age can know who they should marry?" He dropped his gaze to the floor again.

Cole placed both hands on Dillion's shoulders, and even though the boy wouldn't look up at him, he spoke straight from his heart.

"Yes, I do think that in some cases kids your age can know who they should be with for the rest of their lives. I know because it happened to me."

Now he had to fight back his own tears, but he went on. "My advice to you is to never give up if she's the girl you love. Call her today and let her know how you feel. Give her time if she needs it, but don't stop letting her know how much you love her and how much she means to you. You'll be sorry for the rest of your life if you let her go."

Dillion wiped his eyes and smiled weakly. "I'm going to follow your advice. Thanks, Mr. Fisher."

Cole gave him a reassuring smile. "Good. I hope it works out for you—honestly I do. Hey, would you be interested in helping me put up a basketball hoop over the garage door right now if you aren't needed in here?"

"Okay, I can do it. No problem."

They walked out the front door together, and Cole asked, "Have you played basketball before?"

"A little," Dillion answered.

"Well, after we get the hoop up, maybe we can shoot a few baskets. I have a basketball in the SUV."

"The trucks would be in the way." Dillion glanced at the garage door and the trucks parked in the driveway.

"Well, I'm sure we can get everyone to move their trucks out to the curb. I'm the boss, well, next to your dad."

"That'd be great, Mr. Fisher."

"You can call me Cole. I think we're on a first name basis. After all, we've known each other quite a while now."

A beam of happiness spread over Dillion's face. "Okay, Cole."

When he came back from retrieving the wall-mount basketball hoop from his SUV, he was surprised to see Phil standing next to the garage with Dillion. Cole walked slowly up the driveway wondering why Phil was outside. What kind of reception would he get? Phillip looked relaxed, and was smiling at something Dillion said. He hoped his good mood wasn't because he was finished with the job and anxious to get on his way.

"Hey, Cole. I hear you're putting together a little basketball game and didn't invite me to join in." Phil acted insulted, but a playful smile curved his mouth.

"Well, first off we have to mount the hoop." Cole glanced down at the hoop in his arms.

"How are you planning to do that with no tools? Or are they still in your SUV?" Phil asked.

"Uh, yeah, I've got tools—of course I do." Cole hoped he wasn't blushing.

"I can help you guys. I've got tools, and I'm all done in the kitchen."

"Cool," Dillion said, and Cole readily agreed to the help, wondering why Phil had come out to join in like this. He was glad, so he didn't think too hard on the reason—just let it happen.

"What kind of stucco is on the house?" Phil glanced at the garage wall.

Cole set the hoop down. "It's hard cement stucco."

Phil disappeared into the house and came back wearing a tool vest. He carried a wrench, tape measure, and a level, which he set down in the driveway.

He walked toward his truck and said over his shoulder, "I need to get my hammer drill and a masonry bit. Dillion, there's a tall ladder in the backyard. Will you bring it out here, please?"

When Dillion was halfway to the gate, Phil added, "Bring the battery off my drill too."

Cole followed Phil to the truck and looked over his shoulder. "Is this going to be complicated?"

Phil rooted around in his toolbox. "No, piece of cake. All I need are the right tools."

Cole rubbed his chin. "I guess I didn't really have this planned out too well. Do you have to use a hammer drill?"

"It'll make it easier. How about opening the box so we can get the measurements for the mounting brackets?"

The three of them worked together for two and a half hours through many curses, a lot of sweat, and effective teamwork. Finally, by late afternoon, Phil deemed the basketball hoop good to go, and was the last to come down the ladder to join Cole and Dillion in the driveway. All three admired the hoop.

Cole clapped his hands together. "Ready to try it out?" He looked from Dillion to Phil.

"Sure, I thought that's why we put the thing up," Dillion said.

"Let me put my stuff away and then I'll see if I have any energy left." Phil picked up his tools.

"We'll help you." Cole proceeded to fold up the ladder and carry the empty hoop box to the side of the driveway. Dillion helped Phil carry the tools to the truck.

"How are we going to play when the driveway is full of trucks?" Phil asked, opening the tailgate and placing his tools in the bed. He removed his tool vest and tossed that in too.

"Don't try to get out of this." Cole leaned on the side of the truck.

Phil shook his head and smiled. "I'm not. I'm just asking, that's all."

"Cole's gonna ask them to move," Dillion said.

"We'll start with you," Cole told Phil. "Would you mind moving your truck to the street?"

"No problem." Phil closed the tailgate and climbed in the driver's seat.

Cole and Dillion walked up to the house. "Dillion, how about asking your dad to get the painters to move their trucks."

Twenty minutes later, Cole, showing off some fancy footwork, dribbled the basketball in front of Phillip and Dillion. "Why don't we start off slow with a game of Horse. Phil and I used to play that all the time, remember Phil?" He spun the ball on his finger, earning him a wide-eyed look from Dillion and a slight smile from Phil.

"I'm out of practice but I'm game." Phil rubbed his hands together.

"I don't know what Horse is, but I'm in," Dillion said.

"Okay, I'll start if neither of you has any objections." Cole dribbled the ball again.

"Would it matter if we did?" Phil answered.

Dillion laughed like Phil had told a joke, but Cole detected a hint of disdain. Maybe because of his guilt he imagined the tone in Phil's voice. Anyway, he chose to ignore it.

"Okay, I'm going to do a free throw, and both of you have to attempt that shot after me," he said for Dillion's benefit.

For a half hour, they took turns shooting baskets trying not to accumulate five points because missing five times would spell the word HORSE, and that player would be out. Dillion left the game first, but he cheered Phil and Cole on from the sidelines while they fought it out. Cole came out the victor in the end.

He bounced the basketball to Dillion and stuck his hand out to shake Phil's. When they shook, Phil said, "I'll bet you've kept in practice all these years, haven't you?"

He smiled. "You haven't?"

"I'm sure you could tell I haven't," Phil said dryly.

"Well, I was always a better player than you anyway." He grinned and lightly bumped Phil's shoulder with his. Elated was an understatement for how he felt after playing basketball with Phillip again. He couldn't help being overwhelmed by the memory of their perfect friendship of the past.

"It was fun, but I've got to get the rest of my gear and go now," Phil said abruptly. He patted Dillion on the back. "I might not see you again. Thanks for all your help these past weeks."

Cole watched Phillip hurry inside, thinking again about the old saying "one step forward and two steps back." Phillip had a way of jumbling up his head, and he knew his return hadn't been easy for Phil. His stubborn ex would have a hard time giving in even though Cole had seen fleeting signs that his attitude had softened, at least compared to the day they'd come face to face in the backyard when

Phil had cut his hand.

"Maybe we can play again, Cole," Dillion said. "I guess Phil won't be coming back, but I'll be here with my dad helping out until the end."

He looked over at the boy and gave him his attention even though he was preoccupied with Phillip and wondered if he'd ever see him again. Strange. Phil had said goodbye to Dillion, but not to him.

"Sure, we'll play again. I'd like that."

"Great!" Dillion handed Cole the ball. "I'm gonna go make my call now. See you later." He hurried away.

Cole tried to make sense of what happened today and wondered how to make something similar happen again. Time with Phillip was what he wanted and needed—the sooner the better.

Cole tore his eyes away from his phone just long enough to give a quick wave to Tom and Dillion, who were the last ones to leave for the day. Phil had been the first to drive away. Cole wondered if he'd seen him sitting in his SUV as he drove by since Phil hadn't acknowledged him, but that hadn't deterred Cole from the plan he'd formulated just after the basketball game.

As soon as he'd finished checking on the work in his house, he'd sat in his SUV and searched online on his phone for the item he wanted. Having been so excited and proud of himself for coming up with the idea, he couldn't wait until he got home to order it on his computer. This had to be ordered now—before he talked himself out of it.

One minute he was enthusiastic and all gung-ho, and the next, he was second guessing himself. Would Phillip see this as a pathetic attempt to hang on to something he'd let slip through his fingers long ago?

Well, it was worth taking the chance. If Phillip thought he was a pathetic jackass, so be it. He clicked on "submit order" and hoped for the best.

Chapter Fifteen

Phil exited The Cat's Meow Pet Store pushing a cart containing two boxes of cat litter and a twelve-pound bag of dry cat food. He aimed the cart toward his Camaro and spotted Eve walking away from the store.

"Hey, Eve," he called, and then he whistled the best he could to get her attention. Luckily it was loud enough to make her turn around.

She smiled at him and jogged over. "Uncle Phil!"

"What are you doing here, honey?"

"Oh, not much. I just went into the pet store to look at the cats up for adoption and then I was going to go to the mall for a while."

"How'd you get here?"

"On the city bus."

"You're all by yourself?"

Eve stared down at the ground and mumbled, "Jennifer left today. I said goodbye to her, and I didn't feel like going back to the apartment to sit around alone, so..."

"I'm sorry, honey." Phil pulled her close for a quick hug. "Hey, why don't you come over to the house and you can visit Batman and Robin."

Eve lifted her chin up and smiled weakly. "Okay, I'd like that.

You're not working today?" They walked toward the car.

"I'm between jobs. I finished up at Cole's yesterday. There's a good possibility I have a new job building closet organizers for an elderly lady a couple streets over from me. Just waiting on her final decision."

"I hope you get the job."

"I do too."

He put the cat supplies in the back seat, and they got in and buckled up. Twenty minutes later they pulled into his driveway. Eve took the cat food out of the car, and he picked up the litter by the handles, and they headed into the house through the back door.

"We'll put this stuff in the laundry room." He walked past the washing machine and placed the containers in the corner. Eve handed him the cat food and he stuck it into a cabinet above the dryer.

"Shall we have something to drink while we play with the cats?" He put his phone and wallet on the countertop.

"What have you got?"

"I have sun tea, Coke, and coffee." He smiled.

"Tea is good," Eve said. The sparkle in her eyes reminded him of the mischief maker she'd always been.

After stirring sugar into their tea, they took the drinks into the living room. Both cats were snoozing on the cat tree.

"Evidently they didn't even hear us. Maybe we'll have to watch them sleep. This time of day is basically their nap time."

Eve giggled. "Most every time of day is a cat's napping time, unless we're talking kittens."

"Kittens sleep a lot too. Cats aren't much trouble since they sleep their life away." He sat down and stretched his legs out, resting them on the foot stool.

"Tell that to Mom." Eve looked longingly at Batman and Robin before sitting down.

They sipped their tea in silence for a few moments, and then Eve cleared her throat and looked Phil in the eye. "Will you see Cole again even though the job's over?"

"I have no plans to," he answered.

That earned him a disappointed frown from Eve. He sat up straighter. "There's really no reason for us to see each other. You know I've been dating someone else."

She scrunched up her nose. "Oh, yeah, *him*."

He raised one eyebrow. "What's that supposed to mean?"

"Nothing. Just that Mom and I have never met him, so I didn't think he was anything to write home about." She pursed her lips.

Eve was so perceptive, but he wasn't going to get into this with her. The doorbell rang, and he jumped up from the couch, grateful for the interruption. Eve whispered comforting words to the cats when they opened their eyes and perked up their ears. They didn't much care for the bell.

He swung the door open, widening his gaze at the woman holding a giant wicker basket adorned by a huge blue bow. At first, he thought she was at the wrong house, but she confirmed his name and address and placed the delivery into his arms.

"Eve," he called out.

"You don't have to yell, Uncle Phil. I'm right here."

He turned to find her standing right behind him. "I see that now. Can you run and get my wallet from the kitchen counter, please?"

"Sure," she said, dashing away quickly.

"Hang on a minute," he said to the delivery lady as he turned the basket in his hands and tried to determine what the heck it was. "What is this anyway?"

Before she could answer, Eve returned holding out the wallet. He took it from her while balancing the basket, pulled out a few bills, and handed them to the woman. "Thanks," he said.

"Thank you, sir." She turned to leave.

"What is it, Uncle Phil? Who sent it?" Eve bounced up and down excitedly while trying to get a closer look.

"I have no clue. Let's set it down so we can find out."

They went into the kitchen, and he set the basket on the table. He closely inspected the outside for a card, but he didn't see one. "I've never gotten anything like this before."

Eve came closer and tried to peer in, but the contents were covered by clear cellophane. He wondered if the card was inside and noticed the paw prints on the bow. "Look at the bow."

Eve smiled. "Maybe it's something for Batman and Robin!"

He narrowed his eyes. "Why would it be for the cats? Who'd send this to cats? That's crazy."

"Well, open it, Uncle Phil. See if there's a card. Staring at it won't solve the mystery."

This weird basket made him feel like a kid getting ready to open a special gift on his birthday. He tried to pull apart the cellophane to get at the card that must be inside. He hoped it hadn't fallen off. This was quite a mystery, like Eve had said.

All he was accomplishing was making loud crinkle sounds with the cellophane, which drew Batman and Robin's attention. They appeared in the kitchen and promptly jumped onto the table and started sniffing the basket. Their little heads bobbed up and down as they investigated. Soon they were both trying to get inside by pawing at the wrapping.

"Maybe there's cat nip in there," Eve said.

"Yeah, or cat food, or both."

He couldn't wait any longer to see inside, so he reached into the kitchen cabinet, found the scissors, and proceeded to cut a slit down the cellophane. That really got the cats in on the act.

"I'll bet you're right about there being cat nip in here," he said. "I think they can smell it."

Once the contents were visible, he saw cat nip mice, crinkle balls, and furry fish partly hidden in blue crinkle-cut paper shreds.

He lifted Batman from the table and put him on the floor and then did the same with Robin. "Run along. We've got to make sure all this is safe for you first."

"I see human treats in here too." Eve ran her fingers over some of the little bags. "Popcorn, trail mix, tea bags, gum, and chocolates. Wow, Uncle Phil."

"Where's the card?" he asked, annoyed that he didn't know who had sent the gift.

"Here's a little envelope." Eve pulled it out from between two packages of cheesy cat treats.

"Let me see it," he said, as the cats rubbed on his legs.

Eve handed it over, her gaze never leaving him.

He started to open the envelope but paused and looked down at Eve. "You're more excited about this than I am."

"Just trying to figure this out. Maybe grandma and Aunt Ruth sent it."

"Now that's an idea." In his haste to get to the card inside, he ripped the envelope right down the front. When he finally had it in his hand, he read the message to himself.

"What does it say?" Eve asked enthusiastically. "Did grandma send it?"

"No, it's not from her." He drew his brows together, and his chest tightened.

"You look sad, Uncle Phil. What is it? What's wrong?" Eve put her hand on his arm and tried to stretch up to read the note for herself. He passed the card to her, which had a cat's face in the corner, and she read it aloud.

Phillip, I wanted you to know I'm thinking of you. I thought you and your cats would enjoy these toys and treats. Maybe someday we can get Batman and Robin and Moonshadow and Moonbeam together for a play date. Think about it. Love, Cole

"Woweeeee, Uncle Phil!" Eve exclaimed.

"Don't blow a gasket," he said dryly, shocked at this gift and trying to figure out how he felt about it.

"I think it's so cute how he calls you Phillip," Eve said, still looking at the card.

"That *is* my name."

"No one calls you Phillip, not even grandma. You're Phil—Uncle Phil."

"I doubt he's trying to be cute by calling me that."

"Well, you know what I mean. It's his pet name for you. Are you blushing, Uncle Phil?" she teased.

"Blushing? Have you lost your mind? And don't go getting all excited over this, Eve. I have no idea why he sent this. It was nice of him, but..."

"He loves you! Look, it says *Love*, Cole." She pointed to the card. "You should call him right now and thank him for the gift."

Trying not to sigh too loud, he took the card from Eve and stuck it back in what was left of the mutilated envelope. "I'll call him at some point and thank him, but not right now."

"All right, it's better you do it in private anyway." She grinned ear to ear before taking on a more serious expression. "It is kind of strange though—a play date for the cats? Cats don't have play dates, do they?"

Phil chuckled despite himself. The whole thing was bizarre. "He was probably just joking about getting the cats together. He liked to joke around back in school—or maybe not—his cats are used to going out. Maybe he thinks it's a normal thing."

"Sit down, Uncle Phil. I think you need another iced tea or coffee. Or maybe this calls for a beer?"

They both laughed.

CHAPTER SIXTEEN

COLE SAT down on the edge of Dana's new panel bed and studied the room for about the fiftieth time since hanging the last picture of a driftwood-style wooden sign laser engraved with her name. He hoped he hadn't gone too rustic. Maybe he should have gotten her input, especially on the sheets and bed quilt, but he'd wanted everything finished before her arrival, so he'd done it himself. But according to Meredith, he didn't know anything about picking out furniture for their daughter. When she'd laughed at him on the phone about purchasing Dana's bedroom set, he'd held his annoyance in. Getting a rise out of him hadn't worked. He wouldn't give her that satisfaction.

He'd fallen in love with the sturdily made bedroom set with the weathered pine finish. Hopefully, it was feminine enough for his little girl, and he wondered if he should have consulted the interior decorator he'd hired for the window treatments to help with Dana's room. The designer had done a fantastic job choosing what she'd called modern rustic for the windows throughout the house.

But this was his home—and Dana's, and he knew a thing or two about decorating as well. Architecture wasn't his only interest. In all the years he'd spent in his profession, he'd taken a big interest in the other aspects of making a beautiful and comfortable living space.

From the beginning of this project, he'd decided to do all that he could on his own. For more years than he could remember, he'd dreamed of one day building and decorating his own home.

He lay back on the bed and stared up at the high ceiling. If Dana didn't like the room, they'd change it. To him, the room looked outstanding, but he hoped he wasn't pushing his personal taste onto her. After all, the entire house was decorated in the style of her bedroom—a difference of night and day from what she'd grown up with in her fancy city home.

He sat up again, removed his glasses, rubbed his eyes, and then he glanced down at the paisley quilt on the bed. He hoped the pattern wouldn't be too vintage for her taste. At least the pink and magenta color scheme was right. Dana loved those colors.

Getting the place ready for Dana had taken many hours of work with no time to do much of anything else, but Phillip hadn't been far from his thoughts.

He hadn't seen or heard from him since their brief conversation on the phone when Phil had called to thank him for the gift basket, and that was three weeks ago to the day. He'd wanted to follow up and do something else for him, but he hadn't come up with any good ideas. Besides, Phillip hadn't sounded all that warm on the phone—hadn't given him any encouragement, so he'd let the time go, throwing himself into putting the finishing touches on the house and moving Moonbeam and Moonshadow in. He'd left their cat tree at the rental—maybe the landlord or the next renter could use it because his cats hadn't wanted anything to do with it.

In the back of his mind, he entertained the thought of buying one of Phillip's cat trees for the house. That would serve two purposes—getting the cats something they might actually use and being able to interact with Phillip again. He wondered why he'd purchased that contemporary style cat tree in the first place. Besides being totally useless, the design was more suited to his New York home. When he'd first moved to California, he'd still been in New York mode but that had quickly worn off. Wine didn't even appeal to him anymore—beer was his go-to drink.

Dana would arrive tomorrow, and thinking about the day ahead made him extremely nervous and excited. He needed a good night's sleep, but he would be too anxious to sleep soundly. After standing up from the bed, he smoothed the bedcovers and went to the door. He turned and gave the room one more glance. Satisfied, he flipped the light switch off and walked down the hall.

Instead of heading to his bedroom, he went downstairs. He didn't see Moonbeam and Moonshadow, so he figured they'd already gone to his bed where they'd been sleeping at night. When Dana arrived, they would most likely ditch his bed and sleep with her.

He decided to shoot baskets before calling it a night. On his way out the front door, he turned on the floodlight and grabbed the basketball from the entryway closet.

As he worked up a sweat dribbling the ball and working on his technique, he imagined Phillip there with him wearing a pair of sexy basketball shorts, although the jeans he'd had on the day he'd put up the basketball hoop had looked great on him too. He had such a firm butt, and the jeans that fit him so well sure showed it off. He let out a sigh as he made a basket. Playing the game with a friend would be so much better. Life would be so much better sharing it with Phillip. He still longed for him—ached for him—loved him.

As he let off steam, he wondered if the backboard would crack from the ball hitting it so hard. He worked himself into near exhaustion before quitting for the night, resigning himself to the fact he couldn't solve his problem tonight. That didn't mean he'd give up though. His heart wouldn't let him give up on Phillip.

"This is so weird, Father." Dana snapped photos on her phone while looking out the windshield of the SUV on the way home from LAX.

Cole wasn't sure what to think of her reaction to the scenery. *Weird* sounded bad to him, but hopefully she didn't mean it that way. She was texting the pictures to her mother, so maybe she actually liked what she saw, or didn't see. Right now they were driving through wide-open spaces, something that Dana hadn't seen much of in her life.

"Mother won't believe this place." She hit *send* on the phone again.

"Interesting, isn't it? We were in the big city under a hundred miles ago, and now..."

"Now it looks like we're on Mars," Dana said, but she was wearing a bright smile and looked like she was enjoying herself. "Where are the houses? Where do people live?"

He chuckled. "Oh, there are plenty of houses, don't worry. It's just that we have to drive through some barren areas between the communities."

"It's awesome. Mother's going to croak when she sees these pictures."

Cole let out another amused chuckle. Since picking Dana up, he'd laughed more than he had in a very long time.

"She must have unplugged after I told her I landed okay. She's not answering."

"She works a lot, huh?"

"Yes, especially since she got her promotion." She stuck her phone into her purse.

"Are you thirsty, sweetie?" he asked.

"If I was, where would we get anything? Maybe find some cows to milk someplace?" Her infectious giggle was music to his ears, and he joined her in a hearty laugh.

"Actually, there's a McDonald's not too far up the road. We can get something there."

"Really? That's interesting. Is it for travelers or... who else would go there? Is there a town coming up?" She craned her neck and peered out the windows.

"There are some little mountain towns nearby, but yes, it's mostly tourists and commuters who stop there."

"So a lot of people live in the desert and work in the city?" She toyed with a lock of her hair.

"There's a lot to be said for living in a more peaceful place with a lot of space. And, it's not that far to commute."

"I didn't realize we'd be near mountains as well as the city, beach, and desert, and we could see it all in one day. I can't wait to see the house and the cats!"

Dana reached into her purse and brought out her hairbrush. As she brushed her shoulder-length hair she said, "I hope I won't be overdressed." She looked down at her outfit. "Mother helped me pick this out. She said it was perfect for traveling—comfortable but stylish. I told her it was a little fancy, but she talked me into it."

Cole glanced at his daughter. "It looks real pretty on you."

"The bling's not too much?" She fingered the sparkly sequins along the neckline.

"I think it was a good choice."

"Good answer." She giggled again. "Well, I have a feeling that one of the first things on my agenda will be shopping for some new clothes. The people I've seen so far have been dressed quite casually."

Cole smiled. "Well, I'm sure your wardrobe is fine, but if you want to go shopping and buy other clothes that you'd feel more comfortable in, that's fine with me. I have a young lady in mind who I'll bet could help you. Her name's Eve, she's fourteen, and the niece of a friend of mine."

"You're already looking out for me—finding me a friend, but are you sure this Eve person wants to meet me? I don't want to be a bother..." She put her brush back in her purse and folded her hands in her lap.

"Eve's a great girl. I have a feeling you'll want to spend a lot of time with her this summer. Keep an open mind."

"I will. It's going to be a great summer, Father. I'm so glad I'm finally here."

Cole patted Dana's knee and glanced her way. "Me too. I've been lonely without you, sweetie."

"Haven't you met anyone to go out with? You said Eve is your friend's niece. Is it by any chance a *male* friend?"

He felt her gaze on him, so he took a quick look at her again. Sure enough, she regarded him with her big, inquisitive dark eyes as she searched for an answer.

He took a deep breath and flipped on the turn signal, giving her a sideways glance. "Oh, look, we're nearly at the turnoff for McDonald's."

"I think I have my answer." She gave him a sly smile.

"Don't jump to conclusions. I'm perfectly happy to just be your father this summer and concentrate on you and me." He took the off-ramp heading toward the restaurant.

"Whatever you say, Father."

Cole couldn't believe that Dana had already hounded him about dating. Ever since he and Meredith divorced, she'd been concerned about him, even more so after he'd leveled with her about why the marriage hadn't lasted. She was a highly sensitive and mature girl, and she had accepted that he was gay. He couldn't have asked for a better daughter.

He could already tell that this summer with her would be anything but dull.

CHAPTER SEVENTEEN

PUSHING A cart containing a large box, Phil headed toward his truck. He hadn't been able to stop thinking about basketball and how out of practice he was, ever since shooting baskets with Cole and Dillion last month. On the way home from work today, he finally decided to buy a hoop. Having one at home would be a good way to help his game. Why did this matter to him? He'd never play basketball with Cole again, but getting in shape and maybe finding the magic touch he had back in school held some appeal.

That day at Cole's brought back good memories of the game and reminded him why he loved it so much—why he loved Cole so much, and he was certain Cole still loved him. Cole's feelings for him became crystal clear that day at the house when he'd overheard him giving Dillion relationship advice.

His mother's words echoed in his mind. *Are you not able to forgive him?*

He was so lost in thought that he nearly ran the cart right into his truck. Luckily, he came to his senses in time. After dropping the tailgate, he loaded the box into the bed, thinking that he shouldn't have much trouble putting up the hoop since he'd done Cole's a month ago. He'd had help though. Maybe Chuck would be around to give him a hand.

On the drive home, he decided to grab something for dinner. He quickly ran through the choices available on his route and decided on Mexican fast food. Del Taco sounded good so he turned in intending to use the drive-thru, but a Lincoln Navigator in a parking space in front of the building caught his eye. The SUV looked a lot like Cole's, and a closer check convinced him that he was right. He shouldn't care—he should just get into the drive-thru like he'd intended, but something was drawing him inside. Parking where he'd be able to see the truck from the window, he headed for the door.

Once inside, he scanned the small dining area. He spotted Cole across the room sitting at a booth, and he wasn't alone. The girl with him had to be Dana. She was very pretty and had the same dark hair and eyes as Cole.

Coming inside the restaurant had been a dumb thing to do. What was wrong with him? Not wanting to intrude, he put his head down and quickly turned to leave.

Before taking even two steps, Cole called out his name. He didn't want to be rude and pretend like he didn't hear, so he turned and waved at Cole. His ex-boyfriend stood beside the table like he was ready to rush over if he didn't succeed in stopping him. Dana was looking his way too, and he wondered if Cole had told her they knew each other. What had he gotten himself into?

He had no choice but to get in line to order his food, and when he had it in hand, he glanced at the booth again. Cole motioned him over, so he weaved his way through the room to join them. He couldn't help but smile at the sight of his old friend having dinner with his daughter.

"Phil, good to run into you. Will you join us?" Before he could answer, Cole added, "I'd like to introduce my daughter, Dana. Dana, this is Phil Thompson, my old friend."

Dana offered her hand. Impressed, Phil gave her a gentle handshake, smiling the entire time. "I'm pleased to meet you, Dana," he said before releasing her small, delicate hand.

"I'm very glad to meet you too, Mr. Thompson."

"Sit down," Cole said. "No reason to eat alone."

Dana slid over on the bench to make room for him, which made him feel a lot more comfortable than sitting next to Cole, so he set his tray on the table and took the seat. Half-eaten food sat in front of them. They were almost finished eating.

"Dana, uh, Phil's my friend from school, the friend with the niece I told you about."

Dana's eyes lit up and her smile grew. "Oh, yes, Father told me about Eve. He wants to introduce us."

Phil directed his gaze to Cole's smoldering brown eyes. "Right... Well, that sounds like a good idea."

"Dana's only been here for a week, and we're still getting her settled in, but we'll give Eve a call very soon," Cole said with his eyes locked on Phil's the whole time.

Phil looked away and began taking the wrapping off his burritos. He ate a french fry and then tore open a packet of ketchup and squeezed some out onto a napkin. Cole and Dana continued to eat their meals too.

After a short time, Phil started feeling a little out of place. He took a big drink with his straw and then asked, "How do you like Apple Valley, Dana?"

"It's awesome! I haven't seen that much yet, but so far I like it."

"She even likes how I decorated the house." Cole smiled broadly.

"It's a beautiful house," Phil said. "Well, I didn't see the whole thing after you had it all done... not that I expected to." He rubbed the back of his neck and focused on his food.

"Phil built our kitchen cupboards," Cole said to Dana. "He's a great carpenter."

"Wow, you did?" Dana said to Phil. "That's wonderful."

Phil finished his last french fry and smiled at Dana.

Cole rested his hands on the table. "Are you working now?"

"Yes, I'm transforming closets in a house close to where I live. Small closets, not walk-ins like yours. Takes some creativity to use every foot to its full potential with shelves, drawers, and cubbyholes." He sipped his drink.

"You keep busy—that's good," Cole said.

"How are your cats?" Phil asked, before taking the last bite of his burrito.

"Great, real good. Dana pays a lot of attention to them, so they're enjoying that."

"I missed them so much," Dana said.

"I'll bet you did." Phil crumpled up his food wrappers and placed them on his tray.

"Are you going to the cat show in Santa Monica?" Cole asked.

"I plan to."

"I might want to buy a tower for the cats. They never did like the one I bought, so I didn't even haul it to the new house. Dana and I will be showing Moonshadow and Moonbeam, so maybe we can look when we're there."

"Sure. Or..."

"Yeah?" Cole leaned forward ever so slightly.

Phil took a deep breath and let it out. "If you have time, you two are welcome come over. I could show you what I've got in my garage. I have several styles made, but you probably have other plans..."

"No, no. We're just hanging out, no concrete plans. Dana, would you like to go see the cat trees?"

A smile spread across her face. "Yes, that sounds like fun, and Moonbeam and Moonshadow really need something to claw on."

Cole smiled, stood up, and quickly gathered their trash. "Well, okay then. We'll follow you over to your place."

All the way to his house, Phil kept wondering why he'd invited Cole and his daughter over. He was letting his guard down where Cole was concerned, and he wasn't sure if that was smart or dumb.

Well, what harm could it do to show them the cat trees? Maybe Cole would even buy one and that would help both of them out, not to mention Cole's cats. He chuckled to himself. Of course his cats had hated that ridiculous cat tree.

Dana would probably want to see Batman and Robin, so he'd have to invite them into the house. Had he cleaned up well enough this morning to have company in? He tried to remember what junk he might have left sitting around. He wasn't a messy person, but he didn't keep a perfect house either. Cole probably had a cleaning lady.

He parked in the driveway, got out, and waited for Cole to park at the curb. As Cole and Dana walked up the driveway, he unlocked the garage door, raising it up so they could see the four completed cat trees.

Cole and Dana joined him, and he smiled when Cole said, "Nice place you've got here."

"Thanks," he answered, not mentioning that he was just renting the house.

He went into the garage and pulled the first cat tower out onto the driveway. Cole helped him with the others.

"If these colors don't fit your color scheme, I take custom orders. If you don't mind waiting, you can get exactly what you want... that is if you like these." He stuck his hands in his pockets and glanced over toward Chuck's house for no particular reason other than he was nervous as hell.

Dana peered at the top of one of the carpeted trees. "Father, I think Moonbeam and Moonshadow would like to claw on a tree like this. Look at all the places they can sleep." She ran her hand along one of the perches.

Cole stood behind his daughter and put his hands on her shoulders. "I agree. I think they'd probably use something like this. It's worth a try."

Phil cleared his throat. "Would you like to come in and see the one I have for my cats? It's their favorite place in the whole house."

"Yeah, let's do that," Cole said, with a smile that made Phil's heart skip a beat.

Phil walked to the back door, and Cole and Dana followed him. Hopefully, Batman and Robin wouldn't be scared when they realized he wasn't alone because he wanted Dana to see them.

"If you keep your voices low, they'll be less likely to run and hide," Phil said, as he led the way into the kitchen, glad he hadn't left any dirty dishes in the sink.

"Moonbeam and Moonshadow are adventurous and like company," Cole said.

"Yeah, well, they're used to going out and being around a lot of different people." Phil put his keys on the countertop.

"You don't show your cats?" Dana asked.

"No, they're mixed breed from the pound. They just hang out at home."

"I like all kinds of cats," Dana said.

"There's a household pet category at most cat shows." A faint smile curved Cole's lips.

"Yeah, well, my cats told me they'd rather stay home." Phil shifted his weight from one foot to the other.

Dana giggled and Cole snorted out a laugh.

"I guess you have your hands full with hauling the cat trees to the shows without having to take the cats too," Cole said.

"Does Eve go to the cat shows?" Dana adjusted the Siamese cat pendant dangling on a chain around her neck.

"Yeah, she comes along. She's a big help selling the cat towers." He lowered his voice. "Come this way and I'll introduce you to my cats." He stepped quietly and directed Dana and Cole into the living room.

Batman and Robin were on the cat tree and hadn't bolted. Phil stopped abruptly. "Hey guys," he said gently. "Relax, we've got company."

"They're so pretty," Dana said, but she didn't try to approach. Cole froze in place a couple steps behind her.

"Walk slowly. I think they'll be okay." Phil took the lead and headed over to the cats, who were now wide awake and watching their every move. He scratched each cat's head, and when he was satisfied they were at ease, he stepped aside. "Go ahead. You can pet them if you want. Robin is on the upper perch and that's Batman underneath."

Both Dana and Cole softly stroked each cat's fur, and Batman and Robin seemed happy with the attention.

"You have two real nice cats," Cole said. "And I can see they like their post."

"Were any of the ones outside a style and color you like, or do you want me to build one especially for them?"

"You're very accommodating." Cole locked eyes with him like he had back at the restaurant.

Phil's pulse jumped up several notches under Cole's piercing gaze. He'd never been able to resist those brown eyes.

Cole looked away, and Phil realized that Dana was waiting for her dad to answer his question about the cat tower, so he focused on the cats and waited for Cole to speak.

"What do you think, sweetie?" Cole looked down at Dana.

"I want a big one like this." Dana looked up at the two high perches. "But as for color, that's your specialty."

Cole pursed his lips. "Okay, how about you make us one just like yours, in brown and tan with a splash of green?"

"Sure, I can do that. Do you want any sisal rope, or all carpet? And where would you like the green to go?"

Cole rubbed his chin. "Hum, this gets complicated, doesn't it?"

"Life is complicated." Phil meant it as a joke, but his statement came out far too serious.

Cole laughed it off. "Okay, let's go with all carpet, and I trust your judgment on how to arrange the colors to make it look nice. All your trees look very professional."

"Thanks. Hey, can I get the two of you some iced tea?"

"We don't want to wear out our welcome, but that sounds good," Cole said. "Dana, would you like some?"

"Sure." She was petting Batman and kept her attention on him.

"Okay, I'll get it. Have a seat."

"Need any help?" Cole asked.

"No, I've got it." Phil went into the kitchen and brought three glasses out of the cupboard. He dropped several ice cubes into each, poured the tea from the pitcher, and was glad Cole wasn't in the room because his hands were visibly shaky. Cole and his daughter being in his house made him nervous, but he was glad he'd invited them—having them here seemed right. After pushing Cole out of his mind for so many years, what if he was to begin to forgive him? If that's what he was doing, what then? These thoughts were too complicated for today.

Cole entered the kitchen, and Phil almost jumped.

Cole raised his eyebrows and smiled. "Uh, just thought you might need help carrying three glasses." His lopsided grin was so familiar, so sexy.

"Yeah, thanks." Phil handed one of the glasses to him and carried the other two himself.

In the living room, Dana was intently staring at family photos on a table across from the window.

"Is this Eve?" She accepted the glass of tea Phil offered her.

"Yes, that's her, and this is her mom—my sister." Phil picked up a photo of Gail and Eve together.

"They're very pretty," Dana said.

"Your sister hasn't changed much." Cole studied the photo. Then he gazed into Phil's eyes again. "In fact, the years have been good to you both."

Batman jumped onto the couch as Dana sat down with her tea, creating a good distraction so Phil didn't have to respond to Cole's compliment.

"He likes me," she said, grinning as he rubbed against her.

"You have a way with cats." Cole sat next to her.

"Eve loves cats, but she can't have pets in the apartment. She comes over here a lot to see Batman and Robin." Phil sat down in a chair across from the couch.

Dana stroked Batman's fur while she drank her tea. Soon, Robin joined her and his brother.

"Do you want payment for the cat tree now?" Cole asked.

"You can pay me when it's finished. I know you're good for it."

Cole smiled. "Okay, that sounds good. Dana, I guess we'd better get going."

She untangled herself from the cats and set her glass on the end table. "Thank you for the tea, Mr. Thompson."

"Call me Phil. Mr. Thompson is too formal."

"Okay," she said shyly.

Phil walked them out, and Cole stopped at the cat trees in the driveway. "Let me help you put these away."

"Okay, thanks." His fingers brushed against Cole's as they maneuvered the towers back into place, and a pleasant tingling shot through his body. Wow, he hadn't experienced a sensation like that since school, since he'd been with Cole.

Phil glanced at Cole. Had he felt that too? Disappointment filled him when they finished moving the last cat tree. Having Cole and Dana there had made his day, and now it was time for them to go.

As the three of them stood in the driveway, Chuck's screen door slammed shut. They turned and looked at him as he walked across the lawn to join them.

"Looks like you've got company," Cole muttered.

Cole's expression changed from relaxed and friendly to a half scowl. Maybe he resented the intrusion. Chuck sure wasn't much to look at, and he was quite a few years their senior. Cole couldn't possibly be jealous, could he?

"Chuck, this is my old friend Cole Fisher and his daughter Dana. This is my neighbor Chuck Larson."

Cole gave a nod and a half smile, but he didn't offer to shake hands.

Phil cleared his throat. "Chuck helps me load the cat trees when I take them to the cat shows."

"Is that so? Well, that's nice. We'd best be on our way," Cole said curtly, continuing to wear an unfriendly frown. He put his arm around Dana, and they walked toward their SUV.

"Real nice meeting you," Chuck called after them.

"I'll let you know when I've got your cat tree built," Phil hollered.

He wished Cole hadn't left so abruptly. If the reason was because of Chuck, what must Cole think of Brad? Although he'd never flaunted the relationship with Brad, he should have been more aware of Cole's feelings. He let out a long breath and tried to shake off the melancholy mood that had settled over him.

After Cole drove off, Phil turned to Chuck. "Hey, if you're not doing anything, I've got a little job you might be able to help me with."

"Oh yeah, what's that?"
"You know anything about putting up a basketball hoop?"

CHAPTER EIGHTEEN

"I THINK it'll be perfect here, don't you?" Cole looked at Moonshadow and Moonbeam curled on the sofa snoozing. "Don't you care enough to open your eyes?"

He smiled and picked up a couple of their toys from the floor, making sure the area was clear for the cat tree when *Phillip* arrived with it.

No wonder he was so nervous. Phil would be here any minute, and not only was he excited over that, but also because he'd get to show him the house. "I want you two on your best behavior, hear me?" Neither cat moved a whisker.

He hoped the cats would jump right onto the cat tower to show their appreciation and make Phillip happy. A lot of love went into those towers, and it couldn't hurt his cause if his cats acted excited.

After sitting down on the sofa beside the cats, he glanced around the family room. This house was truly a home now, just like he knew it would be after Dana arrived.

He'd set up the meeting between Eve and Dana, and the girls had hit it off just like he'd hoped they would, and they'd been texting and talking ever since. Today was their third time going out together. Gail and Eve had picked Dana up and headed off to the movies. Gail had been friendly and warm to him and being around her made him feel closer to Phillip. Even though he'd wanted to, he'd refrained from asking her any questions about Phil—like how serious he was about Brad, and a lot more.

During the past couple weeks, he'd been busy working and spending as much time with Dana as possible. But today with Dana out of the house and a well-deserved day off, he'd be able to spend time with his old friend, and he hoped they could continue building on their new relationship, whatever that was. From his perspective, they'd made some progress the other day when they'd spent time together at Del Taco. And Phil inviting him and Dana over to his house was a big step in the right direction. He'd been so annoyed that day when the neighbor had butted in and messed up his opportunity to say a proper goodbye.

Anxious for Phillip to arrive, he got up, walked out of the family room and into the entryway, crossed over to the front door and looked out the sidelight. Not speaking to him for the past couple weeks was hard, but finally Phil had called to say the tree was done. That had been a short conversation, but he hoped today would be better.

Was he making more of this than there was? Almost three months had passed since they'd met out in the backyard, and they still hadn't been able to get anything going between them. He'd tried—maybe not hard enough—but Phillip hadn't given him any encouragement, so what more could he do?

He didn't want them to just be acquaintances, or even just friends. He wanted them to go back to the way they used to be. His feelings for Phillip were strong, no question about that, but he wasn't sure if Phillip could ever forgive him and give them a chance.

The sound of a truck snapped him out of his thoughts, so he turned the doorknob and stepped out onto the porch, his heart pounding. The mere sight of his ex through the truck's windshield was enough to make him stir below the belt. He took a deep breath and strode over to the truck, intending to make the most of this time with Phillip.

Standing there with his thumbs hooked in the pockets of his jeans, he waited while Phil got himself ready to get out of the truck. He seemed to be fiddling with the radio. After a few moments, he got out with an envelope in his hand.

"Hi," Cole said, wishing he felt confident enough to say something more personal.

"Hey." Phil handed him the envelope. "Here's your invoice."

Cole took the offered paperwork and stuffed it in his pocket, disappointed that Phillip was acting so businesslike.

"Let me unload the tree, and we'll see how you like it." Phil moved to the back of the truck.

"I'll give you a hand." Cole followed behind, anxious to get a look at his cat's new tower. The view he had of Phil's backside wasn't bad either.

A thin tarp secured with ropes covered the tower, which Phil began untying. "Where's Dana?"

"She's out right now... With Eve, in fact."

"Is that so. I heard the girls had met and were getting along. Eve said she liked her."

"Dana really likes Eve too. It's working out good."

Phil pushed the tarp off the bottom of the cat tree, and Cole got his first look at the color of the carpeting—brown on the base and up the middle post. Phil removed more of the tarp, revealing the tan perches, and then he yanked the entire tarp off.

"Looks great. I like the way you did the colors, and I love the green accent." Cole ran his hand over the carpet, smiling while imagining his cats napping on the perches and digging their claws into the carpet.

"Let's get it out and stand it up." Phil lowered the tailgate and pulled the tree until it hung over a few feet.

Cole stood shoulder to shoulder with him, grabbing the bottom while Phil reached for a high perch. He grimaced as they kept the heavy and well-constructed tree balanced until the tower stood proudly upright in the driveway.

"That's impressive." Cole looked from top to bottom. "You did a beautiful job."

"I hope your cats will like it."

"I don't see why they won't. Let's get it carried inside and see firsthand."

"We'll use the dolly to save our backs." Phil pulled the dolly from the back of his truck.

Cole helped him ease the tower on and get it balanced before he hurried ahead to open the door. Phil navigated the giant tower toward the house. Once at the threshold, he helped Phil jockey the awkwardly shaped tower into the entryway.

"Where to?" Phil asked. "I think the wheels are clean enough not to mark your fancy hardwood floor."

"Don't worry about that. It's durable."

He briefly laid his hand on Phillip's back to direct him toward the family room. That firm, taut muscle under the material of the soft T-shirt brought back memories of long ago. He wished he could wrap his arms around Phillip right now. The wonderful memory of holding Phil washed over him and sent quite a jolt zinging through his body.

He stayed next to the cat tree as Phil rolled the dolly along just in case the tower should start to shift, but Phillip seemed well skilled maneuvering the load.

"Are your cats in here?" Phil asked when they reached the doorway to the family room.

"They were earlier." Cole grabbed on to the side of the dolly to help it through the entry.

"If they were here, we probably scared them and they split," Phil said. "Where do you want this?"

"Over here by the end of the couch." Cole walked over to show him where to place it.

Phil wheeled the dolly over. "Okay, if they don't take to it here, you might consider moving it near a window."

Cole rubbed his chin. "I thought they could watch us sit on the couch but maybe watching birds outside would be more interesting to them."

"Go ahead and try it here if that's what you'd planned." Phil slid the tower off the dolly. "Let's see...maybe point it this way?"

Cole looked up at the perches as Phil adjusted the direction of the base. "Yeah, that looks good. I can't wait for them to see this." He laced his fingers together, palms out, and stretched his arms downward while glancing around the room. "I wonder where they went. Have a seat. I'm going to find them."

"It's probably better to let them find this on their own—don't force anything."

"Well, I want you to meet my boys. I'm going to get them. Sit down, uh, on the couch."

Phil glanced at the cat tower. "As if I was going to sit on this thing?"

He took Phillip's humor as a good sign, which spurred him on. "Well, I don't know, maybe you're part cat." He stepped up to Phil and patted his head. "You don't have any pointy ears up here, do you?"

Phil squirmed out of his reach. "You're crazy."

"Maybe." Cole didn't move for a few long moments, preferring to look straight into Phillip's blue eyes instead. Phillip's magnetic gaze right back at him gave him hope, but he didn't want to ruin the moment by doing something stupid, so he slowly backed away, turned and headed off to find Moonbeam and Moonshadow.

The cats were in Dana's bedroom, where they'd been hanging out a lot since she arrived. He grabbed their soft-sided carrier out of her closet, scooped both of them up, stuck them into the enclosure, and headed for the stairs.

"I want you to meet a friend of mine. Be on your best behavior. We're just going on a short walk," he said to the pair on the way down the stairs.

He entered the family room with the carrier in hand, proud to show off his Siamese cats. Phil stood up from the couch, his full attention directed to the cage. Smiling, he peered through the mesh material.

"Who have we got here?"

"This one's Moonshadow and this is his brother Moonbeam." Cole indicated which was which.

"Moonshadow—the escape artist." Phil smiled slightly.

"He had help," Cole said. "I got a lock for the show cage so that won't happen again."

"Good idea."

"Sit down. I'll let them out of the carrier to see how they react to you."

Phil did as he was told, and Cole opened the cage. Phil encouraged the cats with soft murmuring, and they came right out, one after the other, going straight to him. He let them sniff his hands and jeans, appearing to enjoy their attention.

"They're beautiful." Phil stroked Moonshadow's head. He moved on to Moonbeam then, making fast friends with both cats.

Cole sat down on the couch. "Let's see if they notice the tower."

"If they don't notice it, I'll have to assume they have vision problems."

Cole laughed. "Yeah, it's big."

"It's supposed to be big. Cats like to climb."

"I know. Big is good." Cole waggled his eyebrows.

Phil swallowed hard. "Uh, I rubbed cat nip on it before I loaded it into the truck, so that will help attract them."

The cats jumped up on the couch and proceeded to sniff Phil's shirt.

"Are you sure you didn't rub cat nip on yourself?" Cole gave Phil a sideways glance.

"They probably smell Batman and Robin on me. That's probably what's got them going."

"Cat nip didn't help on the other tree I bought."

"Yeah, well... " Phil rolled his eyes.

"Don't say anything."

"Don't worry. I'm not like my niece."

Cole chuckled. "I hope the girls are having fun today."

"Where are they?"

"At the mall for a movie and shopping."

Moonshadow stepped gingerly over Phil and onto the arm of the couch. The cat stretched his neck, fixated on the cat tree. Phil stayed still and kept his eyes on the cat.

"Is Moonshadow usually the more adventuresome?" Phil asked quietly.

"Most of the time," Cole answered.

They waited and watched while Moonshadow stepped onto the lowest perch and looked up to the higher ones. Moonbeam soon followed his brother, and it wasn't long before both cats had chosen a perch and were rubbing on the carpet and testing it with their claws.

"Couldn't hope for anything more than that," Cole said, more than satisfied with his cat's reaction.

Phil turned his attention from the cats to Cole. "What made you decide to adopt Siamese cats?"

Cole looked down at his hands in his lap and softly said, "Their eyes reminded me of you." He hadn't intended to say that—it had just slipped out, and he regretted the statement, but what the hell, it was true. Reaching under his glasses, he rubbed his eyes, and then he chanced a glance at Phillip to gauge his reaction.

Phil's arms were folded across his chest, and evidently, he was at a loss for words, so Cole changed the subject.

"Do you have time for a beer and some basketball?" His heart sped up as he waited for an answer. If wishing hard enough could make this happen, Phillip would say yes.

Phil let out an audible breath, and he prepared to hear a negative response from this stubborn man he loved so much it hurt. He'd write a check for what he owed, and then he supposed Phillip would be on his way.

"Okay," Phil finally said.

"Okay? Okay you'll stay?" Cole asked, not quite trusting his ears. He sat up straighter.

Phil stood up. "Which way is the beer?"

Cole quickly got to his feet. "Come this way, I'll give you a mini tour."

"Well, I already know where the kitchen is."

"Right, well, then you know where the beer is."

Cole led the way to the kitchen and grabbed a can out of the refrigerator for each of them. "You still drink Coors?"

"Yeah, that'll do."

"Let's take it outside with us and have a game of one-on-one. There'll be some shade at this time of day." The thought of getting in Phillip's space while following him around with a basketball was extremely appealing.

Once outside, Cole opened the garage door and came out with the basketball. "Just set your beer down on the porch. Let's get started."

Phil took a long drink and then put his can down next to Cole's. "Okay, let's get this game going."

Phillip sounded genuinely glad to be there about to play basketball, and Cole wondered if he was dreaming. This was the absolute best way to spend a summer day.

"Take your best shot to see who goes first." He bounced the ball to Phil.

Phil made a basket easily, and when it was Cole's turn, he did so as well. They kept that up until Cole finally missed. "You were holding back the day we played with Dillion," he said.

Phil laughed and grabbed the ball, dribbled for a few quick seconds and made a jump shot.

Cole narrowed his eyes. "I wasn't even ready."

"Don't whine. Your turn." Phil snickered and handed off the ball, bounding around Cole with his arms in the air.

Cole snorted and dribbled low, shifting his weight, trying to get a clear path to make his shot. He attempted a hook shot but missed.

"Good try." Phil sounded slightly out of breath.

"You're going to wear out if you keep this pace up, buddy," Cole said, while trying to block Phil's next shot. Shivers shot through him each time his hands came into contact with Phillip's muscular body.

After just a few minutes of play, Cole's focus shifted to trying to win the game. Maybe he'd been paying too much attention to how sexy Phillip looked—how he pushed his hair back from his face and how he'd kept himself in good shape all these years—because he'd quickly fallen behind in the score by double digits. Being a competitive person, he couldn't let that go unchallenged. He needed to step it up and be more aggressive.

Their touches became more energetic and spirited, which was turning Cole on so much he was glad he had on jeans and not thin shorts despite the hot July temperature. But his jeans were getting more and more restrictive, which was taking a toll on his game. By this point, none of that mattered—the only thing he cared about was that Phillip Thompson was at his house and they were playing basketball together almost like old times.

Cole was flying high after the game. He drank the last of his beer on the porch with Phillip. Their afternoon had gone so well, especially being in such close proximity during their impromptu basketball game. While much of their touching had been inadvertent, he'd sensed Phillip getting into his space a little more than necessary, and he'd gladly reciprocated.

Maybe they were on their way to resurrecting the good old days.

CHAPTER NINETEEN

"I'LL SEE you in the morning to load up the towers," Phil called out to Chuck before getting into his Camaro. He fastened his seatbelt, started the car, cranked up the AC, adjusted the radio dial, and once on the street, he stepped on the gas and headed toward the Breezeway Pub to meet Brad. He turned the music up loud, trying to drown out his troubles.

It wasn't working.

He was mad at himself for refusing to give Cole a break when he'd called a couple days after they'd played basketball and asked if they could get together again. His answer had been no, but he wished he'd said yes.

Delivering the cat tree and then playing basketball with Cole ten days ago had been a real good day. Truth be told, he wished he was on his way to meet Cole rather than Brad. His attraction for Cole was strong, and he'd had a great time with him, but something still held him back.

Thinking about Cole every day since he'd found out he'd come back to town had given him time and perspective to work on getting rid of most of his anger. He'd come to realize that Cole was guilty of loving his mother—that's what it boiled down to, and how could he fault him for that? But the way Cole had handled the whole situation had ruined both their lives, and he was having a hard time getting past that.

Brad was a nice diversion for as long as it lasted and then he'd find someone else. Cole had no right to expect him to welcome him with open arms after what he'd done.

He didn't want to become a bitter old man, but if he kept closing himself off, that's exactly how he'd end up—like old man Fisher.

The cold blast of air shooting out of the vents raised goose bumps on his skin, so he turned the air conditioner down a couple notches.

Arriving at the Breezeway Pub was a relief because he was forced to think of something else. He needed to stop overanalyzing the situation with Cole before he drove himself crazy.

Brad was always early, so he wasn't surprised to see his truck in the lot. He parked the Camaro and headed for the entrance, glad that Brad already knew this would be an early night because of the cat show in Santa Monica tomorrow.

When he didn't see Brad at the bar, he searched for him and found him sitting at their favorite table sipping a beer. He was halfway to the table when Brad noticed him. His dimpled smile lit up his face and when Phil reached the table, Brad stood up, pulling him in for a quick hug.

"How's it goin?" Brad sat back down, relaxing in his seat with his legs stretched out.

"It's going." Phil took the seat across from Brad and glanced around, hoping a server had seen him come in. He rubbed the back of his neck, which he hadn't realized was stiff until he sat down. His back didn't feel too good either. A waitress appeared and took his drink order, slightly improving his mood.

He focused on a baseball game playing on the TV near their table. He didn't feel much like talking, and Brad must have figured that out because he came over to sit next to him and settled in to watch the game. The waitress brought his beer, and she set down a bowl of peanuts too.

A commercial came on, and he let his mind go blank as he stared across the room at nothing in particular. He noticed someone who looked like Cole sitting at the bar, and he did a double take. His stomach clenched, and he leaned forward, zeroing in on him. What the hell is Cole doing here? He watched him for a while, and he seemed to be alone.

"Isn't that Cole Fisher over at the bar?" Brad asked.

The sudden voice so close to his ear startled him out of his deep thoughts. He turned to Brad and narrowed his eyes at him.

Brad pulled back and raised his eyebrows. "What's that look for?"

"Sorry, but you spoke so loud right in my ear."

"Loud?" Brad ate a couple peanuts and took the last swig of his beer. "I wonder why Cole is in a place like this. Doesn't he have his daughter living with him?"

"Yeah, his daughter's staying with him for the summer, but I'm sure they aren't together 24/7."

"You seem bothered by him being here."

"I'm not bothered." Phil drained the last of his beer.

"Okay, whatever you say. Maybe we should order dinner."

Phil barely registered that Brad had said anything. All he could concentrate on was Cole looking so sexy and confident sitting there on the barstool in a blue and grey T-shirt. His hair appeared freshly cut. Seemed like he'd come here hoping to make a good impression on someone. Phil never would have pictured him in a gay bar, and he wondered if he'd been here before. Just then a good-looking blond slipped onto the stool right next to Cole. The guy had a mile wide grin plastered on his face. He sat facing Cole and leaned in to converse with him. Cole was smiling and seemed receptive to his company.

"Phil, shall we eat now?" Brad asked. His unusual gruff and annoyed tone brought Phil back to reality.

He stared at him and wished he'd stayed home tonight.

"I can see by the blank expression on your face that you aren't really present," Brad said.

"Uh, yeah, well, maybe we should just call it a night."

"Look, Phil. I think I've been pretty patient with you all these months."

"What?"

"I don't regret our time together, but I think our relationship has run its course." Brad pushed his beer bottle away and cracked a couple peanuts, throwing the shells onto the floor.

"What are you talking about?" Phil sat up straighter, his gaze remaining on Brad.

"All these months and you've not once invited me over to your place—do you think I haven't noticed?"

"Where's this coming from? I didn't know you wanted to come

over."

"Don't act stupid, Phil." Brad slammed his hand on the table. "We always go to my place or get together in one of our trucks. You've held back letting me into your life fully. I know we'd agreed from the start that neither of us wanted any strings, but this friends with benefits is getting old. Now tonight, well, it's plain as day you want Cole Fisher, and you wish you were with him, not me. Do us all a favor and admit that to yourself and do something about it."

Brad stood up and tossed some bills onto the table, glanced over at Cole and then back at Phil. "Would have saved us a lot of wasted time if you'd have just acknowledged your feelings from the start. See ya around."

Phil sat in stunned silence as he watched Brad stomp out of the bar. He'd handled their relationship poorly, and he hoped to apologize at some point. This day was bound to come sooner or later, although he had no idea it would go down like this. Nervously tapping his foot, he wished the damn waitress would come with another beer. He chanced a glance over to the bar, and Cole and the blond guy were still chatting. In fact, it looked like they were deep in conversation. Hopefully, Cole had not seen him and Brad.

After waiting a few minutes for a waitress and deciding that if he wanted a drink, he'd have to go get it himself, he left the table and headed for the bar—straight toward Cole and the guy who seemed captivated by him. He reached the two men, looked right at the blond and said, "Mind if I cut in?"

"We're not dancing—yet, so you'll have to wait," the overconfident blond said.

"Look, I really need to have a word with Cole if you don't mind," Phil ground out between clenched teeth.

The guy widened his eyes and arched his eyebrows in response to Phil's abrasive tone. He stood up with his drink in his hand. Nodding at Cole, he retreated to the other end of the bar.

Once the guy had taken a seat far out of earshot, Cole spoke. "You mind telling me what the hell that was about?" His tone came across as accusatory, but his face conveyed a different message, the corners of his lips turning up ever so slightly.

Phil opened his mouth to say something, but he couldn't find the words, so he turned his attention to the bartender and motioned him over. "I'll have a dirty martini and one for my friend here." He made eye contact with Cole. "Remember how we used to drink those back in college?"

"Shaken, not stirred," Cole said.

"You do remember."

Cole stood up and patted Phil on the back. "I'm going to pass, and maybe you should too. We have an early morning tomorrow."

Phil took a deep breath and looked at the bartender. "We'll take a raincheck, thanks." He sat down on the barstool where the blond had been, and Cole took his seat again.

"Shit, I at least need a beer, how about you?" Phil asked.

"I need to pick Dana up soon, so I'm stopping at one tonight. Where's Brad?" He glanced around the room.

"Oh, he had to leave. Family emergency." Phil reached for a pack of matches on the bar and began fidgeting with them.

"Are you okay?" Cole asked.

"Yeah, why?"

"You're acting a little strange."

Phil chuckled. "Yeah, maybe so. This has been a weird night. First I chased my date off, and then yours."

"I thought you said Brad had an emergency, and that guy wasn't my date." Cole leaned his elbow on the bar as he gazed at Phil. "Dana is having dinner at Gail and Eve's tonight, so I stopped in here for a quick beer and to relax a while before I go pick her up. I wasn't looking for a hook-up."

"Yeah, not your fault that someone found you irresistible," Phil said, smiling slightly.

"Oh, I don't know about that." He sat up straight and rubbed his chin. "I must have a five o'clock shadow by now."

"I don't need to worry about that. That's one reason I went with the scruffy look."

Cole shook his head and smiled. "Have you eaten?"

"No. In all the excitement of the evening, I haven't gotten around to that yet."

"Well, I have time for a quick bite. Would you like to have dinner with me?"

That caught Phil off guard, and he didn't know what to say at first, but it didn't take him long to figure out his answer. "Sure. Shall we stay here or find a table?"

"May as well get comfortable. Let's sit at a table."

Fortunately, the table Phil had been sitting at with Brad wasn't available. Instead, they found one clear across the room.

"We're lucky to get a table on a Friday night," Cole said, getting comfortable in the seat across from Phil.

"Sounds like you've been here before."

"A time or two."

Phil tried not to stare, but Cole was so easy on the eyes and extremely appealing. He was having a hard time wrapping his head around this man who'd had both feet in the closet back when he'd known him, now totally comfortable in his skin. That, among other things, was a huge turn-on.

"I'm not going to be able to spend a lot of time." Cole motioned for a server. "Not that I don't want to."

The waitress came to take their order. Phil followed Cole's lead and ordered Coke to drink, and they decided to share a pepperoni pizza.

Cole seemed quite relaxed, as if he was completely satisfied just sitting at the table with him. Phil had no interest in the baseball game anymore. Looking at Cole was much more interesting, although simply staring at the man soon became uncomfortable. His throat was dry and he was too overwhelmed to talk. The waitress set their drinks down on the table, and he welcomed the interruption.

Phil took a refreshing drink of his Coke. "So, how are Moonbeam and Moonshadow doing?"

"They're fine and enjoying their tower a lot." Cole swirled the ice cubes in his glass with his straw.

"Glad to hear that. Is Dana looking forward to the cat show tomorrow?"

"She sure is, and with her and both of the cats along, it'll be an adventure." Cole took out his phone and checked the time. "I'll send a text and let her know I'll be a little late picking her up."

"Gail won't mind having her longer," Phil said.

"I don't want to take advantage." He quickly typed out the text and returned his phone to his pocket.

The server arrived with the hot, steamy pizza, placing it down in the middle of the table along with two plates. "Parmesan cheese?" she asked.

"Sure," Phil answered.

She set the container down. "Be right back with a drink refill."

Phil waited for Cole to take the first slice before taking one for himself. He sprinkled Parmesan cheese onto his slice and then passed the jar to Cole.

"Looks nice and hot," Cole said, before taking a bite.

Phil picked off a piece of pepperoni and ate that first while watching Cole to see if he burned his mouth or not. Satisfied the pizza was the right temperature, he dug in too.

The server brought more Coke and left them to their meal.

"Do you cook?" Phil asked.

"Sure, a little, especially since Dana's been here."

"I don't cook much," Phil said. "I'm tired when I get home, and I usually work on the cat towers in the evenings, so I don't have that much time."

"I work from home a lot, so it's not as hard for me," Cole said. "This is nice—having dinner with you."

"Yeah, this sure wasn't the way I thought the evening would go, but I'm not complaining." He wiped his mouth with a napkin.

"Some other time we should go to a quieter place." Cole leaned across the table ever so slightly.

Phil looked around. The place was getting crowded and noisy. Maybe he noticed it more because he was stone sober or because he didn't want to miss anything Cole said.

"I'd better send another quick text to Dana." Cole gave the phone his attention for a few seconds and then pushed it away. "There, that should do." He put another slice of pizza on his plate and sprinkled it with Parmesan cheese.

"You're a good dad. I can tell you love having Dana with you," Phil said before taking another bite.

"To tell you the truth, I don't want the summer to ever end. And she loves it here. Eve is a big part of that, and Gail has been really good to her."

"Has Gail shown you her paintings?"

"Yeah, well, it's kind of hard to miss them when you walk into the apartment. She has talent, that's for sure."

"I'm hoping someday she'll get a showing at a gallery."

"I wish her luck. She'll need to start selling some or she'll run out of space in the apartment."

"That's a fact. She has all this energy and all those ideas for paintings that she just can't seem to stop."

"Creativity runs in your family. Your cat trees are really amazing."

Insanely happy with the compliment, heat rushed to Phil's face and he had the sensation of butterflies in his stomach. "Thanks," he managed to say.

Cole finished off his Coke and checked his phone. He grinned slightly after glancing at the screen.

"Is that a text from Dana?" Phil asked.

"Yeah. She's a great kid."

"Is she waiting on you?"

"She's okay, but I'll have to get over there soon."

Cole gathered up his napkins, wadding them into a ball. Phil put his used napkins onto his plate and pushed it away, sorry the time had passed so fast and that Cole would have to leave.

But instead of signaling for the check, Cole sat back quietly as if thinking hard about something, glancing from his lap to around the room. Phil wondered if he was going to say something, but the moments ticked by with nothing forthcoming.

Finally Cole sat forward again and their gazes connected. Cole's pupils were so dilated that his eyes looked even darker than usual. So mesmerized by the moment, Phil didn't notice Cole reach across the table until Cole's strong, warm hand covered his. A gentle squeeze came next, and then Cole used his thumb to rub light circles on the back of his hand. Tenderness like this was something he'd never thought would be possible again in his life. He let it happen, relishing in Cole's touch, their eyes still locked.

"I don't know about you, but to me it doesn't feel like fifteen years since we've held hands," Cole murmured.

Phil wished he could think of something to say, but he was at a loss for words. All he could do was gaze at the most handsome man he'd ever known, who was holding his hand and regarding him with love. He never wanted to see that look in another man's eyes.

Cole began to speak again, and Phil leaned in to catch every word over the music and loud voices in the room.

"The reason I feel so close to you is because you've been with me all these years even though you didn't realize it." He paused and looked down at the table. "Everywhere I went and everything I did, you were there..." Cole gazed at Phil again, tapping his heart with the fingers of his free hand. "Right here." He let go of Phil's hand and sat back in his seat as if uncomfortable he'd let himself be vulnerable.

Phil wanted to tell him how he'd been completely gutted and thought he might die back when Cole left him. He wanted to tell him that he'd hoped and prayed that maybe in a year he'd be able to recall their time together and smile at the good memories, but how even after fifteen years, those memories were few and far between. He wanted to tell him that he was still working through his bitterness. But he couldn't get the words out. Phil looked down at the tabletop afraid that if he tried to speak, he'd break down.

Cole put his phone away and caught the attention of their waitress, and she promptly came and cleared the dishes and set the check down between them. Phil took his wallet out, and so did Cole, and they stood up and tossed bills down on the table as they turned to walk out together.

Once outside in the fresh air and away from the noise, Cole stopped on the landing and turned to Phil. "I need to get over to Gail's now and pick Dana up. Guess we'll run into you and Eve at the cat show tomorrow."

"Yeah, we'll be there. Just look for the cat towers and we won't be far."

"We'll do that."

Phil wasn't sure who initiated the hug, but his stomach did flip-flops as he melted into Cole's embrace. He wished they could stand there with their arms wrapped around each other all night, caressing each other's backs, but all too soon, Cole pulled away and the contact ended. Smiling slightly, Cole turned and headed to his SUV, leaving Phil basking in the glow of that perfect goodnight hug that left him calm and content.

Two hugs with two different men—one to begin the evening and one that brought the night to an end. That was a first. Clearly there wasn't a hug that could ever compare with the one that came second, or a man who could compare with Cole Fisher.

CHAPTER TWENTY

"WE'LL BE at the cat show soon. You'll be able to talk to Eve face-to-face in a little while, so why all the texting?" Cole glanced at his daughter in the passenger seat.

Dana looked at him shyly through her bangs. "Just catching up on news."

She sounded so serious he had to wonder what kind of news they were discussing. He'd told her last night about his dinner with Phil. Was that one of their topics of conversation?

"How are the cats doing?" he asked.

Dana turned to check on them in the back seat. "They're fine. They look a little tired. How far are we from Santa Monica?"

"We'll be there within ten minutes barring any unforeseen traffic problems. Are Phil and Eve there already?"

"Yes. They have the cat towers almost all set up."

"They have quite a job with those," Cole mumbled.

After a few seconds, Dana hadn't said anything, so he glanced at her again. She stared at him with a wide grin spread across her face.

"Are you enjoying yourself?" he asked.

"Yes, it's a great day," she answered.

He turned back to the road. Phillip and their time together last night filled his thoughts. There was no question that Phillip had been jealous of the blond at the bar, and Phil was so sexy wearing that hostile stare that disappeared as soon as he'd chased the guy to the other end of the bar. That look was replaced with a soft, affectionate gaze that had melted Cole's heart. God, how he had wanted to kiss him.

Later, while they'd said goodnight, he'd been so tempted to try for that kiss, but all he'd managed was the hug, and what a hug it had been. Not a friend-hug like the previous ones they'd shared since he'd been back, but a romantic hug, nice and long with their hips pressed tight. He could almost feel the sensation of Phillip's arms around him now.

He came back to the present, focusing on the freeway signs to make sure he didn't miss their off-ramp. The thought of seeing Phillip again made him want to drive faster but that was impossible in the heavy traffic. At least they were moving along, inching closer to the auditorium where they'd all have a chance to spend some time together.

Hopefully Phillip was in the same mood as last night.

Dana stepped back from Moonshadow and Moonbeam's large show cage and gave it a long look.

"Satisfied with what you've done?" Cole asked.

"I think so. What do you think?" She looked up at him.

"I think it looks absolutely wonderful, and I don't know how I ever did this without you."

Dana fixed her gaze at the floor, her face flushing pink.

Cole put his arm around her. "Moonshadow and Moonbeam like it too. You made it real comfortable for them."

His attention was diverted to the man and little boy across the aisle busy setting up their own cage. He caught the man's eye, smiled and gave a half wave.

"Is that someone you know?" Dana asked.

"That's Jim and his son Brian." After a pause, Cole bent down closer to Dana's ear and said quietly, "Brian is the one who opened Moonshadow's cage at the last cat show. He's the reason we have this." He flicked his fingers across the padlock hanging on the cage door.

"Oh yes. I remember when you told me about that on the phone. He's pretty young. His dad must not watch him very well." She gave the father and son the once-over.

"It was an accident. He just wanted to pet Moonshadow, but I agree. Jim should have been watching him closer, especially when he'd assured me that he'd watch the cat for me. I think the boy learned his lesson, but I'm not taking any more chances."

"At least it ended well. I'm glad I'm here to help you now."

"I am too. You're the best helper." Cole gave her a big squeeze.

"Better than you know." Dana looked up at him with a big smile.

Cole picked up the program and scanned through the show times and the schedule of events.

"Can I see?" Dana asked.

"Sure." He handed the brochure over. "I'll go get us something to drink. Are you okay waiting here with the cats?"

"Sure, go ahead. I'm fine."

As Cole stepped away, he saw Dana pull out her phone. He had an idea who she was texting, and it wasn't her mother. Wondering how Phillip was doing and where he and Eve had set up their booth, he was tempted to try to find them, but he decided to stay focused and get back to Dana as soon as possible. There would be time to visit at some point during the day.

Cole carried Moonbeam from the show ring, making sure the path was clear for Dana following close behind with Moonshadow. Once back at their spot, they placed each of the cats back inside their safe and secure cage.

"I'm going to add more food and top off their water bowls," Dana said.

"Looks like they have plenty, sweetie."

Ignoring what he'd said, she poured water out of their thermos and sprinkled some cat food in their bowls.

Smiling, he watched her fuss over the pair.

Dana checked the time on her phone. "Well, we don't have to take them back to the judging ring for quite a while so..."

He waited for her to finish her sentence, but all she did was grin at him with a twinkle in her eye.

"Let's secure the cage." She focused on the padlock, clicked it closed and then glanced around the area. "Maybe you should ask Jim to keep an eye on them."

"Well, okay, but they're locked in so they should be all right. Shall we wander over to get ourselves some lunch? Are you hungry?"

"Ask Jim and then we'll go." She motioned toward their

neighbor sitting on a stool next to his cat's cage.

Cole stepped across the aisle toward Jim and did as Dana wanted. When he returned, she took his hand and did a little hop. She was almost vibrating with excitement.

"What's gotten into you, sweetie?" He couldn't help but grin at her.

"We're going on an adventure. Don't say no."

"How can I say yes or no when I don't know what you're talking about?"

She tugged on his hand. "Come with me, Father."

He raised one eyebrow. "Where are we going?"

Dana smiled as she pulled him along, and he had a pretty good idea they were going to see Phil and Eve, which suited him fine. He'd been looking for Phillip all day among the throngs of people passing by, but he hadn't really expected to see him since he was busy selling his towers.

He hoped Phillip hadn't gone from hot to cold overnight, but that had happened before, so he wasn't sure what to expect when they saw each other. By the time Dana led him past numerous tables of various cat-related items, his heart was pounding, and then the familiar tall cat towers loomed ahead of them, and his stomach started to churn.

They got closer, and Cole sucked in a breath. Phillip looked so handsome and confident in his element surrounded by the cat trees. He was busy talking to a customer, so Cole hung back while Dana and Eve greeted each other excitedly. Eve then acknowledged him with a little hug, which helped to calm him down.

"How are you, Eve?" he asked.

"Great, it's a fun day so far and promises to get even better." She turned to Dana, and they chattered in each other's ears. He couldn't make out what they were saying.

The customer left, and Phil turned toward them. His bright blue eyes locked on him, and Phil sent him a friendly, welcoming smile that put him at ease and weakened his knees. Did Phillip know what that smile did to him? He was probably grinning back like a fool, but that was okay. He was a fool in love.

Phil joined them. "Hey, how has the day been so far? Are you having a good time, Dana?"

"Yes, it's fun. I love it here."

"Good to see you, Cole." Phil swept an admiring gaze up and down Cole's body. "How are the cats?"

"Great, great," Cole answered, feeling tongue-tied because all he could think about was how Phillip was ogling him and how much he liked that.

Eve stepped closer and pulled Dana along with her. "Well, we don't have a whole lot of time, so we'll come to the point."

Furrowing his brow, Cole glanced at Phil, and he looked just as confused. "What's going on?" Phil asked.

"Yeah, what's going on?" Cole echoed.

"We had this great idea that the four of us could get away from here for a little while—have lunch, take a short walk. Dana and I are treating you," Eve said, her big smile matching Dana's.

Phil narrowed his eyes. "Leave here? But we have work to do, and Cole and Dana are showing Moonshadow and Moonbeam."

"We've got it all planned out. Betty is going to watch the towers while we're gone... "

"And, Father and I left the cats with food and water all locked in safely, and we're not due in the show ring until late this afternoon." Dana took a deep breath and looked up at Cole. Excitement sparkled in her wide eyes.

"Can't we have lunch here?" Phil asked.

Cole joined the girls in a stare down aimed at Phil. None of them averted their eyes until he held out his hands in surrender. "Well, okay, I'm game if you are," he said, directing his comment to Cole.

"Good. I'm glad you're not going to be a party pooper," Cole said.

Dana and Eve giggled, and Betty appeared from around one of the biggest towers. She smiled and gave Eve a quick hug. "Introduce me to your friends."

"This is Dana and her dad Cole Fisher. Cole and Uncle Phil are old friends, and Dana and I are new friends."

"It's wonderful to meet you," Betty said.

"Same here," Cole said with a nod of his head.

"Nice to meet you," Dana chimed in.

"Dana and I are going to take a look at your T-shirts when we get back," Eve said.

"Well, that would be nice." Betty clasped her hands behind her back.

"Father, we should have T-shirts like Eve and Phil." Dana glanced at Phil's shirt.

Cole took a step closer to Phil, zeroed in on his shirt and read aloud, "This Guy Likes Cats." He smiled. "That's a good one."

Dana's eyes lit up. "We can get you one like it."

"We'll have to see." Cole rested his hand on Dana's shoulder.

"Betty, I don't want to impose on you..." Phil said.

"Nonsense, I'm glad to do it. You four go out and have some fun. I'll take care of everything here." Cole noticed Betty wink at Eve. He shared a knowing look with Phil. He'd seen the wink too.

"Well, if we're going, we'd better get moving," Phil said. "Who's driving, or are we walking someplace?"

"We can go in my SUV if we need to drive somewhere." Cole pulled his keys out of his pocket.

"Great, this is going to be so much fun!" Eve exclaimed. She and Dana slapped hands as the four of them walked down the aisle toward the door.

"When are we going to find out where we're going?" Cole asked, once they were outside.

"I thought Dana would love to see the pier. It's close, and we can have lunch and then ride the Ferris wheel." Eve's enthusiasm was contagious.

Cole stole a glance at Phil, wondering if he was thinking about when they'd driven to the Santa Monica pier in Phil's Camaro right after their high school graduation. They'd bummed around the pier, rode the Ferris wheel, and camped on the beach. Phil didn't hold his gaze, but he looked upbeat and agreeable.

When they reached the SUV, the girls rushed to the back doors. They wanted Phil to ride up front, and that was great as far as Cole was concerned. Phil climbed into the passenger seat without any hesitation. Once they were all buckled in, Cole backed out and headed out of the parking lot.

"Remember the last time you rode in here?" he asked Phil.

"Yeah, that was quite a day." He held out his hand and flexed his fingers.

"What happened that day?" Dana asked.

Phil turned slightly in his seat to speak to Dana. "I had a slight accident at your house while I was working on the kitchen cabinets. Your dad had to drive me to the hospital to get stitches."

"Wow." Dana's eyes widened.

"He had a huge bandage on his hand." Eve indicated the size with her thumb and finger.

"It wasn't that big," Phil said, shaking his head. He turned back to the front.

"He didn't miss any work over it. In fact, he went right back that day and finished up what he'd been doing." Cole glanced at Phil and smiled.

"That was the first day they met after fifteen years. Oh, except for at the cat show when they thought they saw each other," Eve said.

"Sounds like I missed a lot of excitement. I wish I'd have been here sooner."

In the rearview mirror, Cole caught a glimpse of Dana smiling wistfully. "Well, you're here now and that's what counts."

Cole took a quick look at Phil, who looked relaxed and happy, not stiff and detached like he had on that day three months ago. As for himself, he couldn't be more content than he was on this beautiful summer day driving toward the beach on what seemed like a family outing.

Cole returned to Phil and the girls after tossing the wrappings from their burgers and fries into the trash can. He checked his watch.

"Father, relax," Dana said. "We still have time to walk around a little bit before going back. It's so beautiful here."

And it sure was. He never in a million years thought he'd ever get the chance to spend time with his daughter and Phillip like this. And Eve certainly filled out the group like the icing on the cake.

Lunch had been great—good food, a sunny day, blue ocean, sea gulls squawking, the whole place buzzing with energy—and having Phillip by his side made his heart swell.

"Can we ride the Ferris wheel before we leave, Father?" Dana took Cole's hand as they strolled along the pier.

"Can we, Uncle Phil?" Eve asked.

"If Cole wants to, I'm up for it I guess."

"Fine with me, let's go," Cole answered.

After buying tickets for the ride, they stood in a short line waiting to board. "Maybe we can come back again when we have more time," Dana said while taking in the surroundings and the other rides.

"Yeah, we could come on a day when we don't have anything else to do," Eve said. She whispered something to Dana that Cole couldn't hear, but Dana giggled and whispered back. He was happy to see Dana having so much fun.

"I guess you've been on the Ferris wheel before, Father?" Dana asked.

"Oh, yeah, a number of times over the years. Phil and I used to come down here now and then." He looked over at Phil. "We skipped our high school graduation trip and came here instead, remember Phil?"

Phil chuckled. "Yeah, we planned on going to Mexico, but we took a side trip, and this was as far as we got."

Dana's eyes widened. "Really? Mexico?"

"Why didn't you go?" Eve asked.

"Oh, I don't know. I guess we were having too much fun here, so we just stayed."

"We had a good time that weekend," Cole said softly. A wave of nostalgia swept over him.

"Hey, it's our turn." Eve looked toward the loading platform and then at Dana.

Cole put his hand on Dana's shoulder to guide her toward the ride, with Phil and Eve right next to them.

"Age before beauty," Eve said, when the operator raised the bar and motioned them forward.

"After you," Cole said to Phil with a sweep of his hand. He watched closely as Phillip got on, noticing how well he filled out his jeans.

"Father, you're next," Dana directed. Cole gladly slid in next to Phillip and then looked toward Dana. "There's plenty of room..."

"We'll get on the next one," Eve said to the operator, loud enough for Phil and Cole to hear, and then she and Dana retreated back several steps. The operator quickly secured the bar, and the chair rose. Cole watched as the girls boarded the next seat. "What the heck..."

"What were they thinking..." Phil added.

As the chair rose higher, Cole reached for Phillip's hand and entwined their fingers. "Looks like it's just you and me."

Cole stared off into the distance, intent on the scenery. He was afraid to look at Phillip for fear he'd want his hand back. Hopeful that this day would end on a high note, he tried not to get too excited in case he was wrong. While the Ferris wheel rose higher and higher, he kept a tight hold on Phillip's hand.

He felt exactly like he had back when he was a teenager— completely in love with Phillip Thompson. Now, fifteen years later, being with him was even better because he didn't have to worry about letting his true self be known. His parents were gone, and his daughter knew the real him, and not only that, she was pushing for this relationship.

The warm summer sun on his face made him feel alive and extraordinarily lucky to be here. He welcomed the gentle puffs of air as the Ferris wheel rose higher and higher because he felt like he was on a slow simmer from sitting next to the sexiest man he'd ever known. Smiling, he prayed they'd be able to rekindle their love.

Phillip, with the sun shining on his blond hair and the breeze ruffling it slightly, gazed in all directions, intent on taking in the beautiful view of the pier, ocean, beach, and cliffs of Santa Monica. Cole wished he'd look his way instead and feel what he was feeling. He longed for a kiss from this strong, amazing, unforgettable man.

Phillip finally turned his head toward him, and his eyes landed right on Cole's lips.

Am I imagining this?

Cole's heart began to race at the thought that they might actually kiss up here on the top of the Ferris wheel. Phillip's mouth was pressed tight into a serious expression, but his eyes sparkled as he regarded him with total admiration. Even though it was broad daylight, Cole felt like the stars had aligned, and when Phillip leaned in and raised his chin with his fingers, he knew it was true.

"Kiss me, baby," Phil whispered, his eyes fluttering shut as their lips met.

Cole wanted to keep his eyes open, but he slipped into some kind of trance, and he closed his eyes too. All his other senses came to life ten-fold, and the euphoric kiss transported him back fifteen years. All his emotions bubbled to the surface, and memories of kissing Phillip flooded into his mind. Phillip liked lots of tongue, so he slipped his tongue inside Phil's parted lips and deepened the kiss, his mouth tingling from the graze of Phil's facial hair. All his blood rushed south. Phillip grasped the back of his head and held him there as if he was afraid Cole would get away—jump off the Ferris wheel maybe. Well, he felt like he could join the sea gulls and fly over the water at this point.

When Phil broke the kiss, Cole met his smile and held his gaze. He wanted to remain close, but considering where they were, he settled back in his seat. He took Phillip's hand again and gave him a quick glance, noticing the color in his cheeks. Was it the kiss that had given them the rosy look, or maybe the sun had. He hoped it was the kiss. His face was probably flushed too. His lips felt puffy and his face tingly from the sensation of Phillip's facial hair.

In some ways the kiss was like old times, and in other ways it was brand new, and he couldn't wait to do it again.

CHAPTER TWENTY-ONE

THE SOUND of the ringing phone got louder and louder as Phil hurried toward the house. He stopped at the back door, grasping the handles of two bags of groceries in his left hand and the key in his right as he struggled to open the door, hoping that Cole was on the line. Had he missed hearing his cell phone ring in the store?

They hadn't talked since their day in Santa Monica three days ago, and he'd been anxious to hear Cole's voice again. The heated kiss they'd shared on the Ferris wheel smoldered in his brain.

He got the door unlocked and burst into the kitchen. After hastily depositing the grocery bags on the countertop, he rushed to grab the phone.

Cole's name was in the caller ID.

"Hey, Cole," he said into the receiver.

"Hey, you sound out of breath."

"I just got in from grocery shopping. I rushed in to catch the phone."

"Oh, sorry. Is this a bad time?"

Phil sat down on a stool at the counter. "No, I can talk. What's up?"

"Uh, yeah," Cole let out a breath and cleared his throat. "I've been wanting to call." Phil detected shyness in Cole's voice and that made him smile. Having Cole on the phone was like Christmas in July.

"How'd your cats do at the cat show yesterday?"

"They both did really well. Dana was thrilled. I wish you and Eve had come on the second day."

"I'm not sure how we'd have topped Saturday."

"That Ferris wheel ride was pretty awesome," Cole said, and Phil heard the smile in his voice.

"That it was," Phil said, smiling himself.

"Well, I called because I wondered if you and Eve would like to join me and Dana for a horseback ride at the park tomorrow. If you're working, we can wait until the weekend."

"It so happens I'm not working tomorrow. I'm kind of between jobs right now."

"Great," Cole exclaimed. "Uh, I mean, it'll be fun—glad you're free. Do you think Eve can come? Can you invite her?"

"Sure, I'll call and set it up. What time do you want to go?"

"Can you meet us at the stables at ten? I called and got the ride times, and a group leaves at ten forty-five."

"Sounds good, I'll tell Eve."

After hanging up, Phil sat there a minute looking at the phone, his mood flying high. Maybe it wasn't a real date since the girls were going, but it was close, and that was a good first step. The sparks were still there between them—that was evident when they'd kissed, and he'd come to the conclusion that he wanted to move forward with Cole.

Phil drew in a long breath and sighed in contentment as he watched Eve, Dana, and Cole admiring the horses in the corral. Dana touched one of them on the nose and immediately pulled her hand back and giggled.

"Don't be afraid, he won't bite." Eve patted the horse's forehead.

"His nostrils are so large," Dana said. "And the air doesn't smell very fresh around here. Not that I'm complaining, I'm just saying... "

Eve frowned. "I love the smell of horses."

Dana wrinkled her nose. "I don't think it's the horses that smell bad, but what they leave behind, if you get my meaning."

Phil and Cole laughed. The two girls looked like genuine cowgirls in their jeans, plaid shirts, boots, and western hats.

While waiting their turn with the riding guide, Eve pulled out her phone from her fanny pack. "Let's take some pictures."

"Stand in front of the corral," Dana instructed her dad and Phil.

"Yeah, stand next to each other in front of the horses," Eve said.

Phil stepped over near Cole, suddenly feeling self-conscious and stopping a few feet away from him.

"Get closer, I can't get a good picture unless you stand closer." Eve shared a smile with Dana.

Cole stepped right up next to Phil, their shoulders touching. The horses, tied to the fence, bobbed their heads behind them, and Phil hoped his cap wouldn't get knocked off before Eve took the picture. She was always very precise when taking photos, framing everything just right and making sure the lighting was good. The longer it took, the longer he could stand next to Cole, so maybe her technique wasn't so bad.

Eve motioned with her hand and said, "Stand just a bit closer."

Cole put his arm around Phil's shoulder and pulled them together. Phil loved the feel of Cole's strong, warm arm around his body, and his heart swelled as he pressed against him. He couldn't help putting his arm around Cole's waist to draw them even closer together.

"Perfect," Dana said. "Smile."

Eve snapped several pictures and finally got one that satisfied her. "Thanks, guys, that was awesome. Now let me get one of you, Dana."

Watching Eve and Dana taking pictures, Phil said more to himself than to Cole, "Those two are playing matchmaker."

"I heard that." Cole smiled. "Do you mind?"

Phil looked Cole in the eye. "I guess not. You?"

"I'm glad Dana likes you. The other night when I texted her about being late, I mentioned I was delayed because I was having dinner with you. She sent back every smile emoji ever created."

Surprised, Phil frowned. "Why didn't you tell me that before?"

"I didn't think you were ready to hear it."

"And now?"

Cole gave him a quick one-arm squeeze. "I think we've taken the relationship to the next level," he whispered near his ear.

Phil couldn't keep the smile off his face.

"I've got to get a picture too," Cole called out to the girls, pulling out his phone from his belt clip holster.

Phil noticed the riding guide watching them patiently. "Maybe get one after Dana gets on her horse."

The guide took her cue and brought one of the horses out of the corral. "This is an extremely gentle horse—perfect for a first-time rider. Her name's Baby Doll," she said reassuringly.

Dana didn't flinch as the guide helped her up onto the horse. The guide went through a few instructions with her about how to hold the reins and how to position her feet in the stirrups.

"You look like a natural sitting up there." Eve gazed up at Dana sitting on a horse for the first time in her life. She looked a little apprehensive, but determined too, and she did look good on the buckskin.

"How do you feel, sweetie?" Cole patted her leg.

She grasped one rein in each hand. "Okay. It's a strange feeling, but I like it."

"You'll feel even stranger when you get down after riding for an hour. You'll feel really short, at least I always do." Eve laughed.

"Maybe that's because you *are* short," Phil joked, wiggling her cowgirl hat on her head.

Eve rolled her eyes and adjusted her hat. "Very funny, Uncle Phil."

She then accepted the guide's help to mount her horse. "This is Serenity," the guide said, helping her settle into the saddle of the chestnut mare.

Phil untied the bay horse he'd been assigned and climbed aboard, adjusting himself in the saddle.

"What's your horse's name, Uncle Phil?" Eve asked.

"That one is Biscuit," the guide volunteered.

Phil liked how Cole stood there watching him in his dark glasses, looking sexy as hell. His baseball cap made him look youthful, just like he'd appeared fifteen years ago. Phil wondered if his cap and dark glasses also gave him the look of a younger man. He sure felt young today.

"When are you going to get on your horse, Father?" Dana asked.

Cole jerked his head toward her. "Right now, I guess."

"Do you need help, sir?" the guide asked. "Your horse is named Shadow Dancer," she added, untying the horse.

"No, I think I've got this." Cole mounted the large chestnut horse in one fluid motion.

"You haven't ridden for a while?" Phil asked.

"No, I haven't, but it's like riding a bike—you don't forget." Cole winked at him.

Phil was filled with nervous excitement on this beautiful summer morning. Not only was he about to share a ride with Cole, but they possibly had a future ahead of them.

He caught Cole's attention and tried to make him laugh by sticking out his bottom lip in a pout and asking, "Why did you get the horse with the snazzy name?"

"What do you mean?" Cole snickered.

"Your horse is named *Shadow Dancer* and mine is *Biscuit.*"

"There's nothing wrong with the name Biscuit. Seabiscuit was a racehorse, you know."

"But my house is Biscuit, not Seabiscuit." He slumped his shoulders.

"Do you want to switch? Would that make you happy?" Phil could tell that Cole was having a hard time keeping a straight face.

"Thanks, but the guide might not take kindly to the switch, and I don't want us to get kicked off the ride." He patted his horse on the neck. "I'll manage somehow," he sighed.

Cole shook his head, smiled, and snorted out a laugh. He urged his horse forward to stand beside Dana. "How are you doing, sweetie?"

"Fine so far, but the horse hasn't moved yet." She giggled.

The guide approached Dana, and Cole said, "Looks like you'll get to move now—see how you like it."

"I'm going to have you ride right behind me in line," she told Dana. Sir, I'll want you right behind your daughter." She looked at Phil and then to Eve. "You two can fall in line right behind them, and the others in the group will take up the rear."

The guide took Dana's horse's halter and led her to where the line would form, with Cole, Eve, and Phil following behind. Phil was pleased with how this was going—he'd have a great view of Cole from behind on their hour-long ride.

Once the guide had everyone situated, she mounted her own horse. "Make sure your hats don't blow off. Hold on to them if a breeze comes up. We don't want the horses to spook. If any problems arise, please alert me. Stay in line and enjoy the ride. Let's go."

Dana glanced back and smiled at her dad as her horse took its first steps. She grasped the reins and beamed.

Phil knew how happy Cole was to see her riding a horse for the first time and enjoying it. He was also happy for Eve to have this new friend who seemed to enjoy all the things she liked.

And he was happy for himself, for allowing his walls to come down so he could give Cole this second chance.

CHAPTER TWENTY-TWO

PEERING INTO the refrigerator, Cole double checked that everything was all set for the dinner he'd planned for himself and Phillip. He'd made potato salad and baked beans, as well as bacon, cheddar, and chive biscuits. The corn on the cob and steaks were ready for the grill, and he had plenty of beer. He hadn't made dessert, but there were a couple flavors of ice cream in the freezer. Personally, he'd rather have Phillip for dessert. With Dana tucked safely away at Eve and Gail's for the night, he had high hopes.

He closed the door and rubbed his hands together, feeling all kinds of nervous energy while waiting for Phillip to arrive. Even though the table was all set and ready, he checked it for the tenth time in the last hour.

Was this really happening? Had Phillip forgiven him, and were they going to begin a new relationship? If that's what happened he'd consider himself the luckiest man in the world. He ran his hand through his hair and straightened his glasses, hoping he looked okay in his cut-offs and T-Shirt.

On his way to the front door to wait for Phillip, he stopped in the family room to check on Moonshadow and Moonbeam, and he wasn't surprised they were lounging on the cat tree. That had been money well spent for more than one reason. He smiled. Phillip had built the tree and his kitchen cabinets. There was a little piece of him in the house, and he liked the soothing feeling that gave him. He didn't pet the cats or speak to them for fear of disturbing their nap and causing them to jump down. When Phillip arrived, he wanted him to see how much they liked their tree.

In the entryway, he admired the new painting he'd just bought of two horses in a stable. He'd had it framed and hung this morning. If Phillip didn't know about it already, he would be surprised, but he figured that Gail or Eve would have told him. After all, Gail had been over the moon when she'd said this was the very first painting she'd ever sold.

The familiar roar of Phillip's Camaro dragged him out of his thoughts. Smiling, he should have guessed Phil would drive the car. And from the sound of it pulling into the driveway, he'd driven it with the same reckless abandon of his younger years.

He opened the door to get a good look at Phillip in the car. Phil pushed his sunglasses up onto his head and climbed out of the car, and Cole drew his gaze to Phil's toned arms in the sleeveless pale blue T-shirt, and then down to the camo cargo shorts showing off his athletic legs. Flip-flops finished off his casual outfit. With lots of skin showing, he looked sexy and comfortable—like he was prepared to kick back and enjoy himself. Considering his choice of footwear, Phil hadn't planned on playing basketball. Cole licked his bottom lip. Maybe that meant he hoped they'd be busy doing something else after dinner.

"Hi," Cole said, at a loss for anything coherent to say because Phillip looked so damn hot.

"Hey." Phil reached into the car and came out holding two ceramic containers with grass growing out of the tops. He held the containers out as Cole closed the distance from the front door to the car.

"These are for Moonshadow and Moonbeam." He had the sexiest smile on his face.

"You didn't have to do that." Cole accepted the gift with a big smile of his own.

"Batman and Robin said I should bring something." He stuck his hands into his pockets with his thumbs hanging out.

Standing like that with the bright red Camaro behind him reminded Cole of what had drawn him to Phillip so many years ago—utterly handsome with a bit of a wild streak, smart, and best of all, unassuming. He wasn't that young man now, rather an even better version of who he'd been. Hopefully Phillip saw him that way as well.

"Do you think they'll like it?" Phil asked.

"Oh, yeah, sure I do. Let's take them in and see for ourselves. The cats have been fed and are relaxing on their cat tree." He raised the containers up slightly to get a better look. "Sorry, I was kind of lost in thought there for a minute... I didn't notice the cat faces painted on these. They're great."

"Have you been shooting baskets lately?" Phil asked when they passed under the basketball hoop.

"Yeah, and I've taught Dana too. She's pretty good." He stopped at the door and waited for Phillip to open it.

Once in the entryway, Phil pulled up short across from the wall adorned with Gail's painting. He slanted his head and peered up at it. "I see you've added something new."

"Did Gail tell you?"

"Yeah, she said you'd bought one of her paintings, but I didn't know which one. I saw this when she had it about half done. I thought it was beautiful then, but it's incredible now." He reached out and ran his finger along the bottom of the frame.

"She's a great artist."

"Thanks for doing that for her. It gave her ego a big boost."

"I didn't buy it just to help her out. I really wanted it hanging here. Brings back good memories." His mouth curved into a smile.

"That's how I felt when I saw her working on it." Phil smiled back.

"Well, let's see what the cats are doing and show them the presents." Cole headed for the family room.

Phil followed close behind. "Sounds good."

Cooking on the grill and drinking beer with Phillip was one of the best experiences of the summer. Cole was enjoying every second of the evening even though he had to make an effort to live in the moment and not think of how much he wanted something to happen between them after dinner.

"The meat smells good." Phil eyeballed the sizzling steaks.

"Thanks, I marinated it all day." Cole turned the corn on the cob with the tongs. "I hope you still like your steak well done because that's how I'm cooking it." He met Phil's gaze and smiled.

"Well done is good, you too?" Phillip's hungry eyes caused him to feel flushed, or maybe it was the heat coming off the grill on this warm summer evening. He took a swig of beer.

"One of the many things we have in common." He found himself staring at Phillip, so he blinked and looked back at the grill.

"Do you and Dana cook out a lot?"

"We have a few times. One night we even cooked the fish we caught out at the aqueduct."

"No kidding. How'd Dana like fishing?"

"She got a kick out of it, and she was actually really good at fishing—and she gets a lot of enjoyment from sending pictures to her mother of the new things she's doing... for shock value." Cole laughed.

"I take it Meredith is... how should I put this... more of a city slicker?"

"You hit the nail on the head." Cole laughed again. They'd actually mentioned his ex-wife, and Phillip seemed to take it all in stride. That pleased him, because after all, she was part of his life and always would be because of Dana.

"Maybe before Dana goes back to New York, you can bring Gail and Eve over for a cookout. We can use the pool too."

"I'm sure they'd like that." Phil drained his beer.

Cole tried to shake off the empty feeling he always got when he thought about Dana going back to live with Meredith. More than half of her time in California was already over. Her presence in his daily life had brought so much joy that the thought of her leaving made his heart ache.

"Are you thinking about Dana going back?" Phil asked.

"You know me better than anyone. It's like you can read my mind."

"I know how much being with her means to you. I feel the same about Eve."

The smoke from the grill rose in the air, sending out a delicious aroma. Cole poked the meat with the tip of the tongs. "I think the steaks are just about ready and the corn should be too. I've got beans on the stove, and I'll warm up some muffins in the microwave."

"You went to so much trouble," Phil said.

"Nothing is too much trouble for you."

Throwing caution to the wind and following his heart, Cole stepped forward and pressed his lips to Phillip's. Their sensual kiss pushed all other thoughts, except for Phillip, out of his brain for those few wonderful seconds. They parted, and the surprised smile he received from Phil made the experience all that much better. He wished he'd had time to grab hold of the man and give him a long kiss like the one they'd shared on the Ferris wheel, but with tongs and a potholder in his hands, he'd been a bit unprepared. Besides that, the food might have burnt, and the house might have burned down. There would be enough time later for another shot at a longer kiss. The vibes he was getting from Phillip suggested they'd be doing some serious kissing before the night ended.

Cole had been pleased with how the meal had turned out—he guessed it all tasted good because Phil had said so, but he'd been so excited, nervous, hyped up, and head over heels in love that he hardly remembered eating the food, let alone how it tasted. The food hadn't been burnt or raw, which was about the extent of his awareness.

"Let's quit in here. I'll clean up the rest later," Cole said, after shoving the last of the leftovers into the refrigerator.

Phil set the plates down on the countertop next to the dishwasher. "The food was sure good, but I already said that, didn't I?"

"Yeah, I think you did." Suddenly the distance between the refrigerator and the dishwasher seemed way too far. He'd held himself back all evening, except for the short kiss at the barbecue, and he didn't want to wait another minute to touch Phil again. He took a tentative step toward him.

"Are you okay?" Phil's flirtatious glance and smile set Cole's blood on fire.

"Yeah, I'm good. Are you?"

Phil stepped closer, and Cole's heart sped up. Could Phillip hear it pounding? He didn't understand why he was nervous, because he'd yearned for Phillip's arms around him every day since they'd parted fifteen years ago.

In contrast, Phil didn't look nervous at all as he slowly ran his hands up Cole's forearms. His blue eyes fluttered shut, and he worked his fingers into the arms of Cole's T-shirt, sending chills up his spine. Phillip's hands on the bare skin of his shoulders and upper back made him weak-kneed and lightheaded. Phil's chest pressed against his had Cole's lower half reacting with the beginnings of a hard-on.

He wanted to yank his shirt up over his head to allow Phil more access, but he used what little restraint he had and waited for

Phillip to take the lead, all the while hugging him gently in return. Phil's strong back muscles flexed under the soft material of his shirt, the sensation heightening his arousal.

Phillip pulled him into a stronger embrace, reaching up under his shirt and kneading his back. Cole grasped his hips, and Phil slid his hands downward, stopping at the waist of Cole's cut-off jeans. He sucked in a sharp breath, wishing his hands would go lower. Phil's heavy, warm breathing close to his ear gave him chills. His erection strained against his shorts, and Phillip ground his bulge against his in a sensual rhythm. Cole never thought he'd ever feel this alive again, but here he was in the place he belonged—in Phillip's arms where he should have been all along.

So many wasted years.

Feeling this aroused without so much as a kiss blew his mind. All the memories of how good they'd been together helped to renew their connection and stoke his desire. That desperate ache built, and he needed to either get them to the couch or to the bedroom like ten minutes ago.

Phillip crushed his mouth against his, and the hot, hard, and deep kiss had him moaning low in his throat and praying he'd last until they got to lie down someplace. He pulled back, but Phil landed his lips on Cole's neck for a few soft kisses then found his lips again, stealing his breath and sending shivers through his body.

He used all his willpower to pull away again. "Let's move this to a more suitable place," he whispered breathlessly.

"I thought you'd never ask," Phil whispered back, inches from his lips.

He took Phil's hand and quickly led him out of the kitchen. For a second, the idea of using the couch in the family room held some appeal, but a real bed would better serve the purpose, so he bounded up the stairs with Phil right behind.

Cole reached his bedroom door and pushed it open. "This is my bedroom." He stumbled inside.

"Nice room," Phil said in a rush.

Phil helped Cole take his shirt off, and he tossed it on the floor, and Phil's shirt followed right behind. On the way to the king-sized bed, they pulled off and tossed two pairs of shoes haphazardly against the wall. They dove onto the bed, and the mattress jiggled under their weight and threw them slightly off balance. Phil fought for control and soon Cole was coming unglued with this unbelievably sexy man over him, sucking his nipples and running his warm hands over his chest and stomach. Cole stroked Phil's ass through his cargo shorts, and he slipped his fingers below the waistband.

"Get these off," he rasped.

"I will if you will," Phil said with a sly smile, rubbing the front of Cole's pants and squeezing his hardness.

Cole was afraid he'd come right then and there. He lay back on the bed with his arm over his eyes, trying to get his breathing to slow down so he could regain control of himself.

After a moment, Phil's fingers lightly touched his cheek. "Are you okay?" His voice sounded so soothing.

"I'm fine, I just don't want to finish before we start, if you get my meaning."

Phil lay down next to him, his head pressed next to Cole's neck. He breathed in the scent of Phillip's hair—the familiar smell, a light woodsy evergreen scent, taking him back in time. He caressed his hair, which was much shorter than fifteen years ago, and moved his fingers to the side of his face. The facial hair felt different, but he liked it a lot—devilishly masculine, and after his years with Meredith, extremely desirable.

An awareness of inner peace washed over him, and he became lost in what seemed like a beautiful daydream that brought him to the edge of sleep.

A strong, familiar arm stretching across his chest roused him slightly as he melted into Phillip's pliant, warm body. Wrapping his fingers around Phil's, he realized his breathing had slowed too, and was becoming deeper. He slipped one foot between Phillip's feet like he used to do all those years ago and closed his eyes.

"I've missed you for so long," he whispered, drifting off to sleep next to the love of his life.

Cole woke up still in the same position as when he'd fallen asleep. The room was etched in shadows—evening had turned into night. How long had he slept? Phillip snored softly beside him. He'd disturb him if he tried to look at the clock, so he resisted the urge to check the time. What did it matter anyway? They had nowhere they needed to be except here next to each other.

He couldn't believe how they'd fallen asleep like this right in the middle of such a frenzied sexual encounter, but that was his fault, and he felt pretty stupid about it. Sleeping next to Phillip had been great though, and maybe it served a purpose, making it clear that their relationship was about more than just getting laid, although that would be nice too. Just the thought of continuing where they'd left off before their nap made his dick stiffen.

He wanted to unbutton and unzip his shorts so he'd be more comfortable. Slowly, so as not to disturb Phillip, he reached down with the hand that wasn't buried under part of Phil's body, undid the button on his pants, found his zipper, and gave it a tug, releasing the pressure on his hard-on. That felt a lot better. He remembered when Phillip had grabbed him there—that's when he'd had to stop for fear of shooting off in his pants. That would have been embarrassing for sure.

Fooling around with Phillip was more than enough to get him all hot and bothered, but besides that, it had been a long time since he'd gotten any, which added to the problem. Phil and Brad had probably been...well, he wasn't going to dwell on that because Phillip was his now—no more Brad or anyone else. At least he hoped so after this night together.

Phil stirred and took a deep breath, sounding like he was waking up. A neck nuzzle and then a little kiss left no question that he was awake and still in the mood. He untangled himself from under Phil's arm and legs, and they both shifted on their sides, facing each other. Cole gave him a hug, pushing his hips tightly into Phillip's erection. Cole's eyes widened, and he hardened more, reaching for Phil's zipper to free his dick from the confines of the stiff material. Phil groaned and then laughed softly, helping to slip his pants and jockeys off.

"You're next," Phil said, his voice sounding thick with sleep.

Cole finished undressing, and went straight for Phillip's mouth. The soft kiss soon deepened, and their tongues glided together. Excitement coiled inside of Cole, and he ran his hands over Phillip's shoulders and chest, getting reacquainted with his body and loving every second of the experience.

Their passion still burned, but now it was much more controlled and directed toward one goal—getting each other off—now.

They grasped each other's dicks, and for Cole it seemed like no time had passed since he'd been with Phillip in this way—certainly not fifteen years. He remembered every wrinkle and bump, all the spots that drove Phillip crazy with desire, and he did everything in his power to please the one he loved. With Phillip working on his dick at the same time, he couldn't help but give in to his own desires every few seconds, throwing his head back and moaning, but then he was right back to pleasuring Phil.

At this rate he wouldn't last long, but if he was right, this was only the beginning of their second chance, so he didn't try to hold back any longer. He coated the tip of Phillip's dick with precum and rubbed quick circles around the head with his finger. All his senses were stimulated and had his dick rock hard. Phil groaned and arched his back, muttering that he was close, but still managed to keep up a good rhythm on Cole's throbbing dick.

Their dual releases coated each other's hands, their low inaudible moans the only sound in the room. Afterwards, there were no awkward moments, and after they cleaned each other with a hand towel Cole pulled out of the nightstand, they exchanged kisses on lips, cheeks, and necks.

Phil whispered, "That was awesome." He drew Cole into his arms.

Cole snuggled against him. "I never stopped loving you."

CHAPTER TWENTY-THREE

PHIL'S LOVE life was as hot as August in the desert. He hadn't minded not working for the past couple of weeks because that gave him more time to spend with Cole now that they were definitely a couple. They had spent time together every day since the cookout at Cole's place. Eve and Dana were over the moon, and Gail had been very supportive too.

Phil sat at the kitchen table drinking his coffee and feeling more content than he ever thought possible. Batman jumped up on the table, and he bumped heads with the cat and scratched him behind the ears.

"You and your brother like Cole too, don't you?" he whispered.

He smiled, recalling the first morning he and Cole had woken up in his bed with Batman and Robin meat-loafed at the bottom and staring at them. And when he and Cole had shot baskets in the driveway, the cats had watched them from the window. His cats must have been able to tell Cole was a cat person because they hadn't shied away from him.

He heard crunching from the cat food bowl and looked over at Robin eating a few nuggets.

He stood up, put his cup into the sink, and then went to the telephone to call a customer about his next job prospect. He had worked up an estimate to weather strip windows and install a front and back door, and he hoped to drop it by later today.

After a short conversation with the prospective client, he hung up and almost immediately his phone rang, flashing Gail's name in the display.

"Hi, to what do I owe the pleasure of getting a call from my favorite sister?"

"Your only sister."

"Well, if I had more than one, I know you'd be my favorite."

"Oh, and why's that?"

"Maybe it's because you paint pretty pictures."

Gail snickered.

"Why are you in such a good mood?" he asked.

"Because it's a beautiful summer day, it's Saturday, I'm getting ready to go shopping with Eve and Dana, and I'm happy."

"With all that going for you, why are you calling me?"

"Because I have good news I want to share."

His curiosity piqued, he said, "Well, get to the point so I can be happy too."

"Are you sitting down?"

"Uh, no, but I can be." He sat down, wondering what he was about to hear.

"Phil, I'm so excited..." Then her voice went up at least an octave. "I'm finally getting my first exhibition at a gallery! Can you believe that?"

"Oh my God. Really?" He stood up, smiling ear to ear, having trouble standing still, almost jumping up and down, so he could imagine how she felt. "I wish you were here—I'd pick you up and spin you around."

Gail laughed. "Maybe it's a good thing I'm not there."

"How did this come about? This is such great news."

"You know I've been working hard at getting a following on social media, putting feelers out, and basically talking to anyone and everyone about my art." She took a quick intake of air. "Well, I talked in front of the right person—a friend of a friend—she knows the right people and put in a good word for me, and it snowballed from there. I couldn't wait to tell you."

"Eve must be thrilled too."

"I'm surprised you didn't hear her scream clear over at your place. She, Dana, and I are going out to the mall to shop for outfits to wear to the showing. I have so much to do you wouldn't believe it. I have to put my collection together, have them framed... I've got to write up my artist statement..."

"When is the showing anyway?" He sat back down.

"Three weeks from today."

"Well, I'd better let you go. You girls have fun, and you can fill me in on more of the details later."

"Okay. I've got to call Mom and Aunt Ruth too. Don't tell them before I get the chance."

"My lips are sealed."

"I love you," Gail said.

"I love you too. Talk to you soon."

Phil hung up, leaned back in his chair, and looked up at the ceiling. "Yes!" he whooped.

Before he could let what Gail had said sink in fully, the phone rang again, and this time Cole's name was on the screen. He picked up the receiver.

"Hey, Cole," he said, with a multitude of positive emotions flowing through him.

"Hi, how are you today?" Cole sounded especially upbeat himself.

"Doing great. You sound like you're having a good day too, so far. What's up?"

"I heard some good news today. I thought we could meet for lunch and I'd tell you about it. Are you free?"

"Sure, I can meet you. You can't tell me over the phone?"

"I'd rather talk in person. How about an early lunch, say in an hour?"

"Okay, where?"

"How does Roadhouse Grill sound?"

"Fine with me. I have some news too, so I'll see you then."

Phil pulled into the restaurant parking lot five minutes early, and Cole was standing outside the door wearing an ear-to-ear grin.

He couldn't wait to be with Cole again. After quickly parking, he jumped out of the Camaro and hurried over to him. Stifling August heat swarmed him.

"Hey, you should have gone inside in the air conditioning to wait." Before he could say more, Cole pulled him into a big hug.

"Yeah, between an August day in the desert and you, I'm overheating. I've missed you." He held on to Phil for a long moment. "Let's go in and order so I can tell you my news, and you said you had news too." Cole released Phil from the hug and turned toward the door.

Phil followed, eager to hear what had put the broad smile on Cole's face and had lit his eyes up.

Once inside, Cole said, "I'll give them our name. By the way, this is my treat." He patted Phil on the arm.

"That's an offer I won't refuse." He watched Cole walk away, admiring his sexy man.

Cole returned from the hostess stand and tugged Phil by the arm toward a bench. "Might as well sit down. She said it would be about fifteen minutes."

Phil frowned. "You mean I have to wait all that time to hear your news?"

"Let's gaze into each other's eyes—the time will pass quickly." He winked.

"Come on, can't you tell me what has you in such a good mood?"

"You mean besides I'm here with my..." Cole leaned in and said in a low voice, "*lover*, getting ready to have lunch on a Saturday afternoon?"

"Okay, I'll stop asking. You're crazy you know."

"Crazy about you," Cole whispered next to Phil's ear and scooted closer to him on the bench.

Phil couldn't believe how close Cole was sitting in this normal restaurant in their hometown where anyone could see them. He had also hugged him in front of the building and said all the right things. Cole had matured into the perfect man and it almost seemed too good to be true.

He turned to Cole. "Well, I'll go ahead and tell you my news while we're waiting. Gail called to tell me she's managed a showing at a gallery."

Cole broke into another big smile. "Wow, that's great. I knew she'd do it. She really deserves this."

"She said she and the girls were going out to look for outfits to wear to the show."

"Good for them. Eve must be positively delighted. Lots going on."

"I can't wait to hear your news, but I know you want to wait, so I'll try to be patient." They leaned back on the bench, stretching their legs out in front of them.

The hostess called Cole's name, and they stood up and

followed the perky young woman to their table. She gave them menus and took their drink order. Cole promptly began scanning the list of food items, and Phil did the same.

Phil quickly decided what he wanted for lunch and set the menu aside. He tapped his fingers on the table. "Can you tell me your news now?"

Cole placed his menu on top of Phil's. "I can hardly wait to tell you, but we'd better order first so we won't be interrupted for a while."

Their waitress returned, setting a basket of biscuits and honey butter in the center of the table and a longneck beer in front of each of them.

"Have you decided what you'd like?" she asked.

They recited their orders without delay, and the moment she was gone Cole took a swig of beer and leaned toward Phil.

"Meredith called today. I don't think I ever mentioned that she's a journalist. Anyway, she has a demanding new job and she's being sent abroad for a year."

"She's leaving the country? But what about..." Suddenly it dawned on Phil where the conversation was going, and he broke into a smile. "You're saying you'll be keeping Dana."

"It's fantastic, and I can hardly believe it." Cole grabbed Phil's hand in both of his. "Just trying to let it sink in. You're the first to hear—I haven't even told Dana yet. She'd gone over to Eve's before Meredith called."

Cole looked as if he was ready to jump out of his skin. Phil gave his hand a couple of quick pats and a big squeeze. "I'm really happy for you."

"Thanks."

"Is Dana going to be on board with this?"

"I think so. She's loved her time here. She'll miss her mother, but she always gets sad when she talks about leaving California."

"Eve will be elated." Phil sat back in his seat to rest his back. He took a drink of his beer.

"I'm just so happy about this." Cole leaned back in his seat too.

"I know you are. It's great, buddy."

Cole put a biscuit on his plate, separated it into two pieces, and reached for the butter. "Are you having some?"

"Sure. All this good news has made me hungry."

Cole looked up at him, desire glittering in his eyes. "Aren't you always hungry?"

Phil did a double take. Such an innocent comment, though the look was anything but. Phil locked eyes with him and smiled before taking half of a biscuit, not from the basket, but from Cole's plate. Cole slapped at his hand, and they both laughed, but they quickly suppressed their laughter so as not to draw attention. Phil continued to chuckle softly while buttering the biscuit.

"I like sharing—have all you want." Cole buttered his half.

"I like it when you're in a good mood." Phil grinned.

"I'm always in a good mood." Cole winked at him.

"Especially when you find out your daughter gets to live with you."

"I still can't believe it. Meredith is going to call back tonight to work out the details after I've told Dana."

"Do you and your ex get along okay?"

"Yes, with things that concern Dana." He straightened his glasses.

Phil could pretty much guess there was tension between Cole and Meredith, but that was none of his business, and he didn't want it to be, so he took a drink of his beer and changed the subject.

"After we're finished here, do you have time to come over to the house for a while?"

"I'm ready, let's go," Cole said.

Phil lifted one eyebrow. "Don't you think we should eat first?"

"There you go thinking about your stomach again. Okay, we'll eat first." Cole smiled and bit into his bread.

Phil kept the engine running while he got out of the Camaro to raise the garage door. By the time he parked and came out into the driveway, Cole was standing there waiting for him.

"Are you up for a game of one-on-one?" Phil looked up at the basketball hoop.

"I'd love a little one-on-one... Oh, you mean basketball."

There was that lustful look again, the one Cole had given him back at the restaurant.

"Uh, we could forgo the game and go straight inside." He undressed Cole with his eyes.

Cole paused, and he swallowed hard and wet his lips with his sexy-as-hell tongue before speaking. "And miss the opportunity to stomp all over you?"

Phil laughed. "*You* stomp all over *me*? Dream on, buddy."

"Where's the ball?" Cole stripped off his shirt.

Phil laughed, dashed into the garage, yanked off his shirt, grabbed the basketball, and returned. He dribbled the ball and then bounced it to Cole. The game was on.

Even though basketball was a team sport, these one-on-one games they'd played together during the past couple of months held a lot of appeal, and today's game was turning Phil on more than usual. Maybe because he was thinking about what was going to happen afterward, or maybe because Cole looked so damn sexy without his shirt on—whatever it was, he was enjoying every moment.

"Traveling, traveling," Phil jokingly hollered, trying to mess with Cole's head because he was winning by several points.

Cole laughed and made another basket while Phil stood there taken by surprise. He wasn't paying enough attention, and he hadn't even attempted to block him.

"Another two points for me," Cole panted.

Even though Phil was competitive, he really didn't care anything about the score of this game. He just wanted to have fun.

"Personal foul, personal foul," Phil stated seriously when Cole blocked his shot.

"No way—I blocked you legally," Cole insisted, tapping Phil on the chest.

"Your whole body came in contact with mine—that's illegal." Phil did his best to look dead serious.

Cole laughed. "You're hallucinating."

"I felt your hip bump into me—that's illegal," Phil said, while using exaggerated hand gestures to get his point across, the whole time staring at Cole's lower half.

Cole spun the ball on his finger and laughed some more. "How about we call this a game—I win."

Phil knocked the ball off Cole's finger. "You'll pay for this."

"For what?"

"For not playing fair."

Cole raised a brow. "Say what?"

"Strutting around with your shirt off distracting me..." Phil's gaze dipped to Cole's perfect pecs.

"What about you? You're not wearing a shirt either." Cole tapped Phil's chest with the back of his hand.

"Don't make this about me."

Phil joined Cole in a fit of laughter. The game was over. No way could he concentrate on basketball any more today. He got himself under control and looked over to the window where Batman and Robin watched them.

"My boys got woken up from their nap."

Cole followed his gaze. "Does that mean we'll have an audience?"

"No different than when we're at your house and those Siamese cats of yours come into the room."

Cole laughed again—more of a giggle this time. Phil rolled the ball toward the garage and then slapped Cole on the back, his skin having taken on a sexy glossy shine that Phil found very seductive.

"Shall we go inside?" Phil asked.

"You don't have to ask twice."

Phil hurried in the back door, opened the refrigerator and grabbed two bottles of water, handing one to Cole. They quickly guzzled down the contents and tossed the bottles into the trashcan, and then Phil tugged his man into his arms and kissed him. He walked them toward the living room by feel because he couldn't see where they were going while French kissing Cole and rubbing his lower half against him. Cole's blissful moans put Phil into a trancelike state. He was aware enough to get them to the sofa, and they toppled down onto the soft cushions with Phil on top.

After their long separation, these intimate times together since reuniting were like Christmas morning times a thousand—something Phil never thought had a snowball's chance in hell of ever happening again. Cole's every touch, every sound, every smell was so familiar to him even after so many years apart.

He rubbed the pads of his thumbs over Cole's nipples, loving the sounds he coaxed out of him. Driving Cole crazy was his favorite thing to do. In the process, he drove himself crazy with lust too. No other man had come close to making him feel like Cole did—no one could compare to him. He'd tried all these years to find someone he could relate to, but he had just gone through the motions, spinning his wheels.

He couldn't believe they'd found each other again and were going out on dates, making love, and hanging out like a family with Dana and Eve.

After kissing, licking, and touching as much of Cole's skin as he could get to, he tugged on Cole's belt and received a smile and a hard tug on his own. Cole sat up and undid his pants, but instead of sliding them off, he fumbled with Phil's and pulled them down, underwear and all, having a little trouble freeing the rigid dick inside, but he got the job done. Cole's dark eyes burned with desire, and when he licked his lips, Phil's heart galloped a mile a minute.

Cole nudged Phil back onto the sofa and went straight for his ridged dick. He licked and sucked while Phil's body coiled and tensed from the heavenly sensations coursing through him. He stretched his arms over his head and let out a loud, strangled groan.

When he was about halfway to orgasm, Cole stopped, moved up to his ear and whispered, "I love you, Phillip." Cole sucked on his earlobe while using his hand to bring him to completion.

Phil shuddered and gasped as he exploded. His eyes were squeezed shut so tight he saw stars. When his breathing slowed down and he could think straight, he reached for the small drawer in the end table and came up with a package of cat wipes.

"What the heck?" Cole asked.

Phil opened the package, pulled out two wipes and handed one to him. "For your hand."

Cole snorted. "You want me to use a wet wipe for cats on my hand?"

"Sure, why not?" Phil jerked his head in the direction of the cat tree where Batman and Robin were snoozing. "If they're good enough for them, they should be good enough for us." He lazily cleaned himself off.

Cole wrinkled his nose and wiped his hand. He shook his head and smiled, then wrapped Phil in his arms.

After a few moments, Phil softly kissed Cole's cheek and said, "I love you, always have and always will."

He could easily fall asleep, but he didn't want to until Cole had his turn, but when he tried to sit up, Cole cuddled him tighter and murmured, "There'll be time later. Let's take a catnap."

Phil's last coherent thought was how extremely content he was.

CHAPTER TWENTY-FOUR

COLE WOKE up with the sun, and that was too early considering he had tossed and turned most of the night. He'd finally drifted off in the wee hours of the morning, and now here he was, a little groggy but awake. Ever since last week when he and Meredith had ironed out the details of Dana living in California, he hadn't been sleeping well.

Why did this have to be so complicated?

He and Dana were overjoyed about the arrangement, but there was just one hurdle to get over before it would all be smooth sailing—Meredith's visit to see for herself that all was acceptable for her daughter in California.

Lying on his back looking up at the ceiling, he felt the walls closing in on him. He wished the cats were on the bed to calm him with their soothing vibrations. Phillip hadn't asked about his phone call with Meredith, and all he'd told him was that everything was still on with Dana's move. He should have given Phil all the details then, or when he'd had several opportunities afterward, but he'd kept his mouth shut because he hadn't wanted to ruin anything between them. He was such a coward.

For the past week he'd struggled with the problem and gone back and forth, torn about what he should do. Even though it had been a hard decision, his mind was made up, and he just hoped he could convince Phillip that this was the best way to handle the situation.

Having Phillip back in his life was just so... he couldn't even put into words how great that was. Talking to him, going out together, just kicking back around the house, making love—all of it was more than he'd ever hoped for. Now that they'd found their way back to each other he couldn't lose him, but while Meredith was here... He rested the back of his hand on his forehead and sighed. How was Phillip going to take the news that they wouldn't be able to see each other for a while?

His first concern had to be about his daughter, and what was best for Dana. Living here was the best thing for her, and he couldn't risk doing anything that would make Meredith change her mind.

Despite the early hour, he sat up on the edge of the bed. After yawning and stretching, he stood up so he could get started with his day. There was a lot to do, and the extra time would come in handy. On his way to the bathroom, he pushed away any negative thoughts so he could concentrate on preparing for the barbecue he and Dana were hosting in honor of Gail's good news. Dana was excited to help with the preparations, and this was something they'd have fun doing together.

If only he didn't have this weight on his shoulders.

Cole walked into the kitchen, widening his eyes at his daughter. "You're up early. And you've made breakfast and fed the cats already."

Dana looked up from the juicer. "Good morning, Father. I'm excited to start decorating and making the food for our party, so I got up early to get started. I'm not the only one who's up earlier than usual."

"Yeah, I guess I'm excited too." Cole pulled out a chair and sat down at the breakfast nook.

"Are you ready for your coffee?" Dana wiped her hands on a towel.

"I'll get it, sweetie. You don't have to wait on me. You've done quite enough already." He looked at the bowls, plates, and newspaper she had set on the table for him.

"Well, since I'm now officially living here, not just vacationing, I thought it would be a good idea to get into a routine and help out more."

"It's my job to take care of you, sweetie. Once school starts, you'll be too busy for this." He stood up and went over to the espresso machine.

"Well, I'm not in school now. It's summer vacation, and I want to do this."

Cole smiled at her. "It looks great. This is very thoughtful of you."

"It's just toast and cereal." She blushed slightly. "The hardest part was making the orange juice." She giggled and poured some into two small glasses.

After pulling slices of bread out of the bag and sticking them into the toaster, she grabbed the milk out of the refrigerator and took her seat at the table.

"Mother never wanted me in the kitchen, so I never got to do anything like this."

"Are you interested in cooking?" He carried his cup of coffee to the table.

"Yes, I think it looks fun, and I'm anxious to help with the food for this evening. If I learn to cook a few things, maybe I can make some of the meals while Mother's here. She'd be so surprised." Dana tilted her head, and a mischievous grin spread across her face. "What do you think?"

"I think you've got a good idea there." He winked, and then sipped his coffee. "Your mother won't be here all that long though. We can go out most of the time."

"She's used to going out, so that's why I think it's nicer if we cook at home to show her something different."

"I get it," Cole said. "Show her how we live."

"Right. I think she'll be pleased with how things are going, and she'll be glad she decided to let me stay here with you."

"It's all going to work out just fine." He wondered if he was trying to reassure Dana or himself.

She took a drink of her juice and then poured cereal into her bowl. "I'm glad you have Phil in your life, Father."

Cole rubbed the back of his neck, and heat crept over his face. "I know you like him, Eve, and her mom."

"And you like him too. You make a good couple."

Cole met her eyes. "Is that so?"

"Yes, you know it's so." She poured milk on her cereal. "Aren't you going to eat? I'm starting the toast." She reached over to the counter next to the breakfast nook and pushed the lever down on the toaster.

Cole filled his bowl with cereal, but he didn't add milk yet. He hated soggy cereal, and he didn't feel like eating.

"I've been thinking that you and Phil might take the next step pretty soon."

Cole cleared his throat. "The next step?"

"You know, move in together. You could ask him to move in here. I wouldn't mind, so if you're thinking that because I'm going to be here now you can't move forward, well, that's just not so."

"Sweetie, Phil and I haven't talked about that."

"But you'd like him here, wouldn't you?"

Cole took a deep breath and poured the milk into his bowl. Maybe if he had his mouth full of cereal, she'd end the conversation.

She reached over to the toaster and retrieved the toasted bread. He accepted two slices, and that left one for her.

As they began buttering their toast, Dana said, "I'm sorry if I was too presumptuous."

Cole didn't like seeing the frown on her pretty face. "You weren't. It's fine to say what's on your mind."

"But you don't want to talk about it. I understand."

"Look, sweetie, I need to ask you a favor."

She narrowed her eyes and leaned in as if she wanted to catch every word. "Anything, what is it?"

"When your mother is here, I think it's best we don't say anything about my dating life. Let's not mention Phil at all." He took off his glasses, set them on the table, and rubbed his eyes.

"You think Mother would be upset?"

"I would just rather not give her any reason to change her mind about this arrangement." He put his glasses on again.

"No, I don't want that." Her knitted eyebrows were visible under her long, wispy bangs.

"I don't want you worrying, sweetie. It'll all be fine if we focus on all the positive aspects of you living here."

"I think Eve and Phil are positive aspects, but I understand. Can I at least have Eve over to meet Mother?"

"Sure you can. Just mention the situation to her so she won't let anything slip. I think your mother would like to meet Gail too, since you spend a lot of time over there."

He moved the spoon around in his bowl and figured the cereal was probably mushy by now. After this conversation with Dana, he wasn't going to be able to put off telling Phillip about this any longer, but he couldn't risk putting a damper on the pool party by bringing it up tonight. He'd take Phillip out someplace tomorrow, and they'd talk then.

Maybe he was blowing this out of proportion, and Phillip would go along with his wishes and be okay with it. Once he explained his reasoning, surely he'd understand.

He pushed his cereal bowl away untouched, along with his barely eaten toast, and tried hard to shake off his uneasy feeling. "After we get these dishes cleared away, we'll start on the macaroni salad. There'll be eight of us, so I bought a big bag of macaroni, and we'd better boil six eggs."

Nothing would give his spirits a life like spending the morning cooking with his daughter.

CHAPTER TWENTY-FIVE

A CAREFREE summer day spent at the regional park should have been pleasant and relaxing, but the longer they spent wandering around the grounds, engaging in superficial conversation, the more apparent it became to Phil that something was bothering Cole.

After sitting at a picnic table eating their fast food lunch, they set out on their walk and must have covered a couple of miles so far with no sign that Cole was tired of roaming around the place. Phil figured he was trying to work up the courage to tell him whatever was on his mind.

Lately he'd noticed that Cole wasn't himself. He'd been a lot quieter than usual. Yesterday, Cole had barely spoken to him at the barbecue, but Phil had figured he was busy being a good host and entertaining his guests. But today Cole was more distant than ever.

Phil guessed this had something to do with Meredith. He sure hoped she hadn't changed her mind about letting Dana live here while she was abroad. If that was the problem, Cole probably would have mentioned it unless he was too upset and depressed.

As if Cole could hear his inner thoughts, he spoke up. "How about we go look at the horses in the pasture for a while? There's something I need to talk to you about."

Cole's tense, serious expression gave him a sinking feeling in the pit of his stomach, but at least he'd know what was going on. He walked toward the corrals with Cole, who slowed his pace and didn't seem to be in any hurry to get there. When they finally reached the stable area, they stood side by side in some shade from the corner of the barn. He focused on three horses grazing in the distance while he waited for Cole to talk.

To break the silence, Phil said, "The rest of the horses must be out on the trail ride."

Cole didn't answer.

"It would be nice to go for a ride with the girls again, don't you think?" Receiving nothing more than a half smile and a grunt, he put his arm around Cole's shoulder, hoping he'd start talking.

When he remained silent, Phil asked, "Was everything okay when you and Meredith talked last week?"

Cole pulled back, and Phil dropped his arm to his side, waiting for the answer. At least he'd gotten Cole's attention.

"Uh, yeah, pretty much." Cole made eye contact. "But she's planning to come for a visit to check out the school and everything. Probably be here at least a week." He ran his hand through his hair and turned away, focusing his attention on the grazing horses.

"Oh yeah? When is she coming?" Phil asked, not missing a beat.

Cole glanced back at him and then stared down at the ground kicking at pebbles in the dirt. "That's a good question. She said she'll let me know, but it'll be soon. Gotta get it done before school starts."

"Where will she be staying?"

Cole looked up at him again. "At the house." He cleared his throat and rubbed his temples. "We have plenty of room, and she wants to spend time with Dana."

"Right, of course." Phil crossed his arms over his chest and stared at Cole, a wave of jealousy washing over him. He tried to push the feeling away, but his insecurity threatened to overwhelm him. He didn't know what to say, and that was probably best. Meredith was Dana's mom, and of course she'd want to check out the situation before leaving her daughter here for the next year. She'd come, like what she saw, and go. That would be that.

But then he noticed Cole couldn't seem to look at him. He darted his gaze from the pasture to the stable and off in the distance toward the park.

"What's going on, Cole?" he asked.

Finally Cole fixed his gaze on him and said, "I need to ask you for a favor while Meredith is here."

"A favor? I can't imagine what that would be."

Cole leaned his back against the corral and rubbed his hand over his face. "To be on the safe side, I don't think we should see each other until she's gone back to New York."

"We shouldn't see each other..." Phil compressed his lips, his shoulders tensing.

"Yeah, well, I just don't think it would be a good look if you were around, especially at the house."

Phil tried to hold in his anger, but the memory of Cole breaking up with him all those years ago resurfaced. He clenched his hands into fists at his sides.

Cole started to fidget, running his hands over the corral fence and then he turned around to pick at imperfections in the wood. After a few moments, he rubbed the back of his neck, inhaled a deep breath, and gazed at Phil again.

"I, uh, I just don't want to give her any reason to change her mind. This visit has got to go smoothly. I need her to come and go and that will be it. Dana will get to stay here, and that's what I want. You know how much I need that."

Phil's anger threatened to boil over. "Yes, I do, but what I don't know is what my presence has to do with any of this."

"I don't want to risk pissing Meredith off, Phillip. If she finds out about you, about us, she might change her mind about Dana staying."

"She knows you're gay. You've got a right to have a relationship. What's the big deal?"

"I just don't want to shove this in her face. Trust me. It's best not to push her."

Phil, seething inside, turned and began walking toward the parking area. His anger grew with every step as he picked up his pace.

Cole caught up to him. "Phillip, stop. This isn't how I wanted this conversation to go. I messed it all up and I'm sorry. Let's talk."

Phil stopped in his tracks and turned to Cole. "We just talked. You told me how it's going to be just like you did all those years ago."

"Phillip, this isn't like that..."

"From where I'm standing, it is." Phil began walking again and didn't stop until he reached his Camaro. He dug in his pocket for the keys.

Cole grabbed his arm. "Phillip, we need to talk some more."

He yanked out of Cole's grip and reached for the door handle, not wanting to hear any more of his excuses.

"Come on, Phillip. We can't leave it like this. I need you to understand."

Phil turned and looked Cole in the eye. "What kind of a person is your ex-wife? I don't get it, Cole." He spread his arms out wide. "Why would you have to hide our relationship from her?"

"Meredith and I barely get along. We try our hardest for Dana's sake and that's about it. I wish you could understand why it's best not to involve you. Can't you do this for me and my daughter?" He met Phil's gaze, and they stared at each another for a few beats.

Phil let out a harsh breath. "You and Meredith barely getting along isn't a good reason. All these weeks we've been together I thought you'd changed. I thought you were okay with who you are, but you really had me fooled. You haven't changed at all." He closed his eyes and shook his head, tears stinging his eyes.

"This has nothing to do with my accepting who I am. It has to do with Meredith accepting the fact I'm with a man. She'd be reminded of our marriage—our sham of a marriage—and that would open all the old wounds and could screw up this whole arrangement of Dana living here. Can't you see that?"

"I don't think dishonesty is right."

"Well, I'm being honest with you and look where that's getting me! You have to be selfish, don't you? Think about Dana. She has her heart set on living here. She'd be crushed if she had to go with her mother to a foreign country."

"I don't appreciate being called selfish," Phil said disgustedly.

"I'm sorry, I shouldn't have said that..." Cole reached for him, but Phil jerked away, turned his back, and opened the car door.

He slipped inside as quickly as he could and slammed the door in Cole's face. Without even taking the time to put on his seat belt, he started the car, put it in reverse, and squealed the tires as he backed out of the parking space. The last thing he saw before gunning the engine and heading for the park entrance was Cole standing with his head down, hands in his pockets, and looking as heartbroken as Phil felt.

He composed himself by the time he neared the gate and slowed the car down to exit, his hands shaking on the steering wheel. Wiping a tear from his face, he pushed thoughts of leaving

Cole stranded out of his mind and continued driving. After all, Cole was the one who'd made this choice. Cole couldn't be a man and be upfront with his ex, rather he had the nerve to tell him to stay away while Meredith was there. He couldn't accept that and refused to be with a man who was ashamed of him.

He punched the steering wheel. This hurt like hell—almost as bad as it had fifteen years ago. Part of this was his own fault for giving Cole a second chance.

His heart would pay dearly for this mistake.

CHAPTER TWENTY-SIX

"FATHER, WHY did you come home in an Uber?" Dana asked from the front porch, as Cole slipped the driver a few bills and then joined her in a few long strides.

"It's a long story. I'm tired, let's go inside so I can have a drink."

"What happened?" Dana followed him into the kitchen. "Why didn't Phil drive you home? Is he okay?"

He ruffled Dana's hair before opening the refrigerator and grabbing a beer. "He's fine. Do you want anything, sweetie?"

"No thanks."

After twisting open the bottle, he took a long pull, sat down at the table, and noticed Dana staring at him from the middle of the kitchen.

"What's wrong, sweetie?"

"That's my question to you," she answered.

Cole took another drink and sighed. "It was a rough day, but nothing for you to worry about. What did you do while I was gone?"

"Don't divert the conversation. Tell me why Phil didn't bring you home."

"You're persistent, you know that?" Cole set the half empty bottle down and tapped his fingers beside it.

She came over to the table. "Did you and Phil have a fight?" she asked, her head tilted slightly.

Cole couldn't help but smile at his precious little girl wearing a wide-eyed expression and wanting to help. He owed her an explanation.

"Well... yeah, we did argue a bit. It'll be all right. I'll call him later."

"He was so mad he didn't drive you home? That wasn't very nice."

"Don't blame him, sweetie. You know, there are always two sides to every story."

Dana sat down next to him. She was quiet at first, but then tentatively asked, "Did you tell Phil about Mother, that you don't want her to know about him?"

He didn't want to talk about this with her, but he couldn't just brush her off. She seemed so troubled.

"Well..." His throat threatened to close up, so he took a sip of his beer before continuing. "I hurt his feelings by asking him to stay away." He took a long, slow breath, and his chest tightened.

Dana placed her hand on his shoulder and then got off her chair and hugged him.

Cole turned his SUV onto Phil's street. Since he hadn't called—he'd been too chicken, he didn't even know if Phil was home. Waiting until this morning to apologize for calling him selfish and to try again to persuade him to see his point, had been hard. He'd barely slept all night, longing to hear Phillip's voice and to make things right between them, but Phil needed time to cool down before they could have any form of a meaningful conversation. Hopefully, that would be possible now.

As he pulled up to the curb in front of Phil's house, he spotted the truck parked in the driveway, which probably meant he was home unless he'd gone somewhere in the Camaro. Cole didn't know what he was going to say to Phil, and that was kind of stupid. He'd thought of nothing but Phillip since they'd parted yesterday.

He slowly got out of the SUV and headed straight for the back door. Strangers probably went to the front door, but Phillip used the back because it was closer to where he parked. He took a deep breath before he knocked. What seemed like a full minute passed before the door opened, and the scowl on Phillip's face told him that he wasn't expected or welcome.

Neither of them spoke, adding to the tension, and he wished

he'd prepared something to say. The longer they stared at each other the more uncomfortable the situation became.

He leaned his arm on the doorframe, unwilling to give up. "Can I come in?"

"I was just leaving. I'm starting a new job this morning."

"Well, I won't stay long. Sorry. I should have called first."

"Yeah, well, you'd have saved yourself the trip over because I have nothing to say to you." Despite Phillip's harsh words, he stepped aside to let him in.

He didn't seem as mad as he'd been yesterday, but Cole still had his work cut out for him. He figured that even if Phillip wasn't in a hurry to leave, he wouldn't offer him coffee even though they were standing in the kitchen. He wished they could go into the living room where the cats probably were, but what would that matter anyway. Phil's scowl didn't fade, and he crossed his arms, waiting for Cole to speak.

Cole took a deep breath and let it out as his shoulders slumped. Now instead of annoyance, sadness clouded Phil's features, and knowing he was the one responsible was almost too much to bear.

He had to repair the damage he'd caused, so he tried to sound sincere despite being flustered. "I want to apologize for yesterday. I shouldn't have called you selfish. I'm sorry."

Phil looked at him with narrowed eyes, the pain shifting back to anger. "You're sorry for calling me selfish. Is that all you're sorry for?"

Cole was left momentarily speechless. He blinked a couple times trying to formulate a response to what seemed like a trick question. Phillip's pointed glare wasn't helping.

After a few moments of tense silence, except for the irritating ticking from a clock somewhere in the room, Cole said, "I'm sorry you're upset."

From the deepening scowl on Phil's face, his mood was only getting worse. "It's obvious we're not on the same page. You need to leave now so I can go to my job."

"Surely you can spare a few more minutes so we can talk this out. Don't storm out of here before we solve the problem."

"According to you there's no problem."

"What's that supposed to mean? I came all the way over here so I could apologize. I hardly slept all night!"

"And that's my fault I guess..."

"I never said that. Look, I'm having a hard time even knowing why we're arguing and why you look so damn mad." He tried to press down his own anger before the situation escalated.

"Yesterday you told me to get lost while Dana's mother is here because you don't want her to know about me."

"Yeah... and I explained..."

"No, you really didn't explain. Is she a homophobe?"

"No, that's not the problem. I already explained this yesterday. I don't want to parade you in front of her and remind her of our unfortunate situation of the past. That could very well piss her off, and she might take it out on me by taking Dana away. I don't know why you refuse to see that."

"She'd find out sooner or later, and what would stop her from sending for Dana then? Misleading her is not the answer, and I don't know why *you* refuse to see *that*."

"Phillip, you're the most stubborn person I've ever known," he said in a raised voice.

"I need to leave now, Cole." Phil hurriedly shoved his wallet and keys into his pockets and then reached for papers attached to a clipboard. He stood staring at Cole, clearly waiting for him to go.

There was nothing else for Cole to do but turn and leave. Once outside the door, he stopped and hoped for some kind of miracle—that a few more carefully chosen words might smooth this disagreement over, but of course that was stupid. Phil pushed past him, got into his truck and was gone in a flash.

The conversation had been a disaster and had only made things worse. He realized he'd been the one who'd used a loud tone of voice. Though he had clearly been angry, Phillip had spoken in a calm manner. Why did that stand out to him?

Maybe he was afraid that Phillip had had enough and given up on them, that he didn't care anymore and resigned himself to moving on and leaving Cole behind.

Before he headed out to his SUV, he wandered by the front of the house and saw Batman and Robin at the window. He hoped he'd get the chance to see them again without a window separating them.

Back in the driveway, he stood under the basketball hoop feeling like a total fool. He'd thought the decision he'd made about Meredith and Phillip had been right, but now he wasn't so sure. He loved his daughter so much he'd been scared to death that something might happen to change Meredith's mind, so he'd betrayed Phillip—again. Now the damage was done, and he didn't see any way to erase the mess he'd made.

Choking back tears, he remembered playing basketball with Phillip just ten days ago, and all the good times they'd shared since they'd found each other again. He reminded himself that Phillip hadn't broken up with him—no words like that were said—so he'd hold that thought and hope he could somehow make this up to him.

CHAPTER TWENTY-SEVEN

WITH THE help of a store employee, Phil wheeled the heavy-duty shopping cart containing two entry doors out of the Home Depot. Once at his truck, they unloaded the doors, and when Phil was satisfied that they were tied and secured, he climbed into the truck, fastened his seatbelt, and started the engine.

For the past couple of days, he'd been replacing worn weather stripping on every window in a big two-story house, and now he could get down to business replacing the doors, which required a lot more mental skill than weather stripping. He'd had too much time to think while moving from window to window, mindlessly cutting, peeling away the backing, and pressing in place each piece of stripping. Too much time to think about Cole.

Pulling out onto the main drag, he turned up the radio and tried hard not to think about Cole anymore. He hadn't been successful since they'd parted three days ago, so why did he expect today to be any different? Ignoring Cole's calls, voice mails, and texts had been hard, but he figured that simply drifting apart would be less painful.

Less painful. He didn't really think anything could make this less painful, and he wondered how in the hell he was even functioning. But he'd survived fifteen years ago, so he could do it again. He refused to let this defeat him.

Maybe the Breezeway Pub would help him forget his problems. That seemed like a good idea for tonight.

On the way to his job, he stopped at The Cat's Meow pet store. Luckily, he found a parking space in front. A thief would be hard-pressed getting the heavy doors out of the back of the truck quickly, and with the truck parked by the big glass doors, he felt safe running in to pick up cat food and litter.

He grabbed a shopping cart and took off toward the cat litter aisle. After loading four twenty-five-pound boxes into the cart, he wheeled to the cat food aisle. Halfway down, he stopped and scanned the shelf expecting to find his cats' brand and realized they'd rearranged the aisle.

Studying the multitude of bags was mind boggling. Evidently, they'd added brands to their inventory, and the orange bags he wanted must be blending in. Deep in thought, he barely registered that someone on his right had said his name. He turned, looked down, and Dana was right next to him.

"Hey. What are you doing here?" he asked awkwardly.

"Same thing you are I guess," Cole chimed in, coming to a stop a few feet away with a half-full shopping cart.

Phil gave him a fast glance. Cole wasn't smiling and Phil sure didn't feel like smiling either.

"Moonbeam and Moonshadow are running low on supplies." Dana picked up a couple bags of food off the shelf and placed them in their cart.

She appeared shy, peeking up at him through her bangs. And she was quieter than usual, but he was glad she was there. He gave all his attention to her and tried to forget Cole was there.

"How are the cats? Still using the cat tree?"

"Oh yes, they basically live on it," she answered. "How are Batman and Robin?"

"They're just fine."

All of a sudden, Dana's eyes filled with tears. She stepped closer and wrapped her arms around him in a long, tight hug that left a lump in his throat.

She pulled back and gave him a weak smile, and Cole said, "We'd better get going, sweetie."

Cole gripped the handle of the shopping cart so hard his knuckles were white. "Well, I guess we'll see you around," he said to Phil.

"Yeah, okay." He avoided looking Cole in the eye. "Good to see you, sweetheart," he said to Dana.

He watched them walk away feeling like he had a giant hole in his chest.

By the time Phil arrived home at five thirty p.m., the day had seemed ten days long. Maybe after a quick shower, he'd perk up and feel like driving over to the pub to clear his mind and have a relaxing drink—maybe catch some of the baseball game on the big-screen TV. Nearly a month had passed since he'd been in the place, and he couldn't say that he'd missed it. He'd had other things to occupy his time. He cursed himself for thinking of Cole again. Moving on was all he could do because being with Cole was no longer an option.

He carelessly tossed his phone and wallet onto the countertop. Soon the cats would join him for their food, so he pulled a can out of the cupboard before he sat down in a chair at the kitchen table. This was the first time he didn't even have the energy to get himself a beer after work, or maybe he was just too down and depressed. He stretched his legs out and leaned back as best he could, letting out a deep breath.

Maybe if he hadn't run into Cole and Dana today, he wouldn't feel so bad. That was like ripping the scab off a sore. Even though he'd tried not to look at Cole, he noticed how handsome he was in his white V-neck T-shirt with the brown and tan stripes across the chest. Damn him anyway.

A surprise knock at the back door snapped him out of his thoughts. He got up, walked over, and pulled it open. The sight of Eve and Gail standing there made him do a double take.

"What are you guys doing here? Did I forget something? We don't have a date or anything, do we?"

Eve's bright smile and comforting hug went a long way to bring him out of his funk, and then his third hug of the day definitely made him feel like he was someone special and that his world was a little less bleak. Gail's curly hair tickled his nose as she snuggled against his chest.

"We thought we'd surprise you with an invitation to dinner tonight. You haven't eaten, have you?" Gail released him from the hug.

"Say you'll come with us." Eve took his hand in hers.

He glanced down at himself. "I was just going to shower. I'm in my old work clothes."

"We'll wait, but you don't need to dress up." Gail put her arm around Eve. They both had on jeans, sleeveless blouses, and sandals.

"I need to feed Batman and Robin first," Phil said. "It's their dinner time."

Right on cue, Batman appeared at the entrance to the kitchen, but he didn't approach.

"He's making sure you're friendly," Phil said.

Eve took a step toward the cat, stooped down, and held out her hand. "You know me, Batman."

As soon as Batman relaxed and got close enough for Eve to touch him, Robin crept in to join them.

"Can I feed them?" Eve asked.

"I'll help her, and that way you can go shower, and then we'll be ready to go," Gail said.

"Okay, the can of food is right here." Phil indicated where he'd set it earlier. "Their canned food bowls are here." He pushed two bowls next to the can.

"We've got this," Eve said, sounding pleased.

"If you wouldn't mind, how about cleaning the litter box too."

"We'd be happy to, wouldn't we, Mom," Phil heard Eve say as he headed toward the bathroom.

Phil felt pretty good after sharing burgers, fries, and Cokes with Gail and Eve. They'd talked at length about Gail's art showing just over a week away, and that suited him fine because he didn't want to talk about him and Cole. When Eve had found out from Dana what had gone down, Gail had called him, and after that conversation he'd asked her not to bring it up anymore. So far, she'd respected his wishes.

As they began crumpling up their napkins and other trash, Gail put her hand on his, and pursed her lips. "Before we go, there's just one thing I want to tell you."

"What's that?" He met Gail's gaze after glancing over at Eve, who sat with her hands clasped on the table and her mouth turned down in a slight frown.

"Cole asked me if I'd mind if he brought his ex-wife by while she's in town. It caught me off guard, but I said it would be fine. I wanted to make sure you're okay with it. I think that since Dana spends a lot of time with us..."

"Yeah, sure, that's fine. Whatever's best for Dana," Phil said, hoping that how he really felt wasn't showing on his face.

"Phil, I just feel so bad about..."

He stood up abruptly. "I know, sis. We've said all there is to say on this subject."

Gail and Eve got up, and they all walked outside together. They stopped next to their vehicles, and Gail gave him a big hug. She held him tighter and longer than earlier. After she let go, Eve grabbed him with the same sad look on her face as Dana had in the pet shop earlier.

When Gail had mentioned Cole at the end of their meal, a dark cloud had fallen over him and put a damper on the evening. Now having them look at him like they'd come from a funeral, made him wish the evening would end.

After Gail's car finally left the parking lot, he climbed into his truck still tossing around the idea of stopping at the Breezeway Pub before going home. Being a Friday night, all the restaurants were filling up, and he figured the bar would be crowded too. Maybe he could lose himself in the music and noise.

A half hour later he was sitting on a bar stool in the comfortable, dimly lit space with a dirty martini and the baseball game on TV for company. Finally thinking of nothing but what was happening on the TV, someone interrupted his solitude by tapping him on the shoulder and saying his name like a question. That voice was very familiar, but it took a second to realize who it belonged to. He turned slowly and glanced over his shoulder.

Brad looked the same, his long hair loose and wild. "Brad." After acknowledging him, he was at a loss for words.

"You remember." Undeterred, Brad smiled.

Phil was surprised to see a smile, considering how they'd left things the last time they'd been together here.

"Is this seat taken?" Brad glanced around the club, and without waiting for an answer, he sat down. He threw a sideways glance at the martini glass that Phil was moving in circles on the bar. "Looks like you needed something stronger than a beer tonight." Brad caught the bartender's eye and raised his finger to call him over. He ordered a highball.

When the bartender left, Brad leaned closer and said, "I have a confession to make."

Phil looked into Brad's eyes for the first time since he'd shown up. "What's that?"

"I saw you here, and I watched you until I was sure you were by yourself."

He didn't want to talk about being there alone. "It's good to see you again because I'd hoped I'd get the chance to apologize about how things went down with us. I regretted everything about the whole deal."

"You could have called to tell me."

The bartender set Brad's drink down in front of him and placed a bowl of peanuts between them. Phil reached for a handful, mainly for a way to disguise his nervousness. He really wanted to be alone, and he didn't want Brad to bring up Cole's name.

They sat in silence for a moment, each sipping their drinks. "Well." Brad cleared his throat. "I thought you and Cole would last more than a month, but here you are drinking alone in this place..."

"I'm not here looking for a pickup." Phil narrowed his eyes.

"Okaaay..." Brad sipped his drink. "I actually wasn't trying to pick you up. We've been there, done that, but I'd still like to be friends."

Phil widened his gaze at that surprising admission, and his irritation began to fade. As long as Brad didn't bring up Cole again, he didn't mind hanging out with him. He'd been a good sport about their past and hadn't made him feel guilty or anything. Brad was a genuinely good guy. Maybe a night out drinking and watching the game with a friend would help him forget his troubles, at least for tonight.

CHAPTER TWENTY-EIGHT

AFTER SPENDING most of Saturday at the office building complex he'd designed in Pomona, Cole's eyes were getting heavy as he drove toward home. He'd felt pretty good while reviewing the progress of the project and assessing every aspect of it, but now on the slow and tiresome drive back, the day was catching up with him.

Everyone and their brother seemed to be on the freeway, and he'd driven for a half hour and wasn't even a third of the way home yet. On a day without the weekend traffic, he'd be able to drive home in an hour.

Dana was at Gail's with Eve and wasn't expecting him to pick her up until well after dinner, so there was no hurry anyway. He may as well make the best of it and try to shake this gloom that was settling over him with each mile. Hoping some music would help lift his spirits, he turned up the radio.

Passing by the off-ramp for the McDonald's brought back the memory of when he and Dana had driven home from the airport after she'd arrived from New York. Her reaction to seeing a restaurant pop up in what she perceived to be the middle of nowhere had been amusing. He smiled at the memory, which gave him a little surge of energy that he needed to keep driving without drifting off.

What would Meredith think when she experienced the scenery out here tomorrow? Wow, this was finally going to happen. Being here in person would be a lot different for her than seeing pictures of the area that Dana had been sending her all summer. He hoped she'd be tactful in her opinions, but even if she wasn't, Dana would just laugh it off anyway.

What would she think of the house that was completely different from the home they'd shared in New York? She'd probably freak out and envision seeing a snake in the backyard and be afraid to wear her open-toe heels.

Stepping on the brakes for the hundredth time, he wished he knew why the traffic was slowing down again. He did the best he could to look up ahead, but confined by his seat belt, he couldn't see far enough. Someone probably changed lanes and caused everyone to slam on their brakes.

This quiet time sitting with nothing to do only managed to push thoughts of his situation with Phillip into this head. He wanted so badly to find a way to get them back on track, but with Meredith's visit looming, there hadn't been time.

At first, he'd felt like Phil had overreacted to what he'd asked of him, but the more he thought about it and tried to see things from Phillip's point of view, he understood why he was so angry.

That day in the pet store, Phillip had shown no emotion until Dana had hugged him, and then Cole had seen a flicker of the old Phillip, but it hadn't stuck. It had killed him to walk away and leave him standing in the cat food aisle wondering when or if he'd ever see him again. Phillip had seemed lost that day, and knowing he was responsible tugged at his heartstrings. If he was being honest with himself, he'd admit that he'd always taken Phillip for granted, and that wasn't right. Phillip Thompson was the kindest, most loving person he'd ever known, and he deserved more than what he'd given him all these years.

He tapped his fingers on the steering wheel and wished the cars would move. Back in high school, when he and Phillip were driving around in the Camaro, he couldn't recall having to deal with traffic like this. Maybe he hadn't noticed with Phil sitting beside him.

Finally traffic began to inch along again, and after a minute, it actually picked up speed and snapped him out of his depressing thoughts. He started going over the things he and Dana had done to get the house ready for Meredith, and he didn't think they'd forgotten anything. Tomorrow, before leaving for the airport, they'd make sure the litter boxes were clean and spotless, use the lint brush on the couch cushions, and that would be it. Since he had no last-minute chores tonight, maybe he'd stop by the Breezeway Pub for a beer on his way home. He had time before picking Dana up, and that would give him a chance to unwind and clear his mind.

Cole sat down at the bar and ordered a beer. He'd walked briskly in the hundred degree plus temperature from his SUV into the pub, but even in those few seconds, beads of sweat had appeared on his forehead. The air conditioning and the cold beer would rejuvenate him in short order—his body anyway, his mind maybe not so much.

He could almost hear Meredith complaining about the heat. She'd picked the hottest month to visit, so she'd have to deal with it. Dana had told her to bring clothes for hot weather, but he had a hard time picturing Meredith in sundresses, tank tops, and shorts.

The beer mug clinking in front of him interrupted his thoughts. The bartender must have realized he'd forgotten the coaster because he came back and slid one underneath his mug saying, "Here you go. Enjoy."

He took a sip and went back to thinking about Meredith. Her impending arrival had him irritated, not only because they didn't get along very well, but because her visit would slow down his ability to try to make things right with Phillip. And in fact, her trip had caused the problem in the first place. He took another drink and pressed his lips together. Or was it his reaction to Meredith's visit that had really created the whole unfortunate situation?

A loud laugh brought his attention to the bartender talking with a nerdy guy in a sweater, of all things, and a bow tie, who was outwardly flirting with him. For the first time since sitting down at the bar, he noticed how good-looking the bartender was. He didn't think he'd been working on the other nights he'd stopped in. With his bright sleeve tattoo and muscle T-shirt showing it off, he wasn't his type, but notwithstanding, he had kind blue eyes and a dazzling smile. He wondered if his perfect teeth were courtesy of cosmetic dentistry. Yeah, he was nice to look at, but he didn't hold a candle to Phillip. In all these years no man had. He took a long drink and wished he'd gone home to have his beer because being here wasn't helping his mood at all.

The nerdy guy left, and the bartender went back to making and serving drinks. Cole focused on his drink and savored the relative quiet. Being a Saturday, no doubt the noise level would pick up soon. He'd be in and out before that happened, which suited him fine because he didn't want anyone to come over and talk to him. He should have gone home to be with Moonshadow and Moonbeam.

The whoops, hollers, and cheers from across the room grabbed his attention. *So much for quiet.*

He halfheartedly directed his gaze to the pool tables. At least someone was having fun tonight. After watching for a few moments, he noticed that they had formed teams and were playing tournament style. He zeroed in on the group of guys and froze. Phillip was one of the players, and his teammate was wild-maned Brad.

Great, this is just great.

Now he really did wish he'd gone straight home because the evening was going from bad to worse. Not even one week had gone by since he and Phil had argued, and he wasn't even aware that they had officially broken up. Evidently they had, otherwise why would Phillip be here with Brad? Phil sure didn't look lonely tonight.

Anger gripped him, and he felt like swearing and throwing what was left of his beer against the mirror behind the bar, but of course he wouldn't. Being mad at himself, at Phillip, at the whole world, made him sick with frustration, but throwing things wouldn't help. What would? When he'd tried to talk to Phil the other morning at his house, that hadn't gone well. He didn't know what else to say or do, and now seeing him here with Brad...

Why the hell are they together? He couldn't have given up on us just like that... Or have I pushed him too far...

Closing his eyes, he rubbed them underneath his glasses. He pushed on his eyeballs harder than he should, as if poking them out would erase the image of Phillip and Brad out together laughing and having a good time. That wouldn't help anyway because the picture was burned into his brain—and heart.

He opened his eyes and chanced a glance over to the pool tables again. Phil and Brad were standing among the group with their backs toward him, holding their pool cues and watching a couple of the men play. Maybe he was overreacting—maybe there wasn't any more to this than a friendly game of pool. They weren't even touching each other. Neither of them was dressed like they were trying to impress—this all seemed casual. Heck, maybe they hadn't even come here together, maybe they met by chance...

He recalled when he'd been with Phillip on the couch a couple weeks ago, and he'd heard him whisper *I love you, always have and always will.*

He believed Phillip then, and he had to believe that was still true. If only he could find a way to fix the damage he'd done.

He entertained the thought of watching the two of them after the game broke up to see if they sat together and had dinner and if they left together, but he'd run the risk of being seen, and he sure didn't want that. Besides, he was no stalker, and he refused to act like a jealous idiot.

He and Phillip belonged together and that's how they were going to end up—he had to believe that. Whatever was necessary to make that happen, he was prepared to do it. For now though, he was going to slip right out the door and head on over to pick up Dana. Talking with Gail might help him organize his thoughts and form a plan of action.

He stood up, threw down some bills on the bar, and with his head down, he did his best to make a beeline to the front door. The place had gotten more crowded, and that was good and bad because he had to weave around several people, which slowed him down, but that also helped him go undetected. Once he reached the front door, he couldn't help but stop and look back inside for one last glimpse of Phillip—his best friend and the other half of his soul.

CHAPTER TWENTY-NINE

PHIL STEPPED out of the back door of his house to intercept the pizza deliveryman. He hurried over to the car and took the pizza in one hand while handing the guy some money with his other.

"Thanks," Phil said.

"Thank you sir. Have a nice day," the young man answered.

Phil hurried into the kitchen. "Lunch is served," he said to his mom and aunt. He set the box in the middle of the table, opened the lid and passed out napkins.

"This is very nice." Aunt Ruth tucked a napkin into the collar of her blouse.

"It looks as good as it smells." Phil's mom leaned forward in her chair and peered at the pizza.

"Do you ladies need any more iced tea before I sit down?"

"I'm fine," they both answered.

Each of them took a slice and put it on the plates in front of them.

"We won't need anything else until the exhibition this evening. We can nibble there," Aunt Ruth said.

"Yes, according to Gail they'll serve hors d'oeuvres. I'm so excited I can hardly wait." Phil's mom picked up her slice of pizza.

"I'll take you out for dessert on the way home if you're hungry."

Phil smiled and took a big drink of his tea.

"That sounds very nice," Aunt Ruth said. His mom nodded and smiled in agreement.

Phil was busy eating and he noticed his mom staring at him. He stopped chewing, swallowed, and looked back at her, waiting to find out why. When she didn't speak, he said, "You look like you expect me to say something."

"Well, I just expected you to say that you're excited about your sister's exhibition too. After all, this is a very special event."

"Oh, yeah, sure I'm excited. Not looking forward to wearing a tie, but other than that..." He grabbed another slice of pizza.

Aunt Ruth softly chuckled.

"Gail is so nervous. I wish there was something I could do for her."

"Just being here is a big help, Mom."

"Eve wasn't this excited even on her graduation day. The dresses Gail bought them to wear this evening are beautiful." Aunt Ruth sipped her tea.

"I can't wait to see Gail's paintings on exhibit. She spent weeks deciding which ones to put on display," Phil's mom said.

"It's going to be so much fun—the start of more good things to come for her." Aunt Ruth clasped her hands on the table.

"She deserves it." Phil smiled.

"Yes, she certainly does," Aunt Ruth agreed.

After they finished their pizza, Phil stood up and gathered the remaining slices and put them into the refrigerator. His mom started to stand up. "Let me help you."

"Relax, Mom. I'll do this." He took their glasses to the sink.

"Well, since you've got this under control, I'm going to take a little nap if you don't mind." Aunt Ruth slowly got up from the table.

"Go right ahead." Phil handed his aunt her cane. "Make yourself at home."

"I'll need a rest before this evening too, but I think I'll sit here awhile first." Phil's mom sat back in her chair.

Aunt Ruth left the kitchen, and Phil's mom was staring at him again. He had a feeling she was going to bring up Cole, and he dreaded that. He'd already told her on the phone why he wasn't seeing him anymore, but knowing her, she wouldn't leave it at that.

He just couldn't keep Cole off his mind, which annoyed him to no end. Meredith had been in town for nearly a week, but he hadn't asked Gail or Eve if they'd met her, and they'd respected his wishes and hadn't brought up the subject. The less he knew the better anyway, although he couldn't help wondering what Meredith was like. Cole had said she wasn't homophobic, so he still couldn't understand why he hadn't wanted them to meet—why he caused this rift between them over that. The decision to let Dana live in California was all but made, so why was Cole so paranoid? He'd always had the tendency to be an overthinker so maybe that contributed to his actions. Telling himself that, hurt less than thinking Cole was ashamed of him.

When his mom said his name louder than usual, he looked at her and blinked. "Sorry Mom, did you say something?"

"You seemed miles away."

"Yeah, well, I'm back." He winked and smiled at her and then sat down at the table. "Do you want some more tea?"

"No thank you. I just want to talk to you. Talking in person is so much better than over the phone, and we don't get the chance very often."

He took a deep breath and waited to hear what she had on her mind. Whatever it was seemed important to her.

She gently put her hand on his. "I know Cole hurt you deeply and made you angry when he said he didn't want you around while his ex-wife is in town, but do you think you'd feel that way if it wasn't for what happened between you two in the past?"

He was momentarily unable to speak. She had a way of simplifying things, and her question was worth some serious thought.

"I suppose that might have changed how I reacted," Phil admitted to her, and more importantly, to himself. "I still don't like it though."

"Oh, I know. You want to be included in Cole's life—to be a part of it all, but if you allow yourself to think of the situation from his point of view, you can understand his apprehension better. I could tell how important his daughter is to him when he talked about her at Eve's graduation." She patted his hand and said, "What he asked of you seems logical to me."

He tried to imagine how he'd have reacted if the past wasn't a factor.

"Well, that's my two cents' worth," his mom said, her smile caring and kind. She held on to his hand.

"Mom, why did you want to put in your two cents' worth?"

She didn't speak right away, her eyes cast down as if she searched for the right words. Finally she met his gaze and said, "In all the years since Cole left, you haven't once brought a man to meet me, or even your sister. To me that means there is only one man you love and that's Cole Fisher."

Her words were painful to hear, mainly because she was right and hearing them said out loud was hard to face.

She gripped his hand tighter. "He was so nice at the graduation. You shouldn't waste this chance, Phil."

"Well, I asked didn't I..." Unwanted tears welled up in his eyes. He wiped at them and stood up. His mom got up from her chair too.

"I'm going to rest for a short time before getting ready to leave for the big event. Maybe the cats will join me if they aren't already in with Ruth."

He reached out and wrapped his arms around her, pulling her close and releasing his bottled-up emotions. Her muscles relaxed, and she felt soft and warm against his chest. When they parted, she looked up and smiled at him like she could read his mind.

"Phil, you'll never get what you want and need by being stubborn like your dad. Remember that."

"Okay, Mom. I'll see you later. Thanks."

After she'd gone, he grabbed a beer, took a long drink and went outside to clear his mind.

Phil pulled up in front of the High Desert Fine Arts Gallery, put the Camaro in park, and got out to help his mom and aunt out of the car. Once he had the two of them standing on the sidewalk with their canes in hand, he sent them on their way toward the front door while he hurried back into the car. He watched them for a few seconds, and satisfied they'd be okay until he returned, he drove to the parking area.

After parking, he returned to the building. His mom and aunt were out of sight, so he went inside, surprised they'd already proceeded to the large table covered with a black tablecloth, glass dishes, wine glasses, hors d'oeuvres and napkins. Other guests were also milling around the table.

A young woman wearing black pants and a white blouse stepped up to him. "Those two ladies over there asked me to point you in their direction." She nodded toward the table and handed him an exhibit brochure. "This will give you the information about the artwork."

Another woman dressed the same as the first joined them. "You're Gail's brother, aren't you?" Before he could answer, she added, "She described you and said you'd be here with her mom and aunt."

"Right, I'm Gail's brother, Phil."

"We're thrilled to show her art. She's a bright, new talent." She shook his hand. "Have a good time this evening. Help yourself to the food and drink." She and the other woman left to greet other guests, and he headed over to his mom and Aunt Ruth.

As he came up behind them, he overheard them oohing and aahing over the hors d'oeuvres.

"I guess I didn't feed you enough at home." He softly chucked.

"You've been around cats too long. Ruth and I aren't cats that must be fed," his mom said. He could tell she was pretending to be offended, but her smile indicated otherwise.

"Doesn't the food look good, Phil?" his mom continued.

"It's a beautiful table. Look at the centerpiece of lovely flowers." Aunt Ruth reached out and touched the arrangement.

"Everything looks good, but maybe we should find Gail and Eve first," he suggested. "Maybe look at the art."

"Yes, I think that's a good idea. She's probably waiting for us," his mom agreed.

The three of them began viewing the paintings as they meandered along. They hadn't gotten far when Eve suddenly appeared between them smiling ear-to-ear.

"So glad you're here," she said breathlessly. "Mom's answering questions from guests over there." She pointed toward Gail who was chatting with a few people.

Gail looked fashionable in a plain black dress. Her hair was pretty in some sort of braid-pony-tail combo. She must have had it done at the hairdresser.

"Ruth, let me show you my favorite painting." Phil's mom nudged Ruth in the right direction.

As they stepped away, Eve pulled her phone out of her small handbag and checked the screen intently before beginning to text. He didn't know why she couldn't put the thing away for just one evening.

After a few seconds he cleared his throat. "Do you want to look at the paintings with grandma, Aunt Ruth, and me?"

Eve put the phone away. She appeared so grown-up in her red

lace dress. He glanced down at her feet and saw that she had on high heels, which he hadn't seen her wear even at her graduation.

"Okay, let's go." Eve took him by the hand.

They headed over to where his mom and Aunt Ruth were watching Gail answer more questions. Nearby, a woman was waving her arm, pointing, and scurrying about.

"That's the gallery owner," Eve whispered.

By the end of the evening, he figured Gail would be exhausted, but she sure didn't appear to be now. Her nerves that his mom spoke of earlier must have settled down. She seemed so relaxed and at home while speaking about her art that it was hard to believe this was her first show. As they joined his mom and aunt, he was sure they made quite a picture, all of them beaming with pride on this happy day.

Suddenly it occurred to him that Dana wasn't there, and he remembered Gail had shopped for dresses for both Eve and Dana. Maybe Eve had been texting her and she was on the way, but if that were the case, would Cole be bringing her? And if Cole came, would Meredith be with him?

He didn't want to ask Eve and make a big deal out of it—that would draw attention to his anxiety that was bubbling up at the thought of seeing Cole come walking in, let alone him with his ex-wife. But wasn't that what he'd wanted all along—to meet Meredith? No, that wouldn't happen. Cole wouldn't bring Meredith to an event Phil would be attending, would he?

Eve tugged on his arm. "Are you okay, Uncle Phil?"

"Why?" he asked, noticing that Eve, his mom, and aunt were staring at him.

"We were saying your name and you weren't responding." His mom reached out and touched his arm.

"I'm sorry. I guess I was thinking about something else."

"Maybe you'll feel better if you have a bite to eat," Aunt Ruth said.

He rubbed the back of his neck. "Yeah, maybe."

"We're going to wait until Gail takes a break before we eat, but don't let us stop you if you're hungry," his mom said.

He wasn't hungry, but he nodded and headed over to the hors d'oeuvre table anyway. Everything looked appetizing, and he decided to eat cheese cubes on a toothpick and a stuffed mushroom, and then he moved over to the drinks. Wine had never been his thing, so he picked up a glass of the nonalcoholic pineapple-strawberry cooler. He ate another cubed cheese stick with the drink. When he finished that, he thought it best to quit for now and wait until his mom and the others were ready to eat.

He stopped in the men's room on his way back. After washing his hands, he took a moment to check his tie in the mirror, making sure it was straight. He felt less anxious than he had earlier, and he straightened his shoulders. What difference did it make if Cole showed up? Of course Gail would have invited him. After all, he'd bought one of her paintings. He'd put any negative thoughts out of his mind and focus on the reason he was here. This wasn't about him. This was about supporting Gail.

He headed out to join his family.

CHAPTER THIRTY

"DANA IS doing great walking in those high heels I bought her," Meredith said, as she and Cole watched her hurry ahead toward the door of the art gallery.

When he'd seen those shoes on the day Meredith and Dana had come home from shopping, his opinion, which he hadn't shared, had been that they should have chosen lower heels. He hoped she wouldn't break her ankle.

He slowed his pace because he didn't want to get to the door too soon. Dana went into the building, and he was glad she hadn't stopped to wait.

"Why are you walking so slowly? It's hotter than a furnace out here. I've got to get inside asap." Meredith pushed her hair away from her face.

Her satin-trimmed skirt suit looked kind of heavy to him. Why she hadn't dressed in something more appropriate for a hot summer day was beyond him.

"Isn't that suit kind of warm for this time of year, long sleeves and all?"

"I expected to be inside in air conditioning, not standing outside in the sun. And these are three-quarter length sleeves." She glanced at her arm and ran her fingers over the sleeve.

He lightly touched her elbow and guided her in the direction of an oak tree. "How about we stand over here in the shade for a minute. There's something I want to talk to you about. It's cooling down. This isn't the hottest time of the day."

After a few steps, she pulled her arm away but continued following along. "This must be the only tree on this street." She glanced around and over toward the art gallery. "All this desert landscape leaves a lot to be desired."

"Yeah, I agree. That's why I put in grass and greenery at the house."

"Your landscaping looks lovely, Cole. You did a nice job." She lowered her voice and added, "It's a good home for Dana."

He lifted his eyebrows, surprised at the compliment, although she'd seemed to like the house okay—perhaps not the décor that much, and certainly not the location, but the house itself.

"What about apple trees? I haven't seen one apple tree in this..." She paused, maybe trying to come up with the right word, or biting her tongue before saying something rude—he wasn't sure which.

At least she'd stopped insisting they rush indoors. "Meredith... I need to tell you something before we go inside."

"What would that be?"

He looked down at the ground and then at her. "There's someone I'll be introducing you to..."

"Well, I figured I'd meet Gail's family. Who else?" Her stare was intense.

Why couldn't he just tell her? He'd waited as long as he could, and time had run out. He had to tell her now, but the words weren't coming. He rubbed the back of his neck.

"Please, go on." She waited all of three seconds, and then snapped, "If you don't get to the point soon, I'm going to have to get a tissue out of my bag to wipe my forehead."

"Maybe we should have sat in the car with the air conditioning on," he said.

"You think? It's a bit late for that now," she exclaimed and pursed her lips.

"I didn't think it would be this hot. It's nearly six o'clock."

"If you'd just say what's on your mind we wouldn't have to keep standing here. You're acting like a child, you know that, Cole?"

She reached into her handbag, came out with a tissue and blotted her forehead. "I'm not going to stand out here forever. I came to attend an art showing. Dana is waiting for us. We're late."

"You've always liked being late—I mean fashionably late." He smiled nervously at his lame attempt at a joke.

After another moment of silence, Meredith impatiently said, "Maybe I should help you along if you've gone mute."

Cole felt like a total heel, so he cleared his throat, prepared to finally speak, but before he could, Meredith surprised him by asking, "Doesn't Gail have a brother? Will he be here this evening?"

Cole stuck his hands in his pockets. "How did you know that Gail has a brother? Did someone mention him?"

"No one mentioned him, but when I was at her apartment with Dana, I noticed some family photos displayed on a table, and there was a guy in one with Gail and an older woman. I wondered if they were her mom and brother, that's all, why?" Her eyes narrowed like she was reading his mind and didn't like what she saw there.

"Uh, no reason. I mean, no reason not to mention him."

"Cole, you're not making a bit of sense. You must really think I'm stupid."

"Why would you say that?"

"I know who Gail's brother is. I mean, I think I know who he is *to you.*"

All he could do was stand there in stunned silence with his hands at his sides. He waited for her to go on, but when all she did was stare off into the distance, he spoke up. "I'm sorry, Meredith. Sorry for everything. I hope you know that."

She fixed her gaze on him again, but she seemed to be staring right through him.

Meredith was hot and uncomfortable, and the conversation was a disaster so far. He groaned inwardly, at least he hoped no sound had come out. Peering into her blue eyes, he said, "Yes, Meredith, you're right. Gail's brother—his name is Phil—he and I are in a committed relationship."

She took a deep breath, let it out, and crossed her arms. "When you introduced me to Gail when we met her for lunch, I thought there was something familiar about her last name. I kept thinking about it, and then later when I was at her apartment and noticed the picture, I started thinking about it again. She had said she'd always lived in Apple Valley, and then I thought about the yearbook I sent you last spring."

She paused, her mouth slightly turned down on the corners. "I'd thumbed through the book before I packed it, and I noticed some pictures of you with a boy in your class. I wanted to check the yearbook again to make sure that what I was thinking was right, but I didn't know where you kept it, and I didn't want to ask Dana."

A bus roared down the street, and she stopped talking until it had passed. Cole tried to digest what he'd heard so far.

She let her hands fall at her sides. "I looked up your high school and the year you graduated online, and I confirmed that sure enough, Thompson was the name of the boy in the pictures with you."

She blotted her forehead with the tissue again. "So, anyway, I put two and two together, figured you'd taken up with him again after you moved back here, but I didn't know why no one had brought up his name. I thought maybe he was away on vacation... maybe he died... I was confused, and now here you stand stammering and babbling and taking way too long to just come out and tell me. Why haven't I met him?"

While he tried to formulate an answer, she said, "Look, Cole, we've been divorced for going on four years now, so what's the big deal anyway?"

"Uh, well, you're going to meet him today—inside. Maybe we'd better go in now."

"I've wanted to get in there since we got out of the car."

So far, Meredith seemed understanding about the whole situation. She'd had time to digest what she'd learned after she'd connected the dots, so that had probably helped her get to this point. He'd be optimistic that she wouldn't ask again why she hadn't met him until today. Maybe that could just be swept under the rug.

He walked with her toward the gallery, and he had great expectations for a good outcome when he introduced her to Phillip. He'd practiced what he'd say in the introduction, and hopefully that would be enough to erase the damage he'd done to his relationship with Phillip.

Fingers crossed, Phil wouldn't look angry even though he had every reason to be. He so wanted, *needed,* Meredith to have a good impression of Phillip. She'd sure taken a liking to Gail, so that might help. Asking Phillip to stay away had been a big mistake. He'd created this mess—driven Phillip away—and he had to fix it.

Cole opened the gallery door for Meredith, and the air conditioning was a welcome relief, even for him.

"It's rather spacious considering how the building looks from outside. Maybe it's a mirage. Lord, I think I'm dehydrated,"

Meredith said.

"Is that your way of saying you'd like a glass of wine?" Cole tried to be attentive to her while subtlety glancing around for Phil.

"I'd love one, but perhaps we should look around first, find Dana for one thing. This is really nice. I can't believe we're actually at an art gallery in the middle of the desert."

"This isn't exactly the middle of the desert."

Meredith laughed, and she seemed immersed in the experience of being in the gallery. Evidently, this was the first place she'd been in Apple Valley that made her feel at home.

"Ma'am, would you like a brochure?" a greeter asked, stepping up to Meredith.

"Yes, thank you very much." Meredith accepted the offered leaflet and immediately used it for a fan.

When Dana called, "Mother, Father," Cole pivoted toward the sound of her voice, and Meredith turned too. He spotted Dana standing off to their right in a wide doorway leading to another part of the gallery. Eve, and Phil's mom and aunt, were standing with her. Why wasn't Phil with them? As he and Meredith walked over to greet the group, he kept scanning the area trying to locate Phillip. Since the gallery had multiple rooms, surely he was there someplace. He didn't see Gail either.

Dana gave him a hug, and he was so proud of her looking so pretty in the pink dress that Gail had helped her choose.

He greeted Phil's mom. "Good evening, Mrs. Thompson." Turning to Aunt Ruth, he said, "Ma'am, nice to see you again. I'd like to introduce both of you to my ex-wife, Meredith. She's here from New York."

He turned to his ex. "Meredith, this is Gail's mother and aunt."

"Hello, Meredith. Please call me Elizabeth. I'm Gail's mother."

"Very nice to meet you, Elizabeth," Meredith answered.

"I'm Elizabeth's sister, Ruth. You've come a long way."

"It's nice to meet you, Ruth. I'm in town to look over the school and everything before I leave for Europe. Dana will be staying with her father while I'm away. She enjoyed spending the summer here."

"Eve and Dana have become fast friends," Ruth said.

"Yes, so I've heard and seen." Meredith glanced at the girls and smiled.

"These two girls have formed a wonderful friendship." Phil's mom looked fondly at Eve and Dana.

"I thought maybe Dana could continue with her dance lessons this year, but her interests seem to be evolving. She's started cooking and has made me several dishes while I've been here. She's really good at it."

"How nice." Phil's mom patted Dana on the shoulder.

"And I like horseback riding, fishing, and basketball too," Dana said.

Meredith smiled. "Dressed like you are right now, that's hard to imagine."

While the women talked, Cole kept looking around for Phillip. He couldn't believe he would miss Gail's art debut, but where the heck was he? Surely, he'd show up soon, unless he was sick or something. He heard Meredith and Ruth laughing, so he focused on what they were saying.

"And, what do you think of the desert, Meredith?"

"Well, it's certainly hot enough."

"Oh, but it's a dry heat." Phil's aunt chuckled. "I live in Santa Barbara. I couldn't take this heat every day. It's rather dismal in the desert, at least to me since I'm not used to it."

Phil's mom straightened her shoulders. "I live in Santa Barbara now too, but I lived here for many years, and I liked it just fine."

"Well, it's all in what you get used to." Phil's aunt shared another laugh with Meredith.

Phil's mom rubbed her chin. "Maybe Gail can bring Eve and Dana to visit us in Santa Barbara."

"That would be very nice," Meredith said. "Wouldn't it, Cole?"

"Yes, I'm sure the girls would like that. What do you think, Dana?"

"It's so beautiful there," Eve said to Dana.

Dana nodded. "I'd love to visit you."

"I'm going to excuse myself to view Gail's paintings and say hello if I can find her," Meredith said.

Cole took a step toward her. "Okay, sure. I'll come with you." They left the girls chatting with Elizabeth and Ruth and walked over to the row of Gail's beautifully displayed paintings.

They'd only seen the first one when he heard Eve call out, "Uncle Phil, over here."

Cole jerked his head in their direction, and sure enough, the man he'd been waiting to see was no more than thirty feet away. Phillip looked more handsome than ever in a sky-blue button-down shirt and a dark blue tie. His heart thumped wildly, partly because

Phillip was a welcome sight, especially after not seeing him for a week, and because the thing he'd fretted about was going to come to a head.

He'd been so lost in thought that he hadn't noticed Meredith had also taken her attention away from the painting and had zeroed in on Phil. She took in a noticeably deep breath as she stared intently. He could tell she was scrutinizing Phillip, and he couldn't blame her for that.

Phil said something to Eve, and then Dana joined them, greeting him with a hug. Meredith continued to stare without blinking, and her expression was unreadable until her lips curved into a slight smile, and she whispered wistfully, "She likes him."

When Dana released Phil from the hug, she said something to him, and then she looked at Cole and gave him a nod of acknowledgement.

Keeping his eyes glued on Phil, who turned their way and shot him a glance, he was about to wave him over, but Phil headed toward him and Meredith without any prompting. Cole was relieved that the girls stayed where they were. Drawing in a long breath and letting it out slowly, he squared his shoulders and prepared himself for what was to come.

Phil got within a few feet of them, and Cole couldn't hold his grin in, and he had the urge to grab the man and hug the breath out of him. He reined himself in and settled for a quick side hug that made his pulse skyrocket. Receiving no resistance put him more at ease. They parted, and the smile that crinkled the edges of Phil's blue eyes made him feel even better.

For those few brief moments, it was as if he and Phillip were the only two people in the room. He'd been so lost in their reunion of sorts, that the sight of Meredith standing beside them jarred him back into reality. She was obviously waiting for introductions, and since she preferred being the center of attention, she wasn't pleased. He smiled at her the best he could, and hoped he'd remember the words he wanted to say.

Cole cleared his throat. "Meredith, this is Gail's brother, Phil Thompson... my best friend from way back..." He switched his gaze to Phil. "He's the person I intend to be with for the rest of my life."

He loved the dumbfounded expression his words had put on Phillip's face.

"Uh, Phil, this is my ex-wife, Meredith." Relief washed over him as she politely extended her hand. Her forced smile didn't reach her eyes, but at least she was trying, and he couldn't ask for more than that.

"It's nice to meet you, Phil," Meredith said.

"Same here." Phil gently shook her hand.

"Dana and I have spent some time with your sister and your niece while I've been in town. They've been good friends to Dana. I guess you've gotten to know my daughter pretty well too."

"Yes, she's a great girl. Always up for a new adventure."

"So I've heard. I can hardly believe all she's done this summer."

Suddenly Meredith seemed distracted by something across the room, so Cole followed her line of sight. Dana and Eve stood in the next room gazing their way. Phil must have noticed they'd become preoccupied, so he turned to look too. Both girls were motionless like mannequins, watching them intently. He figured they were trying to assess the situation—wondering if it was okay to come join them, so he waved them over. They smiled and came readily.

"So... Uncle Phil, I see you've met Dana's mom." Eve toyed with a lock of her hair.

Phil smiled at her, seemingly at a loss for words, so Cole asked, "Are you girls enjoying the show so far?"

"It's wonderful," Dana said.

"Yes, it's fun." Eve glanced around the room wide-eyed.

"You must be so proud of your mother," Meredith said. "Shall we go find her so I can say hello?"

"That's a great idea." Eve took a step closer to the row of paintings.

"I'll see you later," Meredith said to Cole. "It was lovely meeting you, Phil."

"Nice meeting you too." He gave a half-smile.

Cole watched the girls walk along the exhibit, gazing at each painting as they continued on. He turned to Phil. "It looks like it's just you and me."

"You and me and a room full of people."

"Yeah, looks like a real good turnout for Gail's exhibition." Phil didn't comment, and Cole noticed him fidgeting with his tie and then putting his hands in his pockets, basically acting like he couldn't stay still.

"Your ex seems very nice."

"She's been on her best behavior on this trip."

Phil chuckled. "Good, that's real good. Dana looks nothing like her."

"Yeah, I think it always irked Meredith that Dana looks like me."

"Well, Meredith is nice looking anyway."

"Yeah, not my type though." Cole smiled nervously. After a moment, he cleared his throat. "You know, it's probably dark outside by now... and cooling down..."

"Are you thinking what I'm thinking?" Phil grinned like a Cheshire cat.

The smile on that handsome face that he'd been afraid he'd never see again filled him with so much emotion he could hardly stand to keep his hands to himself. Knowing that he was the reason for that smile made him weak-kneed, and he couldn't help but smile back so wide that his cheeks hurt.

He had to be alone with Phillip *now*.

He leaned in and whispered, "If you're thinking about us going for a little walk outside, well then, yes, I am."

"Sounds good to me. I wonder if anyone will miss us."

Cole took a half step back, ready to head for the door. "Does it matter if they do?"

"Definitely not. Let's go." Phil bumped him with his shoulder as he aimed them for the door.

Once outside, Cole felt like he was back in high school sneaking away to make out behind the gym. He had to make an effort to keep up with Phillip's long strides as he led them away from the gallery. The quick pace was fine with him. Making the most of the time they had until their families would start wondering where they were was high priority. He soon realized exactly where they were going, and he should have known what Phillip had in mind. Now he really did feel like he was in high school—the memories never having left his mind.

They reached the Camaro, and Phil unlocked the doors. He flung open the driver's side and pulled the seat forward, crawled into the back, and yanked the door closed. From the passenger side, Cole followed Phil's lead, scrambling in next to him. They fell into a fierce hug followed by an exchange of frenzied kisses and roving hands that sent shockwaves to every part of Cole's body. Each time he brushed against Phil's erection his desire intensified. His face would be red from the scraping of Phillip's beard, and that would be hard to explain when they got back to the gallery, but this was worth every second of awkwardness he might encounter later. He yanked at the knot on Phillip's tie, managing to loosen it, and then he got a button on his shirt undone, relieved that it hadn't popped off.

"I went to a lot of trouble getting this damn tie on perfectly, you know," Phil scolded with tongue-in-cheek humor.

Cole chuckled and undid his own tie in a hurry, before pulling open a couple snaps on his shirt and then burying his face in Phillip's neck, breathing in his cologne. The earthy scent carried him to a place he'd thought was lost to him, and he was overcome by intense euphoria.

"Phillip, I love you," he rasped.

Phil softly moaned in response, and he said, "I love you too."

Cole trembled, and his already hard dick stiffened more than he thought possible.

In the tight confines of the back seat, there was no way that Phil hadn't noticed the excited state he was in, just like he'd felt Phillip's hardness a few seconds after they'd started making out. He wondered how they'd ever managed to do the deed in this back seat hundreds of times before because it was sure cramped. Evidently, two grown men compared to two teenagers made a big difference. He smiled in spite of himself. Despite the darkness, the glow filtering in from the parking lot lighting made Phillip's eyes sparkle.

"You forgive me then?" he asked in a whisper, gently running his finger across Phil's lips.

Phil pulled him down and kissed him hard, stealing his breath. By the time they broke the kiss, he felt like the life had been kissed out of him, and he took that as his answer.

Phil squirmed like he wanted to sit up, so he pulled himself off him as best he could. His pants threatened to cut off the circulation to his nether regions. At least he was in soft dress pants rather than Levi's.

As Phil sat up, he wiped away a few beads of sweat on his forehead and rasped through labored breathing, "We have to quit. I've got to drive my mom and aunt home in this car, and if we don't stop now, I'm going to have a big problem."

"Oh, yeah, what kind of problem?" Cole asked, even though he knew full well.

"The kind of problem that would require driving home to change my pants—probably have to loan you a pair too," he said as his eyes swept downward.

Cole chuckled. "They'd be a bit on the large side, most likely we'd have to drive to my place too, and by the time we ever got back, no one would be here anymore." He took a deep breath.

"What's wrong?" Phil asked.

"Just thinking..."

"Thinking about what?"

"What terrible luck that we're making up when I've got my ex-wife at my house and you have your mother and aunt at yours."

"No make-up sex..."

Cole ran the back of his hand down Phillip's cheek. "We have the rest of our lives to be together. You want that, don't you?" He leaned in for a soft kiss. "Tell me you do," he murmured, his lips inches from Phil's.

"I never could erase you. Yes, I want that."

"I'm the luckiest man in the world," Cole whispered.

"No, I am," Phil whispered back.

"Guess we'd better straighten ourselves up and go back inside before someone sends a search party." Cole sat back in the seat and rested his hand on his forehead.

Phil sighed. "Yeah, I haven't even talked to Gail yet."

"Well, I'm sure they aren't worried about us. Here, let me fix your tie." He redid Phillip's tie, and then to his surprise, Phil did the same for him. "You've been practicing, huh?"

Phil shrugged. "If I haven't learned to tie a necktie by now there's no hope for me."

"How does my hair look?" Cole asked.

"Wouldn't hurt to run a comb through it. How about mine?" He ran his fingers through his hair.

"You know I think you're the best-looking man in town, but you'd benefit from a comb too."

Once they checked each other out, making sure they were presentable, they got out of the car, and Phil locked the doors. Cole slipped his hand into Phillip's as they walked toward the gallery. He turned and glanced over his shoulder one last time, hoping that in the near future he'd be making space in his garage to park the shiny red Camaro, and more importantly, making space in his closet for Phillip's things.

No more wasted time—he was ready to start their life together in the house on Shadow Ridge.

EPILOGUE

SEVEN MONTHS LATER...

Riding in Cole's SUV sure beat riding in his old truck, Phil mused as he tied another knot in the tie down rope over the cat trees in his trailer. He threw another rope over the top of the load and continued securing it. The day was warm and calm—a perfect spring weekend to enjoy a peaceful drive and a fun day at the cat show. Every day had been great whatever the weather since Cole had persuaded him to move in last fall.

The ring on his finger caught his eye as he tied another knot. He never thought he'd be a married man, but the gold wedding band glistening in the sun was a symbol of the best day in his life. He had married Cole just a few weeks after they'd moved in together.

Just gazing at the ring made him feel happy and safe. He didn't need the ring to remind him of the deep connection he shared with Cole, but he loved admiring it. No way could he imagine life without him anymore.

Walking around the trailer double checking all his knots and making sure the ropes were snug, he wondered if Cole and Dana had Moonshadow and Moonbeam in their cages yet. Those cats were never a problem getting into their carriers—the opposite of the ordeal he always went through when Batman and Robin needed to go for a ride in theirs.

He'd been surprised at how well his cats had adjusted to the house, and especially to the two Siamese cats who were now their brothers. Cole really had a knack with cats, and he'd been a big help getting them to accept their new home and family. They'd put Batman and Robin's cat tree across from Moonshadow and Moonbeam's, and at first, the cats all used their own while checking each other out from atop their security zone. They'd stayed a safe distance away from one another when slinking through the house too. Now everyone shared, and the two purebred blue-ribbon winners and the two shelter cats were one big happy family.

He checked his watch, hoping that Gail would show up soon to drop off Eve. Gail was focused on her art more than ever, branching out more and more, and he couldn't be happier for her, but she kept herself so busy he didn't see much of her. She used every free minute either painting or posting on her blog.

At least she and Eve had more space now. They had moved into his old house. He'd left his furniture for them, and he'd spent days cleaning the garage so Gail could use it for an art studio. The natural light flooding in from the open door and the overhead florescent lighting he'd installed gave her a great place to work. He'd been so excited to show her what he'd done to the space, especially the bookcase he'd built to hold all her art books. She'd hugged him so hard he almost couldn't breathe.

Phil had built something else too, a special surprise for Eve. He'd left the awesome cat tree with a scratching ramp, perches, and a condo on top standing in the house when he'd left. Eve had called him, thrilled to pieces with the tree, telling him that her mom had agreed to let her have a cat. Soon after that, they'd adopted a pretty Tuxedo cat from the shelter. Now Eve had lots of amusing cat stories to share, and no doubt they'd hear some new ones today on the drive to the Pavilion in Palm Springs.

The sound of a car coming up the street brought him back to the present moment, and he hoped Gail and Eve were arriving. The color of the car was right, and when it got closer, he made out the familiar Toyota. They turned in and parked next to the SUV. Gail and Eve were both smiling, and he smiled back. Eve, as full of energy as ever, threw open the door as soon as the car had stopped and bounded out with her backpack.

"Good morning, Uncle Phil."

"Good morning. You look ready to go."

"First let me show you the newest pictures of Pepé Le Pew. I took them this morning, and I was going to text them to you, but I decided to show you in purrson—get it—purrrrrson."

"What did you have for breakfast this morning? Cat nip tea?" Phil asked.

"Good one, Uncle Phil." Eve giggled.

While she got her phone out and began bringing up the pictures, Gail got out of the car and gave him a hug. "Looks like you're all loaded up." She eyed the trailer filled with cat trees.

"You can still change your mind and come with us. You'd enjoy a day away."

"No, I'll pass, but thanks anyway. I'm working on a very special painting right now and I want to get back to that." She glanced at Eve and smiled. "I'm painting Pepé Le Pew for Eve's bedroom."

"Nice," Phil said. "I bet that'll be amazing."

"I'm also doing a very colorful close-up of a horse. People seem to really like the paintings of horses." She brushed back her hair with her fingers. "Well, enough about me... Eve, did you find the pictures of Pepé?"

Eve stepped closer to Phil and held out her phone. "Look at this one—he's upside-down on the top of his cat tower."

"He's going to fall off on his head one of these days," Gail said. "He likes the roof of the condo better than inside it."

"Cats like to be up high, Mom." Eve playfully rolled her eyes. "Here he is looking into the bathtub filled with water. I thought for sure he was going to dive in."

Gail tapped her chin. "That might be an idea of how to give him a bath."

"Mom, cats are self-cleaning, right Uncle Phil?"

"Brushing and pet wipes do the job as far as I'm concerned. Cole and Dana give Moonbeam and Moonshadow baths before a show though."

Eve finally handed him the phone. "Just scroll through to see them all."

He looked at each one, oohing and aahing at the beautiful long-haired Tuxedo cat, while Eve beamed with happiness like a proud cat mom.

"Okay, all set," Cole said to himself, or the cat, he wasn't sure which. He secured the flap on Moonshadow's soft-sided carrier, jiggling the lock to make sure he'd gotten it latched properly. After taking the cage to the entryway, he set it next to Moonbeam's on the hardwood floor. Bringing the carrying cages out of the closet had caused Batman and Robin to hide someplace. By this evening, after returning from Palm Springs, they would undoubtedly be in the family room on their cat tree.

He called up the stairs, "Dana, are you about ready? I'm sure Gail and Eve will be here any minute."

"I'm putting my stuff in my backpack. I'll be there in a second."

Cole smiled. A second would be at least five minutes. She always took more than she needed in her survival bag—the name she used for her backpack. He walked over to the front door, and through the sidelight he spotted Gail's car parked in the driveway. Peering closer, he noticed Gail and Eve talking with Phil on the other side of the trailer.

He'd helped Phillip load the cat trees earlier, and they were piled high. With all the odd shapes, he marveled at how Phil had gotten them tied down so quickly.

He was anxious to go out and greet the girls as soon as Dana joined him, although watching Phillip from right where he was held a lot of appeal. Anyway, he and Gail could probably use a few extra minutes to talk. Eve seemed to be the one talking though, very animated as she waved her phone around. Eve always put him, and everyone else, in a good mood.

He sighed and gazed adoringly at his family, the family he'd always wanted... The *right* family this time. Took long enough, but with Phillip, he'd finally gotten it right.

When they'd stood in the backyard of their home and slipped rings on each other's fingers with Dana, Eve, Gail, Elizabeth, and Ruth gathered around them, a sense of peace and joy had engulfed him, the likes of which he'd never thought he'd find in this life. He'd actually trembled as he'd placed the wedding ring onto Phillip's finger.

"Are they here?" Dana asked from right behind him. He'd been so deep in thought he hadn't even heard her come down the stairs, and the sudden sound of her voice startled him. He turned and smiled down at her.

"Are you okay, Father?"

"Sure, why do you ask?"

"Because you nearly jumped out of your skin just now." Dana

set her backpack on the floor.

"I did not."

"You did too."

"Okay, maybe I did, but you snuck up on me as quiet as a cat." He winked at her.

Dana giggled. "Next time I'll make more noise."

He pulled her close and gave her a quick hug. "Gail and Eve are out there."

"They are? Well, let's get the cats and go." She picked up her backpack.

"Let me carry that," Cole said, taking it from her.

She picked up Moonshadow in his carrier while Cole set the security alarm. Then he quickly picked up Moonbeam and opened the front door. They stepped outside, and Eve saw them immediately.

"Hey, we've been waiting for you," she called.

Gail walked toward them. "Good morning, you two." They met her halfway to the SUV. "Do you need help carrying something?"

"I think we've got it covered," Cole said.

"How's Pepé Le Pew doing?" Dana asked Gail.

"He's fine—getting more spoiled by the day though."

"I heard that," Eve said, joining them. "He deserves to be pampered after spending so many months in a cage at the shelter."

"Our cats are pampered too," Dana said. "All four of them."

Phil walked up, and Cole couldn't keep from smiling. The love of his life always looked so hot, and he loved being in his presence no matter what they were doing. Even with the girls around, or a room full of people, they had a unique connection, and Phil's lingering eye contact full of tenderness and warmth never failed to ignite a spark.

"About time you got out here. I missed you." Phil flashed one of his irresistible grins.

More and more every day, Cole felt like the luckiest man on the planet. He was excited about today and looking forward to enjoying every minute.

"I've got the blanket on the seat to set the cages on," Phil said. "Let me take Moonshadow off your hands, sweetheart."

"Thanks, Dad." Dana smiled shyly.

Hearing Dana call Phil dad warmed Cole's heart. He followed him to the SUV with Moonbeam.

"I'm going to get going," Gail said, once they had the cats

situated. "You all have a great day." She hugged Eve. "Text me when you get there."

Cole hugged Gail goodbye. "I wish you were coming with us."

"Thanks, maybe next time. I'd need to get a cat T-shirt so I'd fit in with all of you," she said with a smile. "I think yours is my favorite—"Real Men Like Cats, Great Men Clean The Litter Box," she read out loud.

"Dana picked it out for me."

"I'll get you a T-shirt today, Mom," Eve said.

"Don't spend your money on me. Get yourself something instead."

"Buying you a T-shirt will help Betty out. We love buying T-shirts from her, and I have enough right now."

"Well, okay then, as long as it doesn't say *crazy cat lady*." She hugged Phil before hurrying to her car.

After the four of them waved and watched her disappear from view, Dana and Eve climbed into the SUV on either side of the cat carriers, sticking their backpacks behind the seat next to the paraphernalia to decorate the show cage.

Cole stepped close to Phil. "Ready to go?" he asked in a low murmur.

"I'm ready to go wherever you want," Phil answered, wearing a mischievous grin.

"Uh, well, come to think of it, our six-month anniversary is coming up soon. We should make plans to get away, just the two of us." He waggled his eyebrows.

"I like the way you think." He was standing so close Cole could feel the heat between them.

"We could go to Santa Monica—ride on the Ferris wheel. I'd suggest sleeping on the beach in sleeping bags, but I think at this stage in our lives a fancy hotel would suit us better, what do you think?" Cole asked, his eyes never leaving Phil's.

"I think the hotel sounds better. We might end up getting arrested on the beach." Phil's tongue darted out wetting his lips, causing a tug at Cole's groin.

"Oh man... I was thinking more about my aching back, but I like the way you think much better." He glanced at the SUV, relieved that the girl's attention was on their phones. "I think we should continue this conversation tonight after we get home when we're alone."

"I'll hold you to that," Phil said. "I like that you're thinking ahead—wanting to make our six-month anniversary special."

"I have no doubt we'll make it something to remember... six months, going on a lifetime." He moved in and gave Phillip a quick but affectionate kiss. When it ended, Phil responded with one of his dazzling smiles, and Cole was transfixed looking into his beautiful blue eyes.

Eve and Dana's cheering voices brought him back to reality. "Woo-hoo" they shouted, smiling ear to ear, and then the clapping began.

Cole gave them a thumbs-up, and Phil formed an A-Okay sign with his forefinger and thumb.

"It's a great day," Phil said.

"It's a great life," answered Cole. He had never been happier.

Born and raised in California, Leigh Vining has been creating stories in her head for as long as she can remember. Always drawn to male friendships, she believes that loving who you love should never be something to be ashamed of.

She and her husband are stray cat magnets and they share their home with a houseful of rescues. Leigh believes that cats are great companions for people who sit at their desks for long periods of time. A lap full of purring cat has kept her company many a night while agonizing over every typed word.

Her muse often goes into overdrive while working out at the gym. She finds that breaking up the day with physical activity is good for your muscles, including the creative ones.

Her favorite ways to relax are baking sweet desserts, taking long walks, and watching baseball on TV.

Leigh's first book is titled *The Power of Two*.

Follow her at leighvining56 on Instagram.